MW00778313

LOREDAN

AGENT GATZ

R.M. SPENCER

Hardback ISBN: 979-8-9853076-2-7
Paperback ISBN: 979-8-9853076-1-0
Kindle ISBN: 979-8-9853076-0-3
EBook ISBN: 979-8-9853076-3-4
Audiobook ISBN: 979-8-9853076-4-1

Library of Congress Control Number: 2022946783

Printed in the United States of America

For my parents

"There is no greater absurdity than
taking everything seriously."

– Baltasar Gracián

AGENT GATZ

CHAPTER 1

August 1, 1914

Jay stood among the first-class passengers crowding the deck of the RMS *Oceanic*, wearing a borrowed suit. He felt remarkably calm, considering what he was here to do. Of course, he didn't know then that by the time the ship reached England, most of Europe would be at war.

The ship's horn bellowed, scattering seagulls. The passengers on the deck waved, shouting farewell to family and friends on the dock below. Jay removed the handkerchief from his jacket pocket. He held it up, letting it flutter in the wind. No one had come to see him off, but he didn't want to appear out of place.

As the ship pressed away from Chelsea Piers, Jay believed with youthful optimism that everything would go according to plan. He had no idea that by the end of the night, his confidence shattered, he would only know one thing for certain—accepting this job had been a terrible idea.

When only a handful of passengers remained on the deck, he flipped open his gold-plated pocket watch and noted the time. Then, clutching the timepiece in the palm of his hand, he started down the deck. It was time to get to work.

He paused outside the first-class smoking lounge and again consulted the watch. A man wearing oversized spectacles tipped his hat to him before disappearing into the lounge.

As the door swung shut, an inviting chorus of laughter spilled out of the room. Jay reached for the door but stopped himself. There wasn't time for that now.

It would probably take more than today to fully familiarize himself with the layout of the ship, and he wanted to cover as much ground as he could before dinner. Measuring how long it took to get to various points on the ship was a monotonous task, but a necessary one when seconds might make the difference in getting caught.

Jay was no stranger to boats, having spent five years sailing around the globe on Dan Cody's yacht. But this was his first voyage on an ocean liner. Almost everything about the ship was foreign to him.

When he first boarded, he'd tried to strike up a conversation with one of the stewards. Having also crewed a boat, Jay imagined there existed some sort of unspoken maritime comradery between the steward and himself. But the man wouldn't even look him in the eye. He kept bowing in his well-pressed uniform, saying, "Yes, sir. Will that be all, sir?" until Jay finally gave up.

The crew members of the *Oceanic*, it seemed, weren't allowed to consort with passengers. Cody would never have imposed such a restriction aboard the *Tuolomee*. He had treated the crew more like co-adventurers than employees.

If it were up to Jay, he'd still be working on that yacht. But fate had had other plans. And in May of 1912 his voyage aboard the *Tuolomee* had abruptly concluded.

Cody had died, and in an instant, Jay had lost his mentor, his job, and his home. He'd been left with nothing, not even the money Cody had left him in his will. Cody's long-time companion, the famed journalist Ella Kaye, had seen to that.

In his penniless state of despair, the bright future Jay had envisioned for himself dimmed like an oilless lamp. And the conjured persona of Jay Gatsby, which had blossomed under Cody's tutelage, withered until only a vague contour remained.

He didn't know why Ella Kaye had challenged the bequest. It wasn't as though she needed the money. The sum Cody had set aside for him was nothing in comparison to the millions she had inherited.

Jay had almost traversed the entirety of the upper deck when a bugle signaled it was time to dress for dinner. Joining the stream of passengers obeying the musical directive, he shuffled past rows of empty deck chairs in the direction of his cabin.

The suit he wore now was nicer than anything he'd ever owned. The fact he was expected to change into an even fancier getup for dinner amused him. Not that he was complaining. He appreciated the expensive wardrobe he'd been given to wear on the ship. He'd never looked better. And in his own tattered clothes, no one would have believed he was a first-class passenger.

Not that long ago, Jay had imagined he'd soon be wealthy enough to purchase a slew of elegant suits. But that was then. At present, he didn't have the wherewithal for such lofty aspirations. Once he paid off all his debts, maybe that would change. For now, all he could think about was how much money he owed the Eastman gang.

He brushed aside the thought. Now wasn't the time to dwell on that. He might as well enjoy the perks of living like a millionaire while he could.

Stepping inside his cabin on the promenade deck, Jay marveled at the lavish stateroom. Everything glistened with opulence. The carved mahogany furniture was polished to a brilliant shine. Glimmering gold etchings embellished the paneled walls. And outside the porthole on the far wall, the sun-speckled ocean shimmered.

Jay gazed out the thick glass before turning to look in the gilded mirror above the washbasin. The reflection staring back still startled him somewhat. His blond hair was dyed an inky black. Raising a hand to his lip, he touched the thin mustache adorning his ordinarily clean-shaven face. He wasn't completely unrecognizable, but he could pass as someone else. This, of course, was the point.

"Theodore Belmont," he said with a practiced grin. "Please, call me Teddy."

He dressed quickly but took his time with the silk tie, reknotting it to perfection. When he was satisfied, he knelt and meticulously arranged the effects stowed in his steamer trunk. Before lowering the lid, he laid a thin piece of black string across the top layer. If, when he returned, the string was disturbed, he would know someone had searched his belongings.

He waited until dinner was well underway before leaving his cabin. When he reached the floor below, the narrow corridor of cabin doors was empty. At the door marked Nineteen, Jay paused, leaning in to listen. A man and woman spoke in muffled voices. He hurried down the hallway and stepped onto the deck.

Outside, the air was cooler now. He leaned on the rail and gazed out at the dark water. Only a sliver of sun remained. If the Feltons didn't leave their room soon, he would have to do this another time. He couldn't arrive at the table in the middle of dinner. That would make a bad impression.

Earlier that day, Jay—or rather, Teddy—had petitioned the chief steward to seat him at the same table as his dear friend Millie Felton. In truth, Jay didn't know Millie at all. He had never laid eyes on her—it was her father he wanted to be near. He was the reason Jay was on this ship.

Stanley Felton was the owner of the American Cartridge

Company, a munitions manufacturer based outside Boston that had recently developed an illuminated "tracer" bullet. When fired, the bullet produced a small pyrotechnic flare that created an observable trajectory. This allowed the shooter to visibly trace the accuracy of each shot.

For the past few years, manufacturers around the globe had attempted to create tracer bullets without success. The unique chemical composition of ACC's tracers was a well-guarded secret, but that was about to change. The tracers and their design drawings were somewhere on this ship. And Jay planned to steal them.

The sky was almost completely dark now. He sighed. He couldn't wait any longer. He'd have to try again tomorrow night. But just as he turned to leave, two heads passed one of the glass portholes of the corridor. He quietly stepped into the hallway as the Feltons disappeared down the staircase.

Back at the door marked Nineteen, Jay retrieved a slim metal rod from his pocket and knelt before the keyhole. After a few swift twists of his wrist, the lock released. Stepping inside, he closed the door behind him. The cabin was almost identical to his own, except, being a two-bedroom suite, it connected to a shared sitting room and bath.

Jay thought it unlikely Felton kept the tracers, or anything else of value, here. Most likely, they were stowed in the purser's safe, but it was worth checking. Breaking into a cabin was much simpler than breaking into a well-guarded safe.

Jay sifted through a stack of papers on the desk, scanning the text for any reference to the chemical composition of the tracer's pyrotechnic charge. Finding nothing of interest, he turned his attention to the armoire. Something in the bottom left-hand corner wedged behind the row of hanging clothes caught his attention. Reaching down, he extracted a small but heavy wooden chest.

He attempted to lift the lid, but it was locked. He reached into his pocket for the pick but froze at the sound of voices outside the cabin door. It was the Feltons. One of them was inserting a key into the lock. He shoved the chest back into the armoire and dashed into the adjacent sitting room.

He closed the door and crept toward the other bedroom. Finding it locked, he slid into the bathroom and stepped behind the open door, not daring to breathe. Jay pressed the bathroom door shut as the door to the sitting room swung open with a loud creak.

If they discovered him here now, it was all over. He'd spend the rest of the voyage locked in the hold. And then what? His heart beat faster and faster like the chug of an accelerating train.

"Did you leave them in the bath?" Millie Felton was right on the other side of the door.

He clapped a hand over his mouth and watched in horror as the door opened a crack.

"Found them," Stanley Felton's deep voice called from the other room.

The door clicked shut. Jay pressed his ear against it, absorbing the muted thud of retreating footsteps. When they were gone, he doubled over, gasping for air. As soon as his breathing normalized, he slipped out of the room. He'd look in the chest tomorrow.

He charged down the empty corridor. If he hurried, maybe he wouldn't be the last passenger to arrive at dinner. He exited the narrow hallway and hastened down the deck.

By the time he reached the wide oak staircase leading to the first-class dining room, the lobby was empty. Dinner was in full swing. The notes of a violin concerto drifted up the stairs along with the clamor of conversation and clinking of cutlery.

All of a sudden, he was seized with panic. What had he been thinking? Why had he asked to be seated with the Feltons? How was he supposed to have a polite conversation with the people who, minutes ago, almost caught him hiding in their bathroom?

He took a deep breath and pushed back his shoulders. He was Teddy Belmont. He was a respectable young man. No one in this dining room, including the Feltons, had any reason to suspect he was up to anything. He descended the stairs.

Adopting what he hoped was a look of seasoned indifference, he took in the magnificence of the crowded room. With its crystal chandeliers, carved oak panels, and marble statues, it looked more like a palace ballroom than the dining room of a ship. In the center of the high ceiling was a large dome comprised of milky glass panels. Illuminated by a string of bulbs encircling its base, it glowed like a giant pearl. Below, the entire room twinkled as light bounced from metal to glass.

There must have been ten stewards per passenger, each bowing courteously while enunciating "sir" in their refined British accents. Jay was led to a circular table set for six. The steward gestured to the first of the two empty chairs, pulling it out for him.

Once seated, Jay turned to the woman on his left—Millie, he assumed. "Teddy Belmont," he said, extending a hand. "Pleased to make your acquaintance."

"Likewise. I'm Millie Felton." She had kind eyes and a smile to match. After shaking Jay's hand, she dutifully introduced him to the rest of the table.

The deep lines on Stanley Felton's thin face were etched into a permanent grimace. He grunted in greeting. To his right sat Lillian Brightman, an older woman with a long neck and large wide-set eyes that caused her to somewhat resemble an ostrich. Her husband, Captain Cecil Brightman, was dressed in the dark blue officer's uniform of the Royal Navy.

"Do you live in New York, Mr. Belmont?" Mrs. Brightman asked.

"Please, call me Teddy," he said, remembering to smile. "I'm from California—San Francisco to be exact. Were you and Captain Brightman vacationing in America?"

"We lived in Washington for the past two years. Cecil was stationed there as Britain's naval attaché."

"How fascinating." Jay, of course, already knew this information. Captain Brightman was the reason Felton was on this ship. Finishing up what had otherwise been an uneventful posting, he was intent on procuring ACC's tracer technology for the British Navy.

"Yes, indeed. But we're both looking forward to Cecil's retirement."

"Quite true," Captain Brightman said, brandishing his fork with enthusiasm. "Let us hope the Kaiser remains satisfied beating his war drum in Serbia, and England isn't drawn into the fight." Noticing Mrs. Brightman's disapproving stare, he lowered the utensil.

"That isn't likely?" Millie asked. "Is it?"

"One never knows," Brightman said, stroking his chin. "Germany's naval expansion certainly suggests they're preparing for war."

Jay considered this. If war were to break out in Europe, that would make the tracers even more valuable. Did Martin Winter think war probable? Was that why he'd hired Jay to steal the tracers?

When Jay had asked Cody's friend Martin Winter for a job, he'd had no idea this was the sort of thing he'd be asked to do. For as long as Jay had known Winter, he'd worked in the mining industry—first, at a nickel mine in French New Caledonia. After that, Winter had moved to America to manage

Cody's copper operation for a time.

When Jay told Winter he was willing to work underground, he'd meant in a mine. But Winter had taken his words to mean something else entirely. Jay still didn't know who Winter was working for now. This was intentional. It was one of the reasons the job paid so well. If Jay got caught, he was on his own.

"What brings you to England, Teddy?" Mrs. Brightman asked.

Jay smiled. He was prepared for the question. "Why, I plan to visit all the capitals of Europe—Paris, Venice, Rome. I, well . . ." He paused, letting his smile fade. "My parents and I were going to make the trip for my eighteenth birthday. It was all planned, you see." He looked down at the table. "But then they died."

Millie brought a hand up to her chest, regarding Jay with what appeared to be genuine sympathy. "I'm so sorry, Teddy."

"I think it's lovely you're making the trip," Mrs. Brightman said. "You know, Cecil was stationed in Rome. I'd be delighted to write introductions for you."

"Gosh, Mrs. Brightman, that's much too kind."

From that point on, the conversation flowed easily. A team of waiters delivered the first of what was to be a ten-course meal, placing the plates before them in practiced unison. As dinner progressed, Jay found he was actually enjoying himself.

He was so engrossed in conversation he didn't notice the arrival of their final dining companion until Captain Brightman rose to formally greet her. Millie grasped the woman's hand. Apparently, they were old friends. The woman's back was to Jay. But she was striking—her slender, angular frame set off by dark waves of hair pinned up haphazardly.

When she turned, and Millie introduced her friend to Jay,

he stared at her, eyes wide. "Pleased to meet you," he managed to stammer before looking down, fixing his gaze on his plate.

That couldn't be right. He must have misheard. Only—she looked like her. No. He was being absurd. He had been thinking of Cody earlier. And now his mind was playing tricks on him. It couldn't be her. Could it?

With mustered composure, Jay forced himself to look up. He flashed his most charismatic smile and met the gaze of their new dining companion. Seated directly across from him was Ella Kaye.

CHAPTER 2

Ella studied the carved panel on the dining room wall—a gold leaf cornucopia overflowing with grapes, wheat, and fat gourds. Why was the décor on ocean liners always so gaudy? There was such a thing as too much gilt. Not everything was improved by painting it gold.

A waiter deftly placed a plate in front of her. She picked up her fork and contemplated taking a bite. But the ship swayed, and a wave of nausea rolled over her.

Ella always suffered seasickness the first day of a voyage. Apparently, she wasn't the only one. The man sitting across from her, Teddy Belmont, was as white as the tablecloth. He looked as though he might faint.

Who was Teddy Belmont? She couldn't recall Millie ever mentioning him. Was he a family friend? Millie came from the sort of patrician family that considered all wealthy individuals of a certain background family friends. Not that Millie was an elitist herself. Ella wouldn't be friends with her if she were.

Retiring her fork, Ella took a sip of champagne. She had read somewhere that champagne helped an upset stomach—something about the effect of carbonic acid. Cody had sworn whiskey and soda crackers did the trick. Ella didn't care for whiskey but found the crackers helpful. She had some with her now in her handbag, but it would be impolite to take one out and eat it at the table.

The bubbles in her glass ascended in shifting diagonal flurries with the rocking of the ship. Her stomach turned. Why shouldn't she take out a cracker? She wasn't dining with royalty. No one else would mind, except perhaps Millie's father, and she couldn't care less what he thought.

When convincing Ella to come to London with her to cover the Women's Suffrage Conference, Millie had conveniently failed to mention her father would be on the ship. Unlike Millie, he was decidedly a snob. The first time Ella visited the Feltons' enormous Massachusetts estate he'd been appalled to learn Millie's new friend was enrolled at their prestigious academy by way of a charity scholarship. To this day, he made no effort to conceal the fact he disapproved of Ella's unimpressive lineage.

Felton was yelling at one of the waiters, pointing a long finger at a minuscule piece of bone next to his filet of sole. "I could have choked to death," he exclaimed, waving away the waiter and the offending plate.

Had Felton ever made it through a meal without sending something back to the kitchen? She doubted it.

"The service on this ship is abominable," Felton said with a grimace. "Wouldn't you agree, Captain Brightman?"

"Well, I'm not sure—" But before he had the chance to say what he was unsure of, Felton started in again.

Mrs. Brightman turned to Ella in an obvious attempt to extricate herself from the conversation. She opened her mouth to speak, but having nothing prepared, it remained ajar.

"You're a journalist," she said finally.

"That's right."

"For the *New York World*?"

Ella hesitated. She thought everyone on the planet knew

she'd been fired from the *World*. The fiasco had been front-page news, after all.

"Ella's a freelance journalist now," Millie said. "Which is wonderful. Ella can write about whatever she wants."

That part was true. Working as a freelance journalist meant Ella could write about anything she damn well pleased. But it was far from wonderful.

Ella forced a smile. "I'm really enjoying the freedom."

She hated the freedom. She missed the challenge of difficult assignments and multiple deadlines. In the past two years she had only written a handful of freelance articles, none of them very good. The writing was flat and static, like most of her life now.

Because she'd inherited millions of dollars, people assumed her life was one big extravagant celebration, but that was far from the truth. She had barely touched the money. Considering the way things had ended with Cody, something about it felt wrong. She didn't like to think about it too much.

She could do anything she wanted now. But it felt like she'd already done everything worth doing. She'd visited the Metropolitan Museum so often, she could give a tour blindfolded. And she'd attended more plays and performances this past year than an usher at the Globe.

She wasn't complaining. She was perfectly fine. Only, she missed the excitement of her old life. She used to do all sorts of crazy things in the name of journalism. She had gone undercover, assuming a false identity to expose the horrendous working conditions in factories. She had broken a world record by racing around the globe in seventy days. And those outrageous stunts had made her famous.

A few years ago, her name used to grace the front page practically every day. But the spotlight of fame that had once followed her everywhere had since dimmed. When Millie asked Ella to cover the Women's Suffrage Conference in London, it wasn't because she was a sought-after journalist. The invitation was that of a charitable friend.

"Are you attending the suffrage conference as well, Mrs. Brightman?" Ella asked.

"Good heavens, no." She crinkled her nose, then turned to Millie. "No offense, dear. But I'm afraid I don't see the point. You're already in a very fortunate position. It isn't as though having the right to vote would improve your circumstances."

"I am fortunate, and I'm thankful for that." Millie smiled patiently. "But I'm not content to sit back and have all my decisions made for me. I believe there are some things we must fight for in this life. The right to vote is one of them."

Ella could never decide if Millie's idealism was astutely sage or incredibly naïve. The ship rocked, and abandoning her prior decorum, Ella slipped a soda cracker out of her bag and placed it in her mouth. She chewed slowly, looking across the table with interest at Teddy Belmont. He had barely spoken a word the entire meal.

Aside from that terrible mustache, he was rather handsome. Ella had noticed him earlier on the promenade deck. She'd spent the entire afternoon in her deck chair hoping, to no avail, the fresh air might alleviate her nausea. He'd passed her more than once. She recalled thinking he must have recently purchased a new watch, as he kept removing it from his pocket to admire it.

She hadn't noticed him consult the watch during dinner, but if he did, she resolved to admire it. He could use a compliment. He looked miserable.

Ella studied his face. Something about it was vaguely familiar. "Mr. Belmont—"

"Please," he stammered, "call me Teddy."

"Teddy," she said, trying out the name. "Have we met before?"

His mouth fell open. "Not that I recall." He met her gaze for a second, then looked away.

She should really stop staring at him, but the longer she did, the more certain she felt she had seen him before today. Of course, that didn't mean they'd ever been introduced. She might have passed him on a sidewalk in New York or shared a streetcar with him one afternoon. That was probably all it was.

There was a loud knock on Ella's cabin door. The cabin stewardess announced herself and entered carrying a tray. The scent of freshly brewed coffee and warm scones filled the room.

When traveling, Ella always took breakfast in her cabin. The thought of waking early to dress and join others for a morning meal didn't appeal to her in the least. She liked to begin her day by reading the news and preferred to do so without interruption. After pouring herself a cup of coffee, she set to doing just that.

The White Star Line's *Daily News* was slight in comparison to any real newspaper. It usually included a list of onboard events, advertisements, and an assortment of international news collected over the wireless the previous night. Today's paper, however, didn't contain a single news article. Aside from a passenger list, it was entirely comprised of advertisements for hotels and restaurants in London.

Ella tossed aside the paper with an exasperated shake of the head. She bit into a scone. Considering the exorbitant cost of the passage, it was truly shameful to print a paper for the sole purpose of generating advertisement revenue. And she had no intention of spending the next week oblivious to what was going on in the world. She would speak to the captain about this, immediately.

Ella made her way down the deck. Pressing through the strong, humid breeze, she kept a hand atop her hat, lest it take flight. Most of the other passengers were still in the dining room at breakfast. She was therefore surprised when a flushed and somewhat flustered Millie came rushing toward her.

"Did you hear the news?" Millie coaxed a windblown coil of hair back into place, fastening it with a pin.

Ella shook her head. She hadn't been made aware of any news. That was why she was on her way to speak to the captain.

Millie glanced around, as though checking to make sure she wouldn't be overheard. "Germany declared war on Russia."

This didn't come as a complete surprise. The papers back home had been running headlines such as "War in Europe?" for weeks, ever since the assassination of Archduke whatever-his-name-was. But nothing had been certain. Headlines were often exaggerated to sell more papers.

"You're sure?"

Millie gave a solemn nod.

Now, the absence of news in the ship's paper made sense. There were a number of German and Russian names on the passenger list. By withholding news of war, Captain Smith was probably hoping to avoid battle lines being drawn on the ship.

"How do you know?" Ella didn't doubt her friend. Millie wasn't the type to go around spreading unfounded rumors. But Ella was usually the first to learn of things like this.

"Captain Brightman told Father. He received a telegram this morning. And there's more." Millie paused until a group of passengers walked past them. "France is mobilizing its troops."

Ella tried to conceal her excitement. She wasn't happy Europe was at war—she wasn't a monster. But wars needed war correspondents, and Ella was already on her way to Europe. Time was of the essence when reporting on war. Aside from any journalists already stationed abroad, she'd be one of the first American reporters there.

She'd always dreamed of being a war correspondent. Every reporter did, but few got the opportunity. And of those few, hardly any were women.

"What about England?" Ella asked, keeping her face neutral.

"They're still hoping for peace." Millie sighed. "But according to Captain Brightman, if the Germans violate Belgian neutrality, they'll have no choice but to intervene."

Ella attempted to recall the details of Belgian neutrality. She had always had an imperfect understanding of European politics. The boarding school Millie and she had attended had been more interested in teaching the proper wording of formal invitations than anything rooted in academia. Other than French, she wasn't sure she had learned much of anything there.

"What about the suffrage conference?" It was an important conference, but if war broke out, Ella doubted anyone would cross battle lines to get there.

"It's still on, as of now, but . . ." Disappointment crept over Millie's face.

"All we can do is hope for the best." She gave Millie's hand a squeeze. "I'm going to see if I can find out anything else."

As she walked away, Ella forced herself to take slow, measured steps. As soon as she was out of Millie's sight, her gait quickened. She wished she weren't wearing a hobble skirt.

The narrow, ankle-length hem was significantly impeding her stride, making her quick, short steps look comical.

This was her chance to revive her career. She needed to send a telegram to the *World* to let them know she was on her way to Europe and ready to go wherever the fighting was. Over a year had passed since her dispute with the editor. He couldn't still be mad at her. Even if he was, he'd be a fool not to rehire her now. She could see her name on the front page now: Ella Kaye, War Correspondent.

She couldn't get to the wireless fast enough. Cursing, she stopped and knelt. She grasped the fabric at the bottom of the skirt on each side of the seam and pulled with all her strength.

Standing, she surveyed her work. She had ripped a ragged five-inch slit up the left side of the skirt. An elegant alteration it was not. But she was too elated to care. She was buoyant with an enthusiasm she hadn't felt in years.

Racing down the deck, she was so caught up in her new-found purpose she didn't notice the man standing directly in her path. When she looked up, he was staring at her, eyes wide with terror, fixed in place like a statue. It was the man from their table last night—Teddy Belmont. The instant before they collided, he leaped to the side.

All of a sudden, she was overcome with a strange sense of déjà vu. Something about him was so familiar. But she brushed the thought aside. It didn't matter. Europe was at war.

CHAPTER 3

Jay sat on the edge of the small bed in his cabin, trying not to think about Ella Kaye. Outside, a steady stream of passengers made their way down the deck. Snippets of garbled conversation seeped through the porthole into his room.

He had dreaded leaving his cabin this morning. He'd been certain that, after a night to sleep on it, Ella would realize who he was. Then, much to his surprise and relief, Ella had been at neither breakfast nor luncheon. Aside from their brief encounter on the deck midmorning, he hadn't seen her all day. She would, however, most certainly be at dinner, and the nervous anticipation from earlier had returned with gusto.

When she'd charged down the deck straight at him, for one terrifying instant he'd been certain Ella recognized him. But then she'd rushed past him, entirely disinterested. Now he didn't know what to think.

Cody had introduced them once, but that had been years ago. After that, Jay had only seen her in passing. She hadn't stepped foot on the *Tuolomee* since her first voyage. She'd claimed that, even moored, it made her seasick.

To Ella, Jay had been just another faceless member of Cody's crew. Or at least, that was what he wanted to believe. But if that was the case, why had she cut him out of Cody's will?

Jay crossed to the window and pulled back the curtain. The deck was empty now. He stared out at the grey water.

How did Ella know the Feltons? Had Cody known the Feltons? Did Winter? Was that how Winter knew about the tracers? Trying to make sense of it all made his head spin. He felt like he'd just taken a turn on one of those whirly rides on Coney Island.

The *Tuolomee* had been docked in Boston the night Cody died. They were there because a party was being thrown in Ella's honor. Had the Feltons attended the party?

Jay hadn't been invited. He'd spent the evening with Winter, who was in Boston to see Cody about business. A sailing enthusiast like Cody, Winter had sailed his gaff-rigged sloop all the way from Michigan by himself. Unless you were Joshua Slocum, a voyage like that was no easy feat. But, thanks to his time spent in the German Navy, Winter was a prodigious sailor.

It had been Jay's first time in Boston. He'd spent the week exploring the city. He'd even made it out to Fenway Park and watched the Red Sox play the Tigers. It was a swell week . . . well, until it wasn't.

The night Cody died, Jay and Winter dined at one of the seafood joints along the harbor. It wasn't so much a restaurant as a slew of outdoor tables with a kitchen housed in a shack. But the oysters were fresh, the beer cold, and the atmosphere festive.

By the time Jay stumbled back to the *Tuolomee* later that night, he was more than a little drunk. A light was on in Cody's cabin. At the time, Jay didn't think much of it. He assumed Cody had gotten drunk and passed out. It happened often enough.

But when Jay entered the cabin to extinguish the lamp, he didn't find Cody sleeping off a bender. Cody was dead. He lay on his side on the floor, his glossy eyes fixed on some indefinite point. His arm was outstretched, fingers gnarled, as if grasping for a tether to the living world.

The pain of his loss was duller now. It was no longer the hollowing punch to the gut Jay had experienced that night and in the weeks following. But Jay still missed his old friend. He always would. He turned away from the window.

Once inside Felton's cabin, Jay went straight to the wardrobe and removed the wooden box from the lower shelf. In a silver cigarette case in his vest pocket were half a dozen standard .303 cartridges, which he planned to swap for six tracers. The markings differed, but hopefully Felton wouldn't closely examine the bullets until they reached London. If so, by the time he realized the tracers were missing, Jay would be safely aboard a ship, making his way back to New York.

He removed a small crescent-shaped pick from his pocket and carefully inserted it into the lock. After a few slight movements the box clicked open. He lifted the lid and frowned.

Inside was an assortment of neatly arranged cuff links, each pair carefully nestled in velvet folds. Jay ran a finger over one of the rows. There was even a pair made out of bullets. He wondered how much a collection like this was worth. Not that he planned to steal them. He was only here for the tracers.

He performed a thorough search of the cabin but found neither the tracers nor the drawings detailing their design. They were probably in a deposit box in the purser's office. If they were in one of Felton's trunks in storage, that was a whole other matter. Either way, he would have to wait until most of the ship was asleep before attempting anything further.

After making sure everything was back in place, Jay slipped out of Felton's room. As he closed the cabin door, a figure stepped into the hallway. He yanked his hand up from the handle and knocked on the door. Then he took a step back, pretending to wait for someone to answer the door.

When Jay turned to nod in greeting to the approaching passenger, his stomach dropped. It was Ella Kaye. Had she seen him exit the room?

He manipulated his mouth into a smile. "Good evening."

"If you're looking for Felton, he's already at dinner." She examined him with narrowed eyes.

Jay cleared his throat and smoothed his jacket, trying to think. He took out his watch and pretended to note the time. "Why, I suppose he is. It's rather late, isn't it?"

Ella tilted her head, considering him. "Remind me again, Teddy. How do you know the Feltons?"

"I don't. I mean, I met them on the ship." He tugged at his shirt collar. "Millie was on my way—her cabin was, I mean. I thought I might escort her to dinner." He wanted to turn and sprint down the hall. Instead, maintaining his smile, he offered his arm. "May I escort you, instead?"

As they walked down the empty corridor, Jay kept his eyes trained straight ahead, while Ella, disregarding one of the cardinal rules of etiquette, fixed her gaze on Jay's face. Beads of sweat pooled on his brow.

"You don't think Millie's too old for you?" she finally said.

His shoulders relaxed, and an indisputable smile extended across his face. "Why, not at all."

If it was merely his age she was considering, Ella could stare at him all she liked. If she was investigating the nobility of his intentions, he welcomed the inquisition. And if pretending to pursue Millie diverted any other suspicions Ella might have, then Jay would do just that.

He spent most of the next two days with Millie. In that time, they formed something of a friendship. From the start,

Millie had openly dismissed the notion Jay might be pursuing her romantically. This was fine by Jay. He didn't need to start a love affair with the daughter of the man he planned to rob. The situation was already complicated enough.

It was late morning the fourth day of the voyage. The day was warm and beautiful. The sun sparkling on the water seemed more luminous than it had ever been. It was as if the universe had shifted, and now everything was a shade more agreeable. Did the world always look this lovely when you were rich and carefree?

Jay and Millie were playing deck quoits with a pair of slightly inebriated Harvard men. They took turns tossing rings of rope at a short pole. Millie was surprisingly good at the game. Jay got the hang of it, soon enough. And by the third round, they were clobbering their opponents.

After Teddy Belmont let it slip that he was a Stanford man, the game transformed into a spirited collegiate rivalry. Jay didn't know much of anything about Stanford. But he knew it sounded a hell of a lot more impressive than his actual college experience—two miserable weeks at Saint Olaf College in Minnesota. Luckily, they only made vague inquiries as to his time there.

Now that he didn't have to worry about Ella, Jay was thoroughly enjoying his time as Teddy Belmont.

"Why, sure. California's great," he said. "Of course, I spend most of my time on my yacht. She's a real beauty. The Dakota's her name."

He was getting good at keeping up the act. He only stumbled once, when the conversation turned to some society ball he'd never heard of. But he managed to change the subject.

He didn't want this to end. What if it didn't have to end? What if he didn't go back to New York? The only thing waiting for him back there was the thousands of dollars' worth of debt he owed the Eastman gang.

That was the whole reason he'd taken this job. There was no such thing as not paying back the Eastman gang. If you couldn't come up with the money, you paid with your life.

But what if instead of paying them back, he used the money to start a new life abroad? The Eastman gang's reach didn't extend to Europe. Even if it did, that was Jay Gatsby's problem. Teddy Belmont didn't owe over ten thousand dollars to murderous thugs.

Even if he didn't manage to steal the tracers, *especially* if he didn't, he could stay in Europe and start a new life as Teddy Belmont. For a few glorious minutes Jay was drunk with possibility. But he sobered quickly upon hearing Captain Brightman's news.

There was a grim expression on the naval captain's usually cheerful face when he informed them the unthinkable had happened. All of Europe was at war. In less than a week, the conflict between Austria and Serbia had expanded to include most of the Continent. England, France, and Russia had sided with Serbia, Germany with Austria-Hungary.

Jay walked to lunch in silence, shoulders slumped, his ego deflated. Now that Europe was at war, he couldn't stay abroad. Starting a new life in a war zone wasn't very appealing.

Dozens of crew members rushed about the deck shuttering portholes and closing the watertight doors. There was barely a cloud in the sky. Were they sailing into inclement weather? Or were these safeguards related to the war?

Whatever the pretext, Jay needed to act fast. The ship was clearly approaching some sort of danger. If the captain implemented increased security measures, stealing the tracers would be even more difficult.

He was overcome with overwhelming impatience. He couldn't do anything about the tracers until later tonight. He had the sudden urge to race down the deck, as though doing so might coax time to travel faster, turning day into night. Ignoring the impulse, he maintained a slow, steady gait. He would wait until after dinner when most of the ship was asleep. Then, he would begin.

CHAPTER 4

Ella stood alone on the deck as the ship churned through the dark waters of the Atlantic. A long coat was draped over her nightgown. But there was a chill in the air, and a sharp gust of wind caused her to shiver. She gazed up at the bright stars blanketing the expansive night sky. And, for lack of anything better to do, she tried to locate the few constellations she knew.

She couldn't sleep but dared not use the lamp in her cabin to read. All the lights, including those which usually illuminated the deck, had been extinguished by the captain's orders. A lit ship might as well be a flashing beacon notifying German cruisers of their position.

With the news of England's entrance into war, there had arrived a palpable excitement on the ship—the nervous, giddy anticipation that often serves as a prelude to imminent calamity. And in the dim light of the tarp-covered dome, the dining room had become more intimate, lending a conspiratorial nature to the conversation. At the start of dinner, everyone spoke in hushed voices, as though anything above a whisper might also inform the Germans of the ship's position. But by the third course, caution cast aside, the crowded room reverberated with animated chatter.

Even Felton displayed uncharacteristic enthusiasm, ordering two bottles of champagne for the table. Ella supposed war was cause for celebration if you owned a munitions factory. He stood to make a fortune.

Copper would be in high demand as well. It was used to make all sorts of armaments. But the copper extracted from the Platacobre mines wouldn't serve that purpose. Cody wouldn't have wanted that, and when she'd inherited Platacobre she'd vowed to uphold Cody's wishes.

In his older years, his fortune well secured, Cody had decided he didn't want his copper used to make things that killed people. Given the high demand for copper, the restriction hadn't made much, if any, difference in the mine's profits. There were plenty of other uses for the copper mined at Platacobre.

Ella was about to return to her cabin when, further down the deck, the vague shape of a man walking toward her caught her eye. She stepped back from the rail, obscuring herself in darkness.

Earlier that day, the captain had announced a strict 11 p.m. curfew. Among other reasons, he didn't want passengers injuring themselves on the now unlit ship. She wouldn't be in any real trouble for violating the curfew, but she preferred to avoid being escorted back to her cabin by a reprimanding steward.

As the figure drew closer, she strained to make out a uniform, but the darkness precluded this. The man kept glancing over his shoulder, as though to make sure he wasn't being followed. He was probably a fellow passenger. Still, she couldn't be sure. As the figure approached, she pressed her back against the wall and held her breath.

As the man passed in front of her, she almost gasped. It was Teddy Belmont. What was he doing sneaking around the ship at this hour? He hurried past her before ducking into a stairwell. What had he been doing in the lobby this late at night? And why did something about him still seem so familiar?

On her way to lunch the following day, Ella found Millie sitting in a deck chair reading. She sat in the empty chair beside her friend and leaned over to examine the title of the book. It was *O Pioneers!* by Willa Cather. Ella wrinkled her nose.

"It's actually quite good," Millie said, closing the book. "You forget parts of America are practically wilderness. Teddy was telling me about his train ride from San Francisco. All the plains and prairies—"

"You've certainly been spending a lot of time with him."

Millie shrugged. "He doesn't know anyone else on the ship."

"Do you really think that story about his parents is true?" Ella wasn't sure she bought it. It was a rather personal detail to share with strangers. Ella had recently lost someone dear to her as well. You didn't see her blabbing about it all over the ship.

"Of course it's true. Why would anyone make that up?"

"I don't know. There's just something off about him, don't you think?"

"No, not really."

"Well, listen to this." Ella lowered her voice, leaning in. "I saw him sneaking around the deck late last night."

"What were you doing on the deck late last night?"

"I was just standing there. I couldn't sleep. He was slinking around the ship like a thief in the night."

Millie raised an eyebrow. "Perhaps he's Arsène Lupin."

"Who?"

"Arsène Lupin, the gentleman burglar." Millie grinned.

"He's a character in a book. I'm joking."

"Well, I'm not. Teddy Belmont was up to something. I'm sure of it."

As she walked back to her cabin after lunch, a thought crossed Ella's mind. What if Teddy had been sneaking out of Millie's cabin late last night? Was that why Millie had defended him? No. Millie wouldn't so much as consider sneaking a man into her cabin with her father right next door. Nor would Millie consider embarking on an affair with a man ten years her junior.

Still, Millie was in exceedingly high spirits, considering she had just learned the women's suffrage conference she'd spent months organizing was cancelled. And during lunch she had barely glanced at Ella. She'd been too busy smiling at Teddy and laughing at his stories, which, in Ella's opinion, hadn't been at all interesting. And was it her imagination, or had Millie been taking more care with her appearance these past few days?

Millie was wonderful. But why was a handsome, well-off man in his early twenties pursuing her? She was practically a spinster. What if he was some sort of confidence man? Ocean liners were allegedly full of them—so much so that a sign outside the smoking lounge warned passengers of card sharps. What if Teddy Belmont had some sinister ulterior motive? She didn't want Millie getting hurt.

Who was Teddy Belmont? And what did he want with her friend? If Ella were in New York, all it would take was a few phone calls to learn everything she needed to know about the man. Journalists made inquiries like that every day.

There wasn't much she could do at sea. But she could send a telegram to her attorney and have him arrange for a background check on Teddy Belmont. And so, she decided to do just that—for Millie's sake.

The response from her attorney arrived shortly after eleven o'clock the following morning. After asking the cabin stewardess to bring her a fresh pot of coffee, Ella settled at the small table in her room and opened the thin envelope. The telegram read:

> *Hired reputable detective to investigate Teddy Belmont. No criminal records. No address found in San Francisco. Name not listed in directory. Investigation ongoing.*
> *—S.B. Whitebait, Esq.*

Ella wasn't sure what to make of this. If, as her attorney stated, this was a reputable detective, it seemed he would have found something on Teddy Belmont. Even if he wasn't listed in the directory, there had to be some record of his existence. Unless, of course, Teddy Belmont wasn't who he said he was.

Perhaps he'd claimed to live in San Francisco when really, he was from some small town in Northern California that no one had ever heard of. That was innocent enough. Ella herself told people she'd been born in Pittsburgh, rather than the unrecognizable town of Parker.

If Teddy Belmont had lived in San Francisco under another name, that was more troubling. There were all sorts of depraved reasons a person might conceal or change their identity. But before she had a chance to ponder which might apply to him, she was interrupted by a knock at the door.

The stewardess entered, placing the silver tray of coffee on the table. After pouring a cup for Ella, she reached into her apron pocket and produced a second telegram. Perhaps the detective had discovered something after all.

But the telegram wasn't from her attorney. It was from the

New York World. She felt a flutter of excitement and sat up straighter. This was it. She was going to be a war correspondent. But upon reading the note, her smile faded.

Received your offer to act as war correspondent.
We respectfully decline.

She stared at the slip of paper until the words began to blur. Then she clenched it in her fist, crushing it into a tight ball.

When she'd been fired from the *World* she'd been livid. She'd been filled with so much rage she'd wanted to smash something. She felt none of that now. Her hand went limp. The crumpled telegram dropped onto the table.

She stared at her distorted reflection in the silver coffee pot. She reached to pour herself a cup. Then, changing her mind, she shoved both telegrams in her handbag and walked out of her cabin. A few minutes later, she was in the smoking lounge.

She usually avoided this portion of the ship, finding the thick, lurking clouds of smoke oppressive. She couldn't recall ever having visited the smoking lounge of her own accord and certainly never alone. The room, eternally dimmer than other portions of the ship, was even darker today—its skylights cloaked in canvas. Her eyes finally adjusted to the low light. Captain Brightman and Felton sat at a banquet table in the starboard corner. They clicked their glasses together, some grim transaction now complete.

The center of the room was thoroughly monopolized by a sextet of raucous youths—the entitled progeny of America's captains of industry. She'd noticed the group on the ship several times before but had thus far avoided close proximity. She wanted nothing to do with that crowd.

They were a younger generation of the students who'd snubbed her in boarding school. At least the girls had been upfront about it. They'd told her she'd never be a part of their social class. She didn't come from the right sort of family.

The boys had lied, pretending none of that mattered. And Ella had foolishly believed one of them. When he was done with her, when he'd discarded her like a piece of trash, only then had he made it clear she wasn't good enough for him.

Years later, when she'd become famous, she'd started receiving invitations to society events. For a time, she'd thought she'd risen in her former classmates' esteem. But nothing had changed. They didn't consider her their equal. They saw her as something of a novelty. She considered the whole lot of them a bunch of undeserving snobs.

She took a small table in the far corner of the lounge. When the steward inquired if he could bring her anything, she asked for a whiskey, straight. As soon as he turned to go, she regretted her choice.

She hated whiskey—the smell, its taste, everything about it, really. Well, at least it would get the job done. She would drink it in honor of the deceased: Cody and her career as a journalist.

The steward returned, placing a crystal tumbler filled with amber liquid atop a small napkin. When she lifted the glass, she was assaulted by the strong scent of burnt caramel. But the taste wasn't half as bad as she'd remembered. She took another sip, and let it linger, singeing the back of her throat.

If she wasn't a journalist, what was she? What was she supposed to do with her life? Ella didn't need to work. Cody had left her more than she could possibly spend in a lifetime. But she needed some sort of a purpose, didn't she?

She could run Platacobre. Except that wasn't a possibility either. Shortly before he died, Cody had leased the mine to another company. Ella had absolutely no desire to oversee a mine. But in her current state of self-indulgent defeatism that didn't stop her from lamenting the lost opportunity of doing so.

One of the drunk Americans was playing the upright piano in the back of the room. His body swayed to the rhythm as he pounded out a rag. She glanced around. The lounge had emptied. She was the only remaining patron aside from the troupe of inebriated socialites.

"Another bottle of champagne?" the steward asked the group. They were gathered around their table, as drunk and loud as ever.

"Say, now there's an idea," the man at the table wearing glasses replied. He had broad shoulders, an authoritative voice, and a somewhat incongruous mess of wavy hair atop his head.

When he caught Ella staring at him, he flashed her a boyish grin before she could look away. Now, he was striding toward her. She closed her eyes, willing him to go away. The last thing she wanted right now was company. She particularly didn't want the company of an intoxicated fraternity member.

As he got closer, she realized he was older than the rest of the group. He possessed a sort of youthful charm, but his college days were far behind him. He looked about the same age as she was.

"Say," he said, sliding up to her table, "you're Ella Kaye, aren't you?" He was handsome. But that didn't change the fact she wanted to be left alone.

"Sorry, I'm afraid you're mistaken."

"Sure, you are." He adjusted his gold-rimmed spectacles, smiling at her.

It was a nice smile. But it was the kind of smile that, on someone like him, she didn't trust. She wished he would leave.

She wanted to wallow in self-pity and mourn the loss of her livelihood unperturbed.

"You're Ella Kaye," he said again.

"Afraid not. My name is Angela." It was a stupid lie. Her name was printed on the passenger list. He'd probably seen it. And who the hell was Angela? Where had that name come from?

"Angela, is it? Huh." He leaned in, scrutinizing her. "Angela what?"

"Whis—" She was about to say whiskey because she was staring at the glass in front her, but thinking the lie too obvious, she stopped herself. "Whiskers."

His eyebrows quirked. "Your name is Angela Whiskers?"

"It is." She wished she had gone with Whiskey. Angela Whiskers sounded ridiculous.

"Well, Miss Whiskers." He bit his lip. "Would you like to join us?"

"No, thank you."

"You sure? You look like you could use a friend."

When he finally left, she downed the rest of her whiskey and ordered a third hoping, to obliterate the memory of calling herself Angela Whiskers. An hour later, she was still sitting alone at the small table, eating soda crackers from her purse, contemplating various miserable existences.

At some point the door to the lounge swung open, and a familiar figure entered the room. Ella squinted in the dim light. It was Millie. As she approached the table, Ella brushed at the layer of crumbs on her skirt.

"When Father said you were in here, I didn't believe him." Millie took the seat across the from her. She picked up the glass of whiskey, held it to her nose and made a face. "Is everything all right?"

"Never better," Ella slurred. "Just got some news, well . . ."

Rather than explain it, because that seemed like a lot of work, Ella reached in her bag and sifted through its contents for the telegram from the *World.* She extracted the crumpled paper and handed it to Millie.

As Millie read the telegram, her brow furrowed. Realizing her error too late, Ella lunged across the table. But Millie leaned back, holding the paper just out of her reach, an incredulous look on her face. In her stupor, she had passed Millie the telegram from her attorney.

"Have you lost your mind?" Millie waved the offending telegram. "Why would you investigate Teddy?"

"There's something off about him. And, well, look!" She pointed a finger at the telegram. "I wasn't wrong. He's not who he says he is." She was having trouble organizing her thoughts, everything jumbled from the whiskey. "He's a sort of confidence man, I think. That's why he won't leave you alone, because he wants your money."

Millie crossed her arms. "So, you're saying the only reason someone would want to spend time with me is because they're after my money?"

"No. That's not—"

"What, then?" Millie insisted. "Do you just assume everyone is potentially guilty of a crime and needs to be investigated?"

"No. What does that even mean?"

"Don't think I don't know what you told the police when Cody died."

"What are you talking about?"

"When they asked you if Cody had any enemies, you gave them my father's name."

"Oh, that." She actually hadn't thought Millie knew. In retrospect, she probably shouldn't have given them his name. Enemy was probably too strong a word. "I was just answering their questions."

"Well, based on your answers, my father became a suspect. He had to hire a criminal attorney."

"I didn't say I thought he had anything to do with it—"

"You also told them I hated Cody!" Millie was becoming hysterical.

"So, what if I did? It was true." Ella had forgotten about telling the police that. It was starting to make more sense why Millie hadn't spoken to her much after the funeral.

"I thought he was too old for you, but I didn't hate him. Why would you tell the police that?" Millie switched to a loud, angry whisper. "Just so you know, I didn't say a word to them about what happened between *you* and Cody that night."

"I know you didn't." She straightened in her chair, slightly sobered. "I'm sorry about all of that. I am." She was. "And this"—she gestured to the telegram still in Millie's hand—"I was just trying to help."

"Well, don't." Rising, Millie tossed the telegram onto the table and stalked out of the lounge.

When Ella emerged from the room a few minutes later, the bright sun was blinding. She wanted nothing more than to go to her cabin and lie down. Unfortunately, in her disoriented state, she couldn't remember where it was. She stumbled toward the portion of the deck that was canvased in. At least there, out of the sun, she would be able to see.

She was about ten yards from the enclosure when a huge gust of wind lifted a portion of unsecured tarp. One of the lines had come untied. The canvas billowed like a parachute. A deckhand hurried forward and reached up, grabbing the loose rope. He struggled, attempting to pull it down.

One of the passengers, a young man, rushed to his aid. While the deckhand held the canvas down with his weight, the passenger knelt and adeptly secured the line, tying an impressive maritime knot.

As Ella watched this somewhat blurred sequence of events, an odd feeling crept over her. It was as though she were watching an actor perform a scene for the second time. She felt sure she had seen this same man tie a rope like this before. Not here, but on Cody's yacht.

She walked toward the man, trying to remember his name. Yes, she knew this man. She knew his name but couldn't quite grasp it—her whiskey-addled mind betraying her.

Then suddenly he turned to face her, and for a brief second, she doubted herself entirely. She was confused. She was drunk. Then everything clicked into place, and perfect clarity descended upon her.

She was right. Teddy Belmont was not who he said he was. Teddy Belmont had worked for Cody.

How had she not recognized him sooner? His hair and clothes were different, but it was him. She'd only sailed on the *Tuolomee* once. It had been a miserable trip; she'd been seasick the entire week. But she'd seen him on Cody's yacht from the dock on multiple occasions.

His name was Jay. Yes, that was it. How could she have forgotten? Cody was always talking about him. "Good old Jay" this and "good old Jay" that, and then if Cody was drunk, as was often the case, "Jay, my boy," "Jay, the son I never had." How could she possibly forget Jay Gatsby?

It was him. She was certain of it. But what was he doing here? And why was he pretending to be someone else?

None of it made sense. Was he here because of her? Or was it something else entirely? She needed to clear her head. Then, she was going to find out.

CHAPTER 5

Jay paced around his cabin. It was the final night of the voyage. Assuming they weren't captured by the Germans, the *Oceanic* would reach England the following morning. Tonight was his last chance to steal the tracers.

Due to the threat of German cruisers, a strict passenger curfew was in effect. This was not merely a perfunctory suggestion. It was an order. Jay had intended to break into the purser's office late last night. But he'd only gotten as far as the staircase before an alarmed committee of stewards hastily ushered him back to his cabin.

Tonight, having feigned illness and made his excuses to Millie, he planned to steal the tracers during dinner. The purser's office was located on the starboard side of the first-class main lobby by the grand staircase leading into the dining room. Jay didn't want anyone to see him anywhere near the purser's office. So, he waited in his cabin until dinner was well underway. There was always a chance someone might straggle in mid-dinner, having lost track of time in the smoking room. But if that happened, hopefully any such passenger would be too blotto to pay him much mind.

During dinner the lobby was unstaffed. The cabin stewards would be busy performing the night service, tidying the rooms and turning down the beds. The only crew member of concern to Jay was the one who patrolled the upper deck.

The security officer—a nervous-looking young fellow armed with an Ever Ready tubular flashlight—spent most of his patrol in the main lobby. Once or twice an hour he took a lap around the entire deck. As long as Jay made sure his entrance into the purser's office coincided with one of these laps, he would have ample time to break inside.

Once inside, Jay would need to unlock the vault's rotary combination lock. Having observed the assistant purser open it on multiple occasions, he had narrowed down the options for each turn to within a digit or so. This left about ninety possible combinations. Even if he had to go through all of them before finding the correct one, he should be able to unlock the safe within thirty minutes.

After that, he estimated it would take no more than ten minutes to locate Felton's security deposit box. Then all he had to do was switch out the bullets and photograph the tracer designs. If all went as planned, he would be finished in less than an hour and could slip out of the purser's office well before dinner ended.

Shutting the door to his cabin, he strode down the hallway toward the stairs. He was dressed for dinner, having decided formal attire would arouse less suspicion should he encounter any crew or passengers. The bullets he would use to replace the tracers were tucked safely away in the cigarette case in his left breast pocket. The diminutive camera he carried, a Vest Pocket Kodak, was, as its name suggested, in the pocket of his vest.

The expansive main lobby was entirely empty, save for the security guard. Before the man had a chance to notice him, Jay stepped behind a large marble column. Safely out of view, he waited for the guard to begin his lap around the deck.

Music and conversation drifted up the staircase into the

lobby. The final dinner on the ship was supposedly the most extravagant. A part of Jay regretted being unable to attend. He might never again get the opportunity to dine in such splendor. His return ticket to New York was second class, which he appreciated. It was clearly better than steerage, but it would be nothing like this.

The minutes passed slowly. It seemed as though the security guard might never leave the lobby. Finally, after what seemed like an eternity, the guard headed down a corridor in the direction of the smoking lounge.

Jay waited behind the column another minute, then dashed across the empty lobby toward the purser's office. At the rhythmic clatter of footsteps, he paused. He turned, scanning the cavernous room. There was no one there. But someone was ascending the staircase from the dining room.

Jay sprinted across the room and ducked behind another column. The person was in the lobby now. The brisk clack of heels on the marble floor picked up speed. Whoever it was, they were in a hurry.

He waited for the footsteps to pass, then peered around the column. He could only see the back of her, but the woman was Ella Kaye. He let out an exasperated sigh as she entered the stairwell that led to his cabin.

The lobby was empty now—the guard still gone. This might be his only opportunity to get into the purser's office tonight. If he had any sense, he'd be picking the lock of the office door this instant. Instead, he was racing toward stairwell.

Some vague animal instinct propelled him forward. It was as though his mind had no control over his body. She could be going anywhere on the ship, but she was heading to his cabin. He was certain of it.

He paused before reaching the top of the stairs and held

his breath. Up on the landing, Ella turned into the corridor on the port side of the ship—the hallway that led to his cabin.

Earlier that afternoon on the deck, a flash of curious recognition had splashed across Ella's face when he met her gaze. He had tried to push it out of his mind, but there was no denying it now. She had realized who he was.

She was probably heading to his room right now to confront him. What would she do when she realized he wasn't there? Would she notify security? He climbed to the top of the staircase.

Not daring to follow her down the narrow hallway, he peeked around the corner for a quick look. She was knocking on his cabin door. He pressed his back against the wall. Her knocking grew louder and more insistent. He winced.

The knocking ceased. He strained his ears. When he ventured another glance down the hall, his mouth fell open. Ella knelt before the door, removed a pin from her hair, and began to pick the lock of his door.

Should he confront her? He lifted a foot, primed to step into the hallway and rebuke this would-be burglar, but reason prevailed. Nothing in the cabin belonged to him. Every single item confirmed his identity as Teddy Belmont.

It didn't matter if she snooped around his room. As long as she was in there, she wasn't following him. And there still might be enough time to get into the purser's office.

He darted down the stairs, taking them two at a time. But when he raced into the lobby, he stopped short. In the center of the room, staring directly at him, stood the security guard.

For an instant, an all-consuming panic clouded his mind and paralyzed his limbs. Then, yet again, some unknown instinct kicked in. He raced at the guard.

In an unrecognizable, authoritative voice, he said, "You there, guard. There's a thief in my room—cabin C on the promenade deck."

"Someone in your cabin, sir? Are you sure?"

Jay took a deep breath and summoned his best impression of Stanley Felton. "Of course I'm sure! I've got eyes, haven't I? There's some sort of miscreant my room!"

"Are you certain it wasn't a steward, sir? That a criminal should find his way to a first-class cabin is—"

"It was a thief, I tell you! Why are you standing there? Arrest him."

"Oh dear. Well, certainly, sir. If you'll just show me to your cabin—"

"Show you to my cabin? Of course I won't show you to my cabin. I've missed enough of dinner as it is."

"Yes, of course," the guard stammered.

"Well? What are you waiting for? Cabin C on the promenade deck. Go!"

The guard gave an awkward bow, turned and bounded up the stairs. Without hesitation, Jay glided across the lobby to the purser's office. He removed the pick from his pocket, unlocked the door and stepped inside. He switched on the light, and his mind shifted into focus. He knelt and pressed his ear against door of the iron vault. Turning the dial with tender precision, he started work on the lock.

CHAPTER 6

After a few maneuvers with her hairpin, the lock clicked open. Ella opened the door slowly. On the off chance "Teddy Belmont" really was ill and in bed, she didn't want to wake him.

She had intended to confront Gatsby at dinner. She had been planning what she was going to say all afternoon. But her big reveal had been thwarted by his absence. He wasn't sick, as Millie had suggested. He was hiding from her because he knew she had recognized him earlier on the deck. She'd considered telling Millie the truth about him at dinner anyway, but decided against it, given she had no evidence to back up her claim.

Earlier that day, she had attempted to send another telegram to her attorney. She wanted the detective he'd hired to search for proof that Teddy Belmont was Jay Gatsby. But she'd rushed to the telegraph operator, only to find that Captain Smith had ordered the wireless shut down, lest its transmissions give away their location to the Germans.

She'd tried to enjoy herself at dinner. The chef had prepared a celebratory menu for their final evening on board. The orchestra had expanded to include a pianist and a man with a trombone. There was a small dance floor, and couples swayed energetically to the music.

Everyone else in the dining room seemed to be enjoying themselves. But all Ella could think about was Jay Gatsby. Why was he on the ship, traveling under a different name? Was it because of her? Did he blame her for Cody's death? Had Cody told him about their fight?

She sat through the first two courses of the meal—oysters, followed by a chilled potato and leek soup—pushing the food around her plate. She attempted to engage in conversation. But Mrs. Brightman and Millie were discussing a novel by Edith Wharton. Ella hadn't read the book, and it sounded incredibly dull. On the other side of the table, Captain Brightman was reciting an equally tedious monologue about his service during the Boer War.

Unable to stand it any longer, Ella had excused herself from dinner with the intention of confronting Jay Gatsby. She hadn't planned to break into his room. But here she was.

Finding the cabin empty, she stepped inside and locked the door behind her. She needed to work quickly. The bed wasn't turned down, which meant the cabin steward might arrive to service the room at any minute.

Surely there was something in the room—a passport, letters, or some documentation—that proved he was Jay Gatsby. She would find it and show Millie. She would vindicate herself and foil his ploy—whatever it was.

Opening the wardrobe, she pushed aside the hanging suits, but there was nothing behind them. She dug a hand into all the jacket pockets but discovered only lint. She flung open his trunk. Under a pile of *Baedeker* guidebooks for various locales in Europe was a stack of envelopes. She sifted through them one by one. They were letters of introduction, all written on behalf of Teddy Belmont. Digging further in the chest, she grinned as she pulled out a passport. She opened it and cursed. It was in the name of Teddy Belmont.

She took all the folded clothes out of the trunk and tossed them onto the floor. Maybe there was a false bottom.

There wasn't.

There was a knock on the door. She froze. Was it Gatsby? No. He wouldn't knock on his own door. It must be the steward, here to turn down the bed. The knock came again, this time louder.

She cleared her throat, and in as deep a voice as she could muster called out, "Yes? What is it?" She held her breath, waiting for a response.

"Excuse me, sir," a man said.

"You needn't service the room tonight. I've retired for the evening," she bellowed.

"Sir, I'm going to have to ask you to open the door."

"I'm in bed," she called out gruffly. "Please cease disturbing me." She winced at the ridiculous sound of her voice.

"Sir," the man in the hall continued, "I'm the ship security guard. If you do not open the door, I will be forced to open it myself."

"I'm not dressed," she said, trying to buy time. "I'll need a few minutes."

If she had just opened the door, she could have talked her way out of the situation. If her appearance in a man's room at night seemed unsavory, so be it. What could she possibly say now when the security guard opened the door and found her with everything strewn on the floor? Millie was going think she'd lost her mind if she learned she had broken into Teddy Belmont's room.

Moving quickly, she closed the wardrobe and shoved everything on the floor back in the trunk. She crossed to the porthole. Outside the thick glass, she could see only darkness. The deck had been covered with canvas to conceal the cabin lights.

She gripped the lever and began cranking. If she could squeeze through the porthole, she could escape without anyone seeing her. It was stiff, and each rotation caused the glass to open only the smallest fraction of an inch. Her arms burned with the exertion.

"Sir," guard called. "I insist you open the door immediately, or else I shall open it myself."

"And I insist you have some goddamned patience when you rouse a sick man from his bed," she yelled in a deep and aggravated voice.

The window was still only halfway open. She pulled at the lever with all her strength. It wouldn't go any further.

"Sir?"

There was no time. She would have to try.

She climbed up on the small desk beneath the porthole. Grasping the curtains to steady herself, she kicked at the glass, pushing it open further, and managed to squeeze through. As she slid down the outer wall onto the deck, the fabric of her skirt caught on something.

She yanked the ripped material free just as the security guard opened the cabin door. Not bothering to check the condition of her dress, she sprinted down the dark deck. By the time she reached the entrance to the main lobby, she was completely out of breath.

The cavernous room was empty save for a single individual. Standing between her and the entrance to the ladies' restroom was the attractive man with glasses from the smoking lounge early today.

"Well!" A smile crept across his face. "Look what the cat dragged in. A pleasure to see you again, Miss Whiskers."

She cringed.

As he took in her disheveled appearance his smile faded. "Everything all right?"

"I'm fine." Ella brought her hand up to her hair. Most of it had come unpinned. She glanced down. The front of her dress was filthy. "Excuse me." Gripping the back of her skirt, holding the ripped fabric together, she brushed past him into the ladies' restroom.

She darted around the confused attendant into one of the stalls. After locking the door, she twisted to examine the rip in her dress. The slit in the fabric caused it to look like a pair of partially open curtains revealing a glimpse of her backside. She removed a few of the pins from her hair and used them to suture the tear.

What had she been thinking, breaking into his room? What was wrong with her? Did he even look like Jay Gatsby, or was the resemblance merely a drunken illusion?

She had found absolutely nothing to suggest Teddy Belmont was anyone other than who he said he was. But where was he? If he was sick, he would have been in bed. Maybe he was a confidence man after all, a card sharp. He was probably in the smoking room this very moment, cheating someone out of their money.

Wherever he was, she needed to make sure no one found out she'd broken into his room. She needed to get back to dinner. Ignoring the curious gaze of the attendant, she cleaned herself up at the sink as best she could.

When she stepped into the dining room, clenching the back of her dress with both hands, the orchestra was in full swing. The rowdy Americans from the smoking room danced without inhibition as the vocalist crooned.

"By the sea, by the sea
By the beau-ti-ful sea,
You and I, you and I
Oh, how happy we'll be."

At the table, everything was almost as she'd left it. Stanley Felton was scowling at nothing in particular. Captain Brightman was still yammering on about the Boer War, while Mrs. Brightman gazed longingly at the dance floor. There was, however, one glaring difference. Seated in the chair next to Millie was Teddy Belmont.

He was the epitome of good health—glowing and triumphant. He flashed Millie a brilliant smile. She giggled as if he had just said the cleverest thing in the world. Ella lowered herself into her chair with care, still clasping the back of her dress.

Millie eyed her skeptically. "Where were you?"

"I needed some fresh air."

Conversation at the table resumed. No one else seemed to have missed her. Ella downed a glass of champagne, then another, trying and failing to stop staring at Teddy Belmont. He looked like Jay Gatsby. He really did.

"You're feeling better, I see," she said to him.

"I am indeed," he replied with a luminous grin. "Would you like more champagne, Miss Kaye?" His eyebrows rose in exaggerated curves like the tops of mirrored question marks. "We should celebrate—it being our last night and all."

When the waiter finished replenishing her glass, Teddy raised his in the air. "To new friends."

"To new friends," Captain Brightman repeated enthusiastically. The others at the table followed suit.

Teddy Belmont's face was a portrait of sincerity. He appeared genuinely pleased to have had the fortune to come across such good company. Maybe he really was just a young man traveling to Europe. It was possible she had entirely misjudged him.

"To new friends," Ella repeated. But when Teddy's eyes

met hers, she held his gaze. Looking only at him, she added, "and old acquaintances."

For a split second, a flicker of fear danced across his eyes. Or, at least, Ella thought that what it was. It was hard to tell in the dim light.

CHAPTER 7

England was at war, and the bustling port was crowded with men in uniform. The *Oceanic* was one of the last ships carrying civilians allowed to dock in Southampton. From here on out, the harbor was to be used exclusively for military embarkation.

The sun was shining, and Jay was radiant. As he stepped ashore, he couldn't stop smiling. In his jacket pocket, carefully nestled in his silver cigarette case, were six tracer bullets. He made his way to the train station, wading through a sea of khaki uniforms—members of the British Expeditionary Force en route to France. At the ticket counter, he purchased a first-class ticket to Waterloo Station.

Since most of the passenger steamers had been diverted to Liverpool, the train to London was practically empty. Aside from an older gentleman he recognized from the ship, Jay had an entire compartment to himself. He set aside the newspapers he'd bought at the station and fixed his gaze out the window with a contented grin.

It wasn't until he was on his way to the dining car that Jay's smile faltered. Ella Kaye was seated in the compartment adjacent to his. Had she intentionally positioned herself there in order to keep an eye on him?

He tried not to let this bother him. For now, it didn't matter if she was watching him or not. He wasn't planning any covert disembarkation. And, having foolishly disclosed the name of his hotel during dinner one night, she already knew where he was staying. Luckily, he wasn't meeting his contact at the hotel. The important thing was to make sure she didn't follow him tomorrow.

Besides, her choice of compartment may have had nothing to do with him. Some sort of argument had taken place between Ella and Millie. During last night's dinner, the two women had barely looked at one another. That could easily explain why Ella wasn't sitting with the Feltons. Except, of course, this was the same woman who had broken into his cabin last night.

Thankfully, she had found nothing to further her suspicions. Winter had advised Jay not to bring any personal items on the ship that could possibly identify him as anyone other than Teddy Belmont. He had heeded this advice with one exception. The silver cigarette case containing the tracers was engraved with his initials. It was a gift from Dan Cody.

It was foolish to bring it, but he'd allowed sentimentality to prevail over reason. Thankfully, the cigarette case had been in his jacket pocket when Ella searched his cabin. And that was where it would remain.

Back in his compartment, Jay set to reading the newspaper. Not surprisingly, a majority of the news was dedicated to England's entrance into the war. Lord Kitchener, the newly appointed Secretary of War, was calling for one hundred thousand volunteers to join Britain's military forces.

In Belgium, the invading German troops continued their bombardment of Liège, but, thus far, the brave Belgians held their ground. Back in America, the nation mourned the loss of its first lady. Grief-stricken President Wilson had little to say of Europe's current calamity.

An article stating that thousands of American "refugees" were stranded in Europe caught Jay's eye. Would he have trouble getting back, as well? The ship he was sailing home on was an American liner, which meant, unlike the *Oceanic*, it couldn't be commandeered by the Royal Navy. Surely, his return ticket was still valid. At least, he hoped as much. After handing over the tracers, the last thing he wanted was to be stuck in England.

The more he read, the more uneasy he became. Several articles mentioned the prominence of spies in England. According to these accounts, the United Kingdom was potentially teeming with hundreds more enemy spies. Various arrests had already been made. Any suspicious activity, whatsoever, was to be immediately reported to the local police.

Jay shifted in his seat. Had he known England would be at war and enveloped in a paranoid, spy-crazed frenzy, he might not have agreed to do this. The articles in the paper made it sound as though people were being picked up by the police for even the slightest irregular behavior.

What if Ella reported him to the police? He raised the window to get some air. She didn't know anything about the tracer bullets. He wasn't worried about that. But what if she told them she thought he wasn't really Teddy Belmont? She didn't have any proof, but did that matter? Was her word alone, that he was impersonating another individual, enough to warrant arrest?

He dropped the paper on his lap. The print on the edges was smeared where his palms, damp with sweat, had gripped the page. If he was arrested and it was discovered he was using a false passport, that would be bad enough. If the police discovered the stolen tracer bullets, that would be truly disastrous.

The more he thought about it, the worse he realized his

situation appeared. He wasn't just in possession of stolen property—he had stolen ammunition and technology intended for the British Navy. He would be arrested as a foreign spy. And then what?

He removed the handkerchief from his pocket and wiped at his brow. What did they do to spies in England? Did they even get a trial? Or were they locked in the Tower of London until they were shot?

"Everything all right?" the older man in the compartment asked.

"Oh. Just—the war." He hadn't realized how labored his breathing had become.

He folded the newspaper and placed it on the seat beside him, attempting a smile. It was important, now more than ever, to remain calm and keep his composure. The last thing he needed was to attract attention to himself.

He pushed the window all the way up to let in more air. The train sped past the English countryside—undulating meadows of grass interspersed with hedgerows and cottages. He brought his hand to the breast pocket of his jacket, and for an instant considered tossing the tracers out the window.

But then what would he do? He only had ten dollars with him. His hotel room had been paid in advance, but only for one night. And he couldn't to go back to New York without the money to pay back the Eastman gang.

Getting rid of the tracer bullets at this point didn't make sense. It wouldn't even guarantee he was safe from arrest. He was still using a false passport, after all.

He could go into the next compartment and beg Ella for mercy. If he explained everything to her, there was a chance she might understand. There had to exist some sort of kinship between them, born out of their mutual respect for Cody.

The thought was so absurd, he laughed out loud, causing his compartment mate to offer up another concerned look.

If only life were an H.G. Wells novel and there was such a thing as a time machine. He'd travel back to the day he borrowed all the money. In this new version of life, he wouldn't even consider a loan. Instead, he'd punch that crook Walter Chase in the jaw.

When Jay met Walter Chase late that rainy night in February at the Tiptop Bar, he had thought it was the luckiest night of his life. He'd thanked God he'd had the good fortune to cross paths with this shrewd and benevolent man. Walter worked in finance, with or for some Wall Street brokerage house. Jay didn't know much about stocks or bonds, but whatever the means or mode of the transaction, Walter Chase was about to make a load of money.

Walter was excited. The deal he was working on now was "the investment opportunity of a lifetime." He really shouldn't be telling any of this to Jay, he had said, but what the hell. He was about to make a lot of dough. He was celebrating.

Walter had bought Jay a drink, then a second. Jay should have been more wary, but he was celebrating too that night. Well, not celebrating—not exactly.

He was still mourning the loss of Dan Cody. But he was somewhat comforted having just learned Cody had left him a fair amount of money in his will. Jay hadn't received it yet. It took time to settle an estate. But he would eventually. Or, at least, that was what he'd believed at the time.

Twenty-five thousand dollars wasn't enough to live off of for the rest of his life—not in the manner of lifestyle Jay envisaged for himself. But Cody had given him enough to get started, just as he'd promised he would. It was up to Jay to invest that money in a manner that generated more money.

When Jay suggested he might follow in Cody's footsteps and try his hand at mining, Cody had said, "That's one way to go about it. But why tunnel underground when these days there's just as much money to be made sitting in an office perched atop the Manhattan skyline?"

Jay should have been more skeptical. But at the time, it seemed like providence that he'd met Walter Chase the same day he learned of the bequest. When Jay asked if he could get in on the arrangement, Walter had said he'd see what he could do. The thing was, the deal was moving fast. If Jay wanted to be a part of this, he'd have to put up the money in the next couple days.

There was no way Jay would get Cody's money by then, but he hadn't wanted to miss out on the opportunity. So, Jay had gone and done something truly stupid. He'd borrowed money from the Eastman gang.

They'd made no bones about the terms of the loan. They were very clear. If he didn't pay them back in a timely manner, he'd end up at the bottom of the Hudson River. But Jay hadn't worried about that then. Paying them back wouldn't be a problem. He was about to be a part of something big.

The Monday after their conversation, Jay put on his best suit and headed down to Wall Street to meet with Walter. The building itself soared high up into the clouds, but Walter's office was only on the third floor. Jay had been under the impression Walter worked for a large investment firm. But his office, which was really just a small sparsely furnished room, stood alone.

But never mind all that. One needed only to look up at that distinguished degree framed on the wall to be assured of being in good hands. Walter Chase was a Yale man.

But it turned out this Ivy League assurance wasn't worth much. The venture failed, or at least that was what Jay was told. Every penny he had borrowed and invested was gone. So was Walter Chase.

Waterloo Station was crowded, chaotic, and severely understaffed, many of its employees having abandoned their posts to sign up to fight the Germans. It took Jay close to an hour to find a porter to arrange for the steamer trunk to be stored. The task complete, he walked the mile or so to the hotel where a room was booked in Teddy Belmont's name.

Taking up most of a city block, the Hotel Cecil was a stately affair, housed in a majestic redbrick building overlooking the Thames. It was set behind a grand courtyard, the entrance to which faced the heavily trafficked street known as the Strand. As Jay approached the lobby entrance, a bellman in a red-and-white uniform hurried to open the door for him.

Inside, an array of plush antique furnishings and potted palms decorated the elegant lobby. Jay hadn't realized the hotel would be this nice. But he supposed the extravagant accommodations made sense. He was still pretending to be Teddy Belmont for one more night.

The only downside to the hotel, as far as he could tell, was that it was adjacent to the Savoy, where Ella and the Feltons were staying. It would only be a matter of time before Felton realized six of the tracers were missing. There was no reason he should suspect Teddy Belmont. Still, Jay would have preferred to be staying further away.

Jay had promised Millie they would meet up later during the week, but by the time she would attempt to contact him, he would be long gone. He felt a twinge of guilt whenever he thought of this, but he couldn't hang around London waiting to be caught. Besides, he already had his ticket home.

His instructions were to meet his contact at an address in north London tomorrow at ten in the morning. After handing off the tracers and camera film, he would take a train straight to Liverpool, where his ship would depart that evening. When he arrived home in New York, fifteen thousand dollars would be waiting for him in a bank account.

After signing for his room, Jay asked the hotel clerk to confirm his ship was departing from Liverpool tomorrow as planned. But when he handed the clerk his return ticket, the man claimed there was no New York–bound ship called the SS *Hespera* that departed out of Liverpool. Clearly, the man didn't know what he was talking about.

Not wanting to risk running into the Feltons or Ella, Jay didn't leave the hotel until he checked out the following morning. He had half expected Ella to come knocking on the door of his room in the middle of the night, demanding he prove his identity, but he hadn't seen her since the train.

He didn't think she or anyone else was following him when he stepped out of the lobby into the bright morning sun. But just in case, as he crossed the courtyard, he slipped off his jacket and hat and in one fluid motion slid them into his suitcase. He quickened his stride until he fell in step with a group of men and walked alongside them until they were out on the Strand.

A mix of motorcars, bicycles and a few horse-drawn carriages shared the busy thoroughfare. The shops were closed, but the sidewalks were crowded with Londoners in their Sunday best. Every so often cheers erupted on the street, presumably prompted by England's recent entry into war. A slew of freshly hung posters reading, "Your King and Country Need You. Enlist Now," suggested as much.

According to the hotel concierge, if he didn't mind taking the tube, the Piccadilly line of the underground railroad was the fastest way to get to Islington. Upon reaching the tube station, Jay purchased a ticket and descended the large elevator to the train platform. Only a handful of people stood waiting for the train, but among those few individuals was an officer from Scotland Yard.

Upon spotting the uniformed man, Jay was seized with panic. The officer had no reason to suspect he was carrying stolen tracer bullets. As long as he didn't do anything spectacularly peculiar to attract the man's attention, he would be fine. But having drawn his own attention to the act of acting naturally, Jay was now finding it impossible.

The more he focused on walking normally, the more manufactured his gait became. Each step he took felt stiff and ungainly. His arms felt unusually heavy. What did they usually do when he walked? Did they swing? Were they relaxed by his side? Neither felt right.

When he reached the platform, he did his best to strike a breezy, nonchalant pose. He put a hand on his hip, then immediately removed it. He shifted awkwardly, trying to assume the stance of an ordinary person waiting for the tube until it mercifully arrived.

After five stops, he got off at King's Cross. Out on the street, Jay headed north, walking past the Metropolitan Cattle Market. The collection of sheds, stalls, and pens were empty, but the pungent aroma of manure hung in the air. During the week, a variety of livestock was traded here, but, like all the adjacent shops, the cattle market was closed on Sundays.

Next he passed Pentonville Prison, its high stone walls a dreary grey. Through the gate he glimpsed a line of men trudging across the courtyard, their ankles bound in chains. Aside from the prison population, the entire area was eerily vacant. Which, Jay supposed, was why he was meeting his contact here. It was a perfect place to hand over the tracers without being seen.

Jay was a block away from his intended destination when a tall unfamiliar man, who seemed to have appeared out of nowhere, approached him.

"Have you got the time, friend?" the young man asked in a thick Irish accent.

Jay was about to reach into his pocket for his watch when he realized "Have you got the time, friend?" was the phrase his contact was supposed to use to introduce himself.

"I'm sorry, no. My watch is in the shop," he responded—this being the prearranged response.

"Good thing I'm not in a hurry," the man replied in kind. "Good to see you, Teddy Belmont." He clapped Jay on the back as though they were old pals. Then, although there was no one else in sight, he leaned in and lowered his voice. "My name's Connor."

"Nice to see you, Connor," Jay said, playing along.

"Come, let's have a pint together." Connor gestured in the direction opposite the shop. "I know a real good place."

Jay hesitated. His instructions were to meet his contact at the address he'd been given by Winter. He didn't know anything about anyone named Connor. What if this was a trap?

"Come on now," the Irishman said with a nervous grin. "I've lots to tell you."

Jay nodded, and the two men started walking back toward the Tube station. But something about this felt wrong. It didn't help that Connor kept glancing over his shoulder.

Jay stopped abruptly. "Shouldn't we go to the shop first?"

Connor shook his head. "Trust me. We'd better get going. As soon as we get to the pub, I'll tell you everything."

CHAPTER 8

Ella had been sitting in the lobby of the Hotel Cecil for almost two hours. She stretched her arms. A yawn slipped out of her mouth as she surveyed the room for what felt like the thousandth time. She was seated in a velvet armchair under a potted palm with an unobstructed view of the elevator, stairs and the front door. Unless Teddy Belmont climbed out the window of his room, she would see him leave the hotel.

She had decided to allow herself one more day to investigate him. She was fully aware this behavior was obsessive, irrational, and most likely a huge waste of time, but she couldn't push her suspicions out of her head. What if Teddy Belmont really was Jay Gatsby? She'd rather waste a day confirming he was who he said he was, than have the unresolved mystery of his identity haunt her for the rest of time.

Then tomorrow, she was going to make her way to Belgium, where the fighting was. This was her opportunity to be a war correspondent. If the *World* didn't want her, that was their loss. She'd sell her articles to the Associated Press.

Captain Brightman had agreed to help her secure credentials to follow the British Army. But that was before Britain's war secretary, Lord Kitchener, announced that no reporters would be allowed to accompany the British Army into battle.

News of the war would instead be issued by the British press bureau.

Still, Ella was undeterred. She'd find another way to see the fighting in Belgium. She was determined to make her way to the front line.

The lobby of the Hotel Cecil was practically empty. Aside from those few pious guests heading to or from Sunday services, hardly anyone had passed through the hotel's doors. As dull as waiting here was, Ella was thankful she wasn't scanning the crowd for Teddy Belmont at her hotel.

The lobby of the Savoy was a madhouse, overflowing with frustrated Americans unable to book passage home. In an effort to assist the overwhelmed American embassy, the American Citizens Relief Committee, an organization headed by an American millionaire named Herbert Hoover, had established its headquarters at the Savoy. Spotting anyone in that congested crowd would have been near impossible.

When Teddy Belmont descended the grand lobby staircase sometime later, Ella quickly raised the open newspaper resting on her lap to cover her face. Peering over the edge, she watched him cross the lobby and approach a mahogany desk, behind which sat the concierge.

She lowered the paper and craned her neck to get a better view. He was wearing a neatly pressed light grey suit and a felt hat of the same color. In his left hand he gripped the same brown valise he had had with him yesterday on the train.

The concierge retrieved a large map from the desk drawer. He carefully unfolded it and laid it out on the desk. She was too far away to hear what was being said. After multiple swirls and jabs at the map with his finger, the concierge took out a pad of paper and inscribed what she assumed were directions. He tore the page off the pad and handed it to Teddy Belmont.

She waited until he had exited the front door of the lobby.

Then she bounded after him. Outside, it took a moment for her eyes to adjust to the bright morning sun. She scanned the entire courtyard. In the distance, a group of men walked out onto the Strand, but none wore a grey suit and hat. She looked in every direction, but there was no sign of him. It was as though Teddy Belmont had disappeared.

She dashed back into the lobby to speak with the concierge, but his desk was empty. Ella rushed to the reception desk. "Excuse me, where I can find the concierge?"

The woman consulted the large wooden clock on the wall.

"Mr. West has left for the day, but our other concierge, Mr. Owens, should be here shortly. In the meantime, is there—"

"There was a map at his desk. May I look at it?"

"Certainly. Go right ahead."

Ella stared intently at the large map of London. She tried to determine where and to what the concierge had been swirling and pointing, but it was no use. She had just about resigned herself to waiting in the lobby until Teddy Belmont's return, when she remembered a trick she had once used as a young reporter.

Glancing around to make sure no one was looking, she reached into the desk drawer and pulled out the pad the concierge had used to inscribe the directions. She wasn't sure this would work, but it was worth a try. Leaning over the desk, she used a pencil to lightly shade the first page of the notepad with diagonal lines. As she did, letters began to appear, revealing an imprint of what she hoped was the last thing written on the pad. The first few lines were illegible. But at the bottom an address was clearly visible: *402A Caledonian Road, Islington.*

When she arrived at the North London address half an hour later, there was no sign of Teddy Belmont. Other than a man sitting on a bench reading a newspaper, there wasn't a soul in sight.

Number 402A was in the middle of a row of small shops, all of which were closed. A pole with a helix of red and white stripes was affixed to the outer wall of what appeared to be a barber's shop. Ella tried the door. Finding it locked, she rang the bell and waited. When no one answered she peered through the window. The lights were off. As far as she could tell, the shop was empty.

She went around to the back of the building and found another door. But it, too, was locked. She glanced around and, seeing no one in sight, bent to examine the lock. She removed a pin from her hair.

At the pounding of footsteps, she closed her fingers around the hairpin, concealing it in her fist, and stood. The window beside the door revealed the reflection of an unfamiliar man.

She spun. The man who had been reading a newspaper on the bench stood before her.

"Excuse me, Miss . . ."

"Kaye. Ella Kaye."

"I'm PC Parker, Scotland Yard. Mind if I ask you a few questions, Miss Kaye?"

She looked him up and down. "You aren't wearing a uniform."

He reached in his pocket and presented her with a card. The hairpin was still in her right hand, so she accepted the card with her left. It read "Police Constable William Parker—Metropolitan Police."

She handed back the card. "Did a dark-haired man, about your height, early twenties, go into this building?"

Parker cleared his throat. "Miss Kaye, may I ask how you came to be at this address?"

"I'm looking for someone."

"The dark-haired man?"

"So, you did see him?"

"I did not." Parker removed a small notebook and pencil from his jacket pocket. "What's the name of the dark-haired man you're looking for?"

"Teddy Belmont."

He jotted this down. "Would you mind telling me the reason you're meeting him at this particular address?"

Ella looked at him impatiently. "Yes, I would mind." She peered around the man to make sure she hadn't missed Teddy.

He scribbled something on his notepad, then looked up at her. "Who told you to come to this particular address?"

"I don't see how that's any of your business." She needed to check the front of the building. Teddy might be there now. "If you'll excuse me."

"Miss Kaye, I still have a few questions."

"I'm sorry, but I'm rather in a hurry." She began walking around the building.

"Miss Kaye, why were you attempting to break into the shop?"

She paused and faced him. "I don't know what you're talking about."

"Miss Kaye, I'm going to need you to come with me to answer some questions. This address is under investigation, and anyone attempting to enter the premises—"

"Sorry, I don't have the time." She gave an apologetic shrug and started to walk away.

"Stop. That's an order."

She kept walking.

"You leave me no choice. Ella Kaye, you're under arrest."

New Scotland Yard, the headquarters of the Metropolitan Police Department, was housed in a turreted brick building on the Victoria Embankment. The building was also home to the Whitehall Recruiting Office, and scores of eager young men waiting to enlist formed a line that snaked around the entire building.

PC Parker pushed his way through the column of men, guiding Ella into the station. Once inside, he led her through a corridor into a small office. The handcuffs employed during her arrest were removed, and she was informed a detective would arrive shortly to question her.

As she sat waiting, she examined her sore wrists. After a failed attempt to flee the scene, she hadn't been entirely co-operative when PC Parker handcuffed her. She probably shouldn't have resisted arrest, but she wasn't about to allow a supposed police officer hanging around a deserted stretch of shops to take her to God knows where.

It was clear now he really was a policeman. She supposed she should be glad of this fact. At least she hadn't been kid-napped. But she was supposed to be following Teddy Bel-mont, not sitting in a dusty office in the Metropolitan Police Department.

PC Parker returned, accompanied by a detective sergeant who offered her a cup of tea. She answered the detective ser-geant's questions—who she was, why she was in London, what had brought her to the shop located at 402A Caledonian Road—as clearly and courteously as possible. She wanted to resolve this misunderstanding as quickly as possible.

She attempted to explain what had driven her to follow Teddy Belmont in the first place. But as she recounted every-thing aloud—omitting the part where she broke into his cabin and attempted to break into the shop—she began to realize how utterly absurd it all sounded. She had absolutely no proof whatsoever that Teddy Belmont was Jay Gatsby.

When they finished questioning her, she was left alone in

the room. In the minutes that followed, she resolved to forget about Teddy Belmont entirely. Whoever he was or whatever he was up to didn't matter. Once this was all resolved, she was going to go back to the Savoy, take a nice long bath and forget about the whole ridiculous affair.

She may very well have done just that. But when the detective sergeant returned, he did not lead her to the door of the station and bid her farewell as she had expected. Instead, he informed her she would remain in custody overnight, while they verified her story.

She was led to an empty block of prison cells in Cannon Row. There she spent a sleepless night on a hard bed locked in a small cell. She passed the hours mentally composing a scathing exposé on the injustices perpetrated by Scotland Yard. She would have liked to write it down but had not been afforded pen and paper—yet another notable injustice.

The detective sergeant had promised to contact Millie at the Savoy to let her know of Ella's arrest. But if he had, why hadn't she come to get her out of here? They hadn't parted on the best of terms, but their friendship had weathered worse. She must not have received the message.

He'd also vowed to contact the American embassy on her behalf. But they were so busy dealing with all the stranded tourists, she doubted they'd rush to her assistance. Did anyone even know she was here?

The thought nagged at her. She could manage spending the night in this cell. She'd survived worse. On an undercover assignment for the *World*, she'd spent over a week at a women's lunatic asylum feigning insanity. Compared to that hellhole, a night in Cannon Row was like an evening at the Ritz.

But what if it wasn't just one night? She'd been able to tolerate the abysmal conditions at the asylum because she'd known that at the end of ten days someone was coming to get her out. This was different.

Why had she followed Teddy Belmont? What was wrong with her? He wasn't some ex-employee of Cody's in disguise out to get her. It was all in her head. She was tilting at windmills like Don Quixote on some ridiculous imagined quest.

Besides, if Jay Gatsby had wanted to confront her, if he blamed her for Cody's death, he'd have already done so in New York. Ella tugged at the thin pilled bedsheet, pulling it up over her shoulders. She closed her eyes and willed herself to sleep. She didn't want to think about all that now.

CHAPTER 9

The entrance to the King's Prospect Tavern was located in a narrow cobblestone alley off Fleet Street. The doorframe hung low, and both Connor and Jay had to duck so as not to hit their heads. Despite the early hour, the modest, dimly lit establishment was packed with patrons. Their rowdy enthusiasm suggested they'd already enjoyed several rounds of beer.

After ordering two pints at the bar, they made their way to the back of the packed room. Jay trailed behind the tall Irishman as he threaded through the crowd. A heavy-set man stumbled, knocking into Jay's shoulder, spilling beer onto his jacket. He issued a semicoherent apology, before staggering away. No one else in the room so much as turned a head to look at them.

They found an empty table in the back corner. Jay would have preferred the seat against the wall so he could see anyone approaching, but Connor got there first.

Now, his back turned to the entire room, all Jay could see was Connor and the unsettling oil painting on the wall behind him. Like all the portraits crowding the tavern's walls, it depicted a former monarch of England. According to the placard, the man staring menacingly down at Jay, with his pointed auburn beard and long upturned mustache, was King Charles I.

After glancing around to make sure no one was paying them any mind, Connor leaned into the table and lowered his voice. He explained to Jay that the owner of the shop on Caledonian Road had been arrested a few days ago. Since then, the address had been under constant surveillance by Scotland Yard.

As Connor shared this distressing news, Jay tried to keep his face expressionless.

"They sent me to stop you before you reached the shop." Connor paused to take a sip of his beer. "Thank Jesus, Mary and Joseph I found you before you did."

If the shop owner had been arrested, this was very bad. Jay wrapped his hands around the pint of beer in front him, gripping it tightly. Had the owner told the police about Teddy Belmont?

A trickle of sweat dripped down the back of his neck. Was Scotland Yard scouring the streets of London looking for him this very minute? An unintelligible series of shouts rose above the already noisy din of the room. Jay resisted the urge to look over his shoulder.

Connor didn't appear all that concerned. Perhaps Jay was overreacting. He leaned back in his chair, attempting to mimic Connor's relaxed composure. But his mind was racing. Connor—if that was his real name—seemed like a nice enough guy, but could he be trusted?

Connor took another sip of his beer, and Jay forced himself to do the same. It was thick and bitter. He tried not to grimace.

How had Connor known to find him? Who was the "they" who had sent him to find Teddy Belmont? Was Connor also working for Winter? If so, why hadn't Connor intercepted him at his hotel?

What if this was a trap? Jay studied his beer intently, deliberating what to say next. He didn't want to divulge anything to Connor.

"Was he the only person arrested at the shop?" Jay ventured.

"I don't know the particulars." Connor's eyebrows lifted. "Was he a friend of yours?"

"Never met him."

"Me neither."

They sat in silence.

Connor took another sip of beer. "They arrested the man who was supposed to be helping me too," he said finally. "They arrested a score of Germans that day."

"Arrested them for . . ." Jay couldn't bring himself to say it out loud.

"Aye, spying."

He took a moment to let his sink in. It didn't come as a complete surprise. A part of Jay had always suspected Winter was keeping more from him than he'd let on. So, this was what he'd been hiding. It seemed Winter wasn't working for an unscrupulous arms dealer, as Jay had been led to believe. Winter had hired Jay to steal the tracers for Germany.

Connor hunched over, resting his arms on the table. "It's not good. I'm not gonna lie. I've been more than a bit jumpy these past few days."

Jay swallowed. If he was caught, he would be tried as a German spy. Because he *was* a German spy. Thinking back, Jay should have realized it sooner. Winter had been in the German navy, after all. And he'd left for Germany a week before Jay boarded the *Oceanic*.

"I was in a real panic," Connor continued. "Well, until I got the message about finding you."

Jay loosened his shirt collar. "Message?"

"Oh, you know, one of the coded ones."

Winter had taught Jay a code to use, should he need to communicate with him via telegram. But if the telegram was from Winter, why hadn't Jay received a message at the hotel? Winter had known where Jay was staying. He was the one who'd booked the room.

"Who was the message from?" Jay asked.

Connor laughed. "You think they'd tell me? You Germans are very secretive."

Why was Connor working with the Germans? His country was at war with Germany.

A group of men began a boisterous rendition of "God Save the King." Jay turned to watch. As they sang, they swayed with drunken enthusiasm.

"*Send him victorious,*
Happy and glorious,
Long to reign over us . . ."

One of the singers raised a glass to Jay. He quickly turned back around, touching the pocket of his jacket containing the tracers. What would those men do if they knew two German spies were in the room? Connor seemed to be asking himself the same question. His eyes darted around the room.

"What happens now?" Jay asked.

"We get out of England."

"Well, that's a relief."

Connor grinned. "You know," he began, then lowered his voice, "I'd never guess you were German. You've really got the American act down."

"I am American."

"Right," Connor said with a wink.

"Are you German?" Jay asked, unsure what else to say.

"Me? Of course not. I'm bloody Irish through and through." He thrust out his chest and held his chin high. "Not that there's anything wrong with being German," he whispered.

Connor abruptly raised his glass. "Well, cheers to you." He took a gulp. "I'm not sure how we would have gotten out of this if you hadn't come along."

Jay raised his glass, pressing his lips together. He felt almost certain Connor was on his side. He didn't think this was a ruse meant to ensnare him. But he had absolutely no idea what Connor was talking about.

Connor was the one who had saved *him*. Jay had no money, no idea who to contact, and was potentially a wanted man. How could he possibly be of any help to Connor?

"I'm not sure I understand."

"Ah, right." Connor tapped his forehead. "I forgot to mention the boat. They said you'd know how to sail it."

CHAPTER 10

Early the next morning, Ella was released from her cell and brought to the office of Basil Thomson, the head of Scotland Yard's Criminal Investigation Department. Thomson was seated behind his desk when she arrived. He was in his fifties with close-cropped hair and a thick mustache.

To Thomson's left sat a younger man introduced as Major Drake. It was unclear what branch of the service Major Drake belonged to, as he wore no uniform. Like Thomson, he was dressed in a suit.

Thomson's office was much larger than the room she'd been interviewed in the previous day. Two windows on the far wall showcased a view of the Thames. Ella was directed to sit in a noticeably small wooden chair facing Thomson's desk, the seat of which was set uncomfortably low to the ground.

"We're still verifying everything you told the detective sergeant yesterday," Thomson said, flipping through some papers. "Most of it appears to check out, but we must be thorough."

Thomson knitted his bushy eyebrows, then looked up at Ella. "How do you know Karl Gustav Ernst?"

"Who?"

"The proprietor of the shop at 402A Caledonian Road."

"I don't. I followed Teddy Belmont there."

"At what time did Teddy Belmont arrive at the address?"

"Well, I didn't actually follow him there, not exactly. I knew that was where he was going and went there myself."

"And you went there because you believe Teddy Belmont is actually someone else, called . . ." He consulted his notes. "Jay Gatsby?"

"I realize it sounds far-fetched, but—"

"Do you have any reason to believe Teddy Belmont was engaged in espionage?"

"He was certainly up to something."

"What about this Gatsby fellow?"

"I'm not sure."

"Were you engaged in espionage?"

"Of course not." Ella sat up as much as she could in the diminutive chair. "I already told the detective sergeant all of this. Why would I spy on England?"

"That's what we'd like to know." Thomson sat back and tapped his fingers together. "It could be one of many reasons. Maybe you needed money."

"That's absurd."

"Yes, of course." He referred to his notes. "Because you 'own half the copper mines in Montana,' which you inherited from a 'Mr. Dan Cody'?"

"Are you suggesting I'm lying?"

"No. But I am confused as to why a copper magnate and"—he glanced down at his notes again—"'world-renowned journalist' was attempting to pick the lock of a barber's shop in Islington."

Ella crossed her arms.

"Are you being blackmailed?"

"No."

"And you are American, correct?"

"Yes."

"Are your parents German?"

"I have absolutely no affiliation with Germany, nor do I wish to. What they're doing to Belgium is atrocious."

"What about Teddy Belmont?" Thomson asked. "Is he German?"

"I don't think so."

"Does he speak German?"

Before she could answer, a knock on the door announced the arrival of the detective sergeant. He approached the desk. Whispering something, he handed Thomson a stack of papers, then backed out of the room.

Ella waited as Thomson, then Major Drake, took their time looking through the documents. Seemingly satisfied, Thomson straightened in his chair and cleared his throat.

"Well, Miss Kaye, it appears everything checks out. I apologize for this inconvenience. I hope you can understand that with our nation at war, we must be careful."

"Does this mean I'm free to leave?"

"It does."

She started to rise but reconsidered. "Who's Karl Ernst?"

Thomson exchanged a look with Major Drake, who nodded.

"Karl Ernst was arrested four days ago. Ernst's shop was a meeting place and exchange for a ring of German spies. PC Parker's been watching the shop, waiting to see if anyone tried to make contact with him."

Ella's eyes grew wide. "So, Teddy Belmont's a German spy?" Of all the outlandish schemes she'd imagined, she hadn't even considered this possibility.

"This is the first we've heard of him," Drake said, finally breaking his silence.

"Are you going to arrest him?" Ella asked.

"For now, he'll be observed," Drake answered.

"Have you checked the Hotel Cecil? He's supposed to be staying there all week."

"We did," Thomson said. "He checked out yesterday morning."

Drake leaned forward. "Is it fair to say arresting Teddy Belmont is something you'd be willing to help us accomplish, Miss Kaye?"

"Certainly."

After a long bath and a change of clothes, Ella left the Savoy to meet Major Drake. She had told him she'd be willing to help find Teddy Belmont. But having had time to think it over, now she wasn't so sure.

She didn't want to become embroiled in some long, drawn-out investigation. She needed to get to Belgium so she could report on the war. Teddy Belmont wasn't Jay Gatsby. He was a German spy. And that had nothing to do with her. She had no idea where he was now. She'd already told Scotland Yard all she knew.

When she arrived at the nondescript café on the Strand where they had arranged to meet, Drake was at a table in the back corner. As she approached, he signaled for the waiter to bring him the check.

He rose to greet her. "Unless you object, I thought we'd go somewhere less crowded to talk."

They headed down the Strand in the direction of St. James's Park. The street bustled with activity. Car engines rumbled, and exhaust filled the air.

Once they entered the park, the crowd thinned, and the noise subsided. They followed a path along a lake filled with ducks. In the distance, across the water, stood Buckingham

Palace.

Ella took a step closer to Drake and lowered her voice. "Don't look now, but I think we're being followed."

A man in a brown suit walked on the path a few yards behind them. She'd noticed the same man trailing her on her way to the café earlier.

Disregarding her warning entirely, Drake immediately stopped and turned. He nodded to the man.

The man tipped his hat in reply.

"You know him?"

"I asked him to keep an eye on you."

Ella frowned. "I'm not still under suspicion, am I?"

"Not at all. It was merely a precaution." Drake nodded again, and the man turned and left them.

"We wanted to be certain you weren't being followed by anyone else."

"And by *we*, you mean Scotland Yard?"

"Not exactly." He placed his hands in his pockets as they continued walking around the lake. "Scotland Yard serves as a sort of front, if you will, for our organization."

"Which is?"

He paused, glanced around to make sure no one else was in earshot, then faced her. "What I'm about to tell you is highly classified information not, under any circumstances, to be shared with anyone. Understood?"

She nodded.

Drake gestured to a bench on the other side of the path, facing the lake. They took a seat.

"I work with the home Security Service. It's our job to protect the United Kingdom from foreign interference."

"So, you catch spies?" Ella asked.

"Our agency locates the spies who need to be caught. We leave the catching part to Scotland Yard."

"And you want me to help you find Teddy Belmont?"

"Not exactly." He paused, waiting for a woman pushing a pram to pass them. "We want you to let the Germans recruit you as a spy."

Ella tilted her head to the side. This certainly was not what she had expected him to say. "Why would they try to recruit me?"

"Because the German Secret Service is recruiting American correspondents to spy on England. It's not a bad idea. It's a good cover. If a reporter snoops around and asks a lot of questions, it doesn't seem all that suspicious."

"All right, but why would they want to recruit *me*?" They'd gone over this when she was being interrogated. She had no connections to Germany or any other reason to be a German spy.

"Ordinarily, I doubt they would," he admitted. "However, we already have an agent on the inside. The Germans asked him to recruit a fellow journalist to partner with."

"So, you want me to pretend to be a spy for Germany, while really working for you?"

"That's right. You'd be acting as a double agent."

"Who's the other reporter?"

"He's an excellent chap, or so I've been told. I've yet to meet him. I'm afraid I can't tell you his name. Not until you've agreed to everything. You understand."

She tried to organize her thoughts. What Drake was suggesting was outlandish.

"I know it's a lot to ask, and that as an American, technically, you're neutral. But, make no mistake, we're the good guys. The Germans are committing all manner of atrocities in Belgium. Destroying entire towns. Massacring innocent civilians. It's up to us to stop them. And we need all the help we can get."

"I'm on your side, really I am. It's just—"

"We could really use someone with experience like yours. Why, you've even gone undercover before. You're perfect for this."

She was flattered. And she had to admit, she was somewhat intrigued. But if she wanted to report on the war, she needed to get to Belgium.

"I appreciate the offer, but I'm afraid—"

"Hold on. There's something in this for you too. Before you make a decision, there's something I'd like to show you." He reached into the pocket of his jacket and pulled out a folded sheet of paper.

CHAPTER 11

The SS *Providence* was moored at a marina further down the Thames in East London. Eying the assortment of bobbing boats, Jay wondered which vessel Connor was taking him to. Not that it mattered. He would have happily boarded a leaky canoe if it meant getting out of England before Scotland Yard arrested him as a German spy. But it turned out their means of escape was an immaculate fifty-foot gaff-rigged ketch.

"Here she is," Connor said.

Jay whistled. This was a boat any yachtsman would be proud to call his own. And, dressed in the yachting costume Connor had provided him, Jay was about to do just that. They climbed aboard.

As per the ship's forged papers, the *Providence* belonged to an American millionaire by the name of Morgan H. Billingsworth. Jay was to play the part of his son, Morgan Jr., heir apparent to the large fortune his father had acquired manufacturing safety pins. According to the cover story, Morgan Jr. had been sailing the *Providence* around Europe since the end of May. He had convinced his father to loan him the yacht by touting the voyage as an international sales trip. In "reality" this was solely a pleasure outing. Morgan Jr. had absolutely no intention of selling safety pins, nor did he have any intention of cutting short his voyage, despite the war.

Connor adjusted the collar of his crew uniform. "So, if anyone asks, that's what you're to say, yeah?"

Jay frowned. "It's a little convoluted, don't you think?"

"I didn't make it up. Don't go judging me."

"Can't we just say Morgan Jr.'s fictional father loaned him the *Providence*?"

Connor considered this. "I don't know about yours, but my da certainly wouldn't loan me his boat for a summer pleasure cruise. If he had a boat, that is."

Maybe Connor had a point. "What about the safety pins?"

Connor laughed. "That part of the story actually makes some sense. You'll see."

"Where are the others?"

"Down below." Connor shook his head. "I told 'em not to come up. Or at least I tried to. Neither speaks a word of English. I don't know how we're going to pass them off as Americans."

They descended into the ship's small cabin and made their way to the galley. At a small table next to a gas stove sat two men dressed in the same crew uniforms as Connor. They were playing cards, and the older of the two appeared to be losing. He slammed his cards onto the table with a loud thud. The younger man, a hulking blond, leaned back and crossed his arms, smirking.

When they noticed Connor and Jay enter the room, the pair rose to their feet. They stood perfectly straight, clicking their heels together in the Prussian fashion. Connor was right. Everything about the duo looked so thoroughly German, they might as well be wearing the uniforms of the Kaiser's Imperial Navy.

"This is Fritz," Connor said, gesturing to the older man.

"And Horst." The towering blond appraised Jay with narrowed eyes, then gave a curt nod.

Jay responded in kind. There seemed no point in introducing himself. He wouldn't be giving his real name. The Germans resumed their game of cards, and Jay followed Connor into the adjacent compartment.

"See what I mean?" Connor said when they were out of earshot. "Anyone can see they're a couple of Fritzes—literally, in Fritz's case. No offense."

Jay had given up trying to convince Connor he wasn't German.

"Can they sail?" Whether they could pass as Americans or not made little difference if they couldn't.

Connor shrugged. "I assume so, but I don't speak German. Thank Jesus you're here. They were both on the boat when I got here, but I don't know if they're the original crew or not."

Jay sighed. How had he landed himself in this ludicrous situation? He was grateful to Connor for stopping him from going into the shop. This was obviously preferable to being arrested by Scotland Yard. But what if the Germans couldn't sail? What then? It would be nearly impossible to make it across the North Sea on a yacht this size without at least three experienced sailors.

Maybe he should jump ship. These men weren't his problem. As far as he could tell, they had nothing to do with delivering the tracers.

He still had his steamer ticket back to New York. The ship departed from Liverpool this evening. If he laid low, he could avoid being arrested for a day. Once he was back in New York, he would figure out a way to get the tracers to Winter—quickly, before the Eastman gang caught up with him.

Winter wouldn't be thrilled the tracers were back in America, but too bad. Jay had never agreed to transport a convoy of German spies across the North Sea. Winter had never mentioned anything about sailing a yacht to Rotterdam. And he hadn't even bothered to send Jay a message letting him know about the change of plans.

Then again, given the situation, maybe this was the best Winter could do. He had arranged for Jay to get out of England and sail to the neutral Netherlands. According to the message Connor had received, once in Rotterdam, Jay was to go to the German consulate. There, or so Jay assumed, he would hand over the tracers.

If the Germans could sail, and they weren't stopped by a British patrol, it wasn't the worst plan. He supposed the German consulate in Rotterdam was as safe a place as any to hand over the tracers. He walked back into the galley with Connor trailing behind him. Fritz and Horst started to rise, but Jay held up a hand to indicate they should remain seated.

"Can you both sail?" Jay asked the men in fluent German, for although he was indisputably American, he was also the son of immigrants. The small farming community in North Dakota where Jay had grown up had been populated almost entirely by Germans.

"Naturally," Fritz replied in kind. "I was in the navy."

"And you?" Jay asked the colossal younger man.

"*Ja*," Horst said, not bothering to look up.

The cards having been put away, the four men now sat around the table, plotting their course. Jay had never sailed the North Sea, famous for its unpredictable tides and shallow water. Cody had preferred sailing in the southern hemisphere.

Fortunately, Fritz had sailed this route countless time. He

knew exactly how to get them to their destination, a rendezvous point on the outskirts of Rotterdam. There, a tug would be waiting with cargo intended for Ireland.

Fritz, it turned out, had been on the *Providence* when it sailed from Hamburg to London a week ago. He was the only remaining crew member. The others had either deserted or been arrested. Fritz didn't know. Horst provided no details as to how or why he came to be in London. Neither did Jay. Should any of these men get arrested, he wanted them to know as little as possible about Teddy Belmont and the tracers.

They had been sailing down the Thames for a little over an hour. Thus far, the only patrol boat they had encountered had paid them no mind. They'd just passed Gravesend. If the wind kept up, they would be out of England in no time. But just before they entered the estuary leading to the North Sea, a British naval patrol boat waved them down and signaled for the *Providence* to halt.

A portly patrol officer with a sun-weathered face came aboard the yacht. Jay pushed back his shoulders, assuming what he hoped was the confident pose of a defiant millionaire. Connor stood by his side, seemingly unable to control his eyelids, which blinked in rapid succession. Jay wasn't sure where Fritz and Horst were, but he hoped they were somewhere out of sight.

"Good afternoon, officer," Jay said, enunciating each word loudly. "I'm Morgan Billingsworth Jr. Welcome aboard the *Providence*." He extended his arm, gesturing to the entirety of the yacht.

The officer was unimpressed. "You're the owner?"

"I am." Jay cleared his throat. "Well, technically, my father is."

"I'll need to see the ship's papers, registration, cargo, all that," he said glancing around the deck.

Connor gave a quick bow and dashed off.

"Occupation?"

"Businessman and gentleman-adventurer." Jay made an exaggerated flamenco-like flutter with his right hand, which he instantly regretted.

"Destination?"

"We head to Rotterdam next," Jay said, shoving his hands in his pockets.

The officer looked up from his notebook. "You are aware, Mr. Billingsworth, that there is a war taking place, are you not?"

"I am."

"In light of this war, I'm afraid sailing to Rotterdam is highly inadvisable."

"But we haven't got anything to do with this war."

"Be that as it may, your proposed itinerary puts you in danger of having very much to do with this war, in that you may very well become a casualty of this war."

"But we're American!"

"Yes. And assuming your papers are in order, technically I can't stop you from sailing to Rotterdam, but I would caution you—"

"You bet you can't," Jay said indignantly.

The officer shook his head, muttering something under his breath. Connor returned and handed over the ship's papers, which the officer examined briefly before handing them back.

"Very well. Show me the cargo."

"This way, sir," Connor said, leading the officer below deck. Jay followed them into the small sleeping compartment. The two bottom bunks had been replaced with large storage crates. Connor lifted the lids of both, revealing what appeared to be thousands of safety pins. The officer scribbled in his notebook, seemingly satisfied.

Up on the deck, the officer's eyes alighted on the two Germans. When they noticed the man looking at them, they froze in place, staring back at him like angry mannequins. The officer stared back. Behind him, Jay waved his arms to get the Germans' attention. When he finally did, he pointed to his mouth.

The Germans dug in their pockets, retrieving the chewing gum Jay had given them earlier as their American disguises. Each shoved a stick in their mouth, gnashing furiously. Jay cringed. They were overdoing it. Finally, the officer turned away from the two Germans. Shaking his head at no one in particular, he headed toward the gangway.

"Does that mean we're free to go?" Jay asked.

"Not quite," the officer said, then disembarked.

No one spoke or moved in the minutes that followed. Gazing in the direction of the patrol boat, Jay gripped the railing until the knuckles on both his hands turned white. Had the ruse failed? Did the officer suspect Fritz and Horst were Germans? Had he been wrong to assume the rest of the world thought Americans were overly confident gum-chewing idiots?

Apparently not. The naval patrol signaled all clear and waved them through. A few minutes later the *Providence* sailed out of the Thames estuary into the North Sea.

Later that evening, Jay and Connor were in the sleeping compartment, preparing the top bunks. Horst and Fritz were taking the first evening shift.

"What are you planning to do with all those safety pins?" Jay asked Connor.

"Ah. Have a look." Connor lifted the lid of one of the two wooden containers. He reached in and swept the safety pins to the side. Rather than filling the entire container, the safety pins were only an inch deep. Below them was a hidden compartment.

"This is where we'll store the cargo we pick up in Rotterdam."

Jay had assumed whatever the *Providence* was set to retrieve in Rotterdam was some sort of contraband. If they were going to all this trouble to conceal it, he must be right.

"What's the cargo?"

"Three hundred rifles and ten thousand rounds of ammunition." Connor smoothed the layer of safety pins back over the concealed lid and closed the container.

"What for?"

"At this point, I'm not entirely sure. The arrangement was made before we knew we'd be at war with Germany. The guns were supposed to be for protection in case the Ulsters make trouble when Irish Home Rule passes. But now they're saying Home Rule's to be postponed till after the war."

Connor wasn't the first Irish nationalist he'd met. It seemed to Jay most of the Irish immigrants living in New York were of the opinion Ireland should be free from British rule.

"When the war broke out, we figured the deal was off. I mean, Germany's our enemy now. Two of my own cousins signed up to fight the Germans. But a few days ago, they sent a message about honoring our agreement." Connor shrugged. "If they're still willing to deliver the guns, we might as well take them. This war with Germany will be over soon enough. Then we'll be back to battling it out with the British for Home Rule."

Jay lay in his bunk, staring up at the low ceiling of the small cabin. Outside, the weather was fair and the water calm. Ordinarily, the gentle rocking of the boat would have already lulled him to sleep. But tonight, he was wide awake, unable to escape the torrent of unsettling thoughts flooding his mind.

Had things gone according to plan, Jay would now be on his way back to New York, safe and sound, with fifteen thousand dollars in his bank account. If he made it to the German consulate in Rotterdam without issue, he'd be back in New York soon enough. But in the meantime, he was sailing through a maritime battlefield on a yacht crewed by German spies running illegal arms for Irish nationalists. His present situation was far from ideal.

He supposed not everything about his current state of affairs was terrible. At least he was out of England. And he no longer had to worry about Ella Kaye. In fact, this was the first time he had thought of her since leaving his hotel this morning. That was certainly a welcome change. Jay didn't think she'd tried to follow him in London. Even if she had, there was no way she'd find him now. Ella Kaye officially no longer posed a threat. At least there was comfort in that.

CHAPTER 12

Having taken Drake up on his offer, Ella was now an official counterespionage agent of the British Security Service. Her mission: to infiltrate Germany's spy networks.

She had fully intended to turn Drake down. The whole British double agent thing was intriguing. And she was curious to learn what Teddy Belmont had been up to, but she had more important things to do. She needed to make her way to Belgium to report on the war.

But the paper Drake had extracted from his jacket pocket had changed everything. He'd presented her with a unique set of press credentials. They were conditional, of course. She had to work for the Security Service for some time before they took effect. But per this letter signed by Lord Kitchener himself, Ella Kaye was granted permission to accompany the British Expeditionary Forces into battle.

Her Security Service training would begin in two days. The only information Drake afforded her was that meals and accommodation would be provided, and that she should bring comfortable boots for walking. Having traveled abroad to attend a women's suffrage conference, Ella hadn't packed anything of the sort.

As soon as her meeting with Drake concluded, she set to

procuring boots and anything else she might need for training and the battlefield.

In Haymarket she bought a Burberry Tielocken made of waterproof gabardine. The raincoat was intended for men, but the smallest size fit her perfectly. With its long silhouette and belted, cinched waist she thought it rather flattering. At a shop two streets over, in addition to boots, she purchased trousers, a canteen, and a leather-bound officer's field notebook. Aside from artillery, she'd be as well-equipped as any soldier on the battlefield.

Her new wardrobe packed in her trunk, she paced the congested lobby of the Savoy, waiting to be collected for her Security Service training. At half past ten, an unmarked civilian car arrived to retrieve her. She still hadn't been told where the training would take place. The few signs along the empty road provided little information. Perhaps the route was intentionally unmarked. She was heading to a secret military training camp, after all.

She pictured herself alongside men in khaki uniforms aiming rifles at distant practice targets in a grassy meadow. Drake would be pleased to learn she was already an excellent marksman. On the many occasions Ella had gone home with Millie during school holidays, they had practiced shooting. This was not a common pastime among their peers, but other girls' fathers didn't own a munitions factory. Millie's did and had constructed an intricate maze of practice targets in the wooded area of their large Massachusetts estate.

Ella guessed the Security Service training course would be something similar to Felton's, but on a larger scale. She wondered what other types of drills she would have to complete. She anticipated long days of arduous training, after which she would sit with her fellow trainees at a long sparse table. They would eat dinner out of tin mess kits before wearily retiring to a series of rugged canvas tents.

Ella spent the remainder of the drive conjuring the rustic details of this top-secret military training camp. She was therefore surprised when, instead of arriving at a makeshift encampment in a desolate field, the car pulled into a long tree-lined drive that led to a large country estate.

Standing outside the expansive residence, dressed in his usual suit, was Drake.

"Welcome to Ashenden," he said, helping Ella out of the car.

Raising a hand to shield her eyes from the sun, she marveled at the imposing Georgian façade. Drake instructed a footman where to take Ella's trunk, then led her through the estate's grand front entrance.

Inside, most of the furniture was draped with canvas covers. It appeared whoever lived here had not been to the house for some time, as it was in the process of being aired and tidied. Displaced dust hovered in the air.

"Whose house is this?" Ella didn't envy the handful of flustered servants racing about readying the house. It appeared they had been given little notice of the guests' impending arrival.

"Mine," Drake said. "Although, I spend most of the year at my London residence."

"Is this where you train all your agents?" Her voice echoed in the high-ceilinged entry hall.

"I suppose the answer is yes—considering there are only the two of you."

"Certainly, there are others?"

"I should clarify. You're the only *foreign* agents working for us. For the Security Service, I mean. The *Secret* Service, well, that's another matter entirely."

"When will I get to meet my partner?" Drake still had not revealed the other reporter's name.

"How about right now? He's waiting in the library."

The soaring walls were lined from floor to ceiling with an impressive collection of books. Beams of light streamed down from high arch windows. At the far end of the room, in front a large marble fireplace, stood a man with his back turned to them.

He was tall, with a mess of wavy hair. He wore a well-tailored suit and held a nearly empty glass of gin in one hand. The other was lodged in his pant pocket.

Drake cleared his throat.

When the man spun around, his mouth stretched into a wide grin. Ella's stomach dropped, and a flush crept over her face.

"Ella Kaye? Well!" The man's gold-rimmed spectacles glinted in the light. "For a minute, I thought I was looking at my old friend Angela Whiskers."

She winced at the mention of that ridiculous name.

He moved closer. "The resemblance is uncanny," he said with mock astonishment. He extended a hand. "It's wonderful to finally meet you, Miss Kaye."

He was her partner? She was supposed to be partnering with an accomplished journalist, not some pleasure-seeking socialite. There had to be a mistake.

"Mr. Engel is a reporter with the *New York Journal*," Drake said. "And, as of today, so are you. As a part of your cover, you two will be sharing a byline."

Ella smiled at this, despite herself. The *Journal* was the *New York World's* biggest rival. If nothing else, at least the partnership would annoy her former editor.

"Ella Kaye." Oliver flashed her another smile. Then he

finished his gin with a final gulp, setting the tumbler on the nearest surface—an antique writing desk.

"Well then," Drake said, stepping forward to remove the offending glass. "We've a lot to discuss. I thought we could begin over lunch."

It was a breezy summer day, and luncheon was served on the terrace overlooking the great lawn. The ornate table set with silver cutlery and bone china was a far cry from the mess kit meal of Ella's imagination. From what Drake had said thus far, it seemed their training was also to be quite different from what she had envisaged.

Operation Zeitgeist, as their mission was code-named, was the Security Service's first planned insurgence of the German spy network. Ella and Oliver were to be the first undercover British agents recruited by Germany as spies. Drake didn't typically train Security Service agents himself, but given the significance of the operation, an exception was being made.

Although Drake was in charge of Operation Zeitgeist, he could not take credit for its conception. That honor belonged to Oliver's friend and frequent drinking companion, Bertram Scott. Bertie, as friends called him, was stationed at the British consulate in New York. And Operation Zeitgeist had been dreamed up over martinis at a cocktail party in midtown Manhattan.

Earlier that day, one of Oliver's colleagues at the *Journal* had attempted to recruit him. German intelligence was looking to send an American reporter to England as an undercover spy. Would he be interested? Oliver had told the man he'd think about it, but he'd had no intention of taking him up on the offer.

Oliver spoke German, but he otherwise had no connection to the Fatherland. His grandparents had been the ones to emigrate from Germany, and they'd been dead for some time. He'd found the whole idea of himself as a German spy laughable. Which was why he'd shared the story with Bertie at the party that evening. But instead of being amused, Bertie had been inspired.

While the two friends consumed copious amounts of gin, a plan was hatched. The next day, Oliver took his German co-worker up on the offer. Two weeks later, he set sail on the *Oceanic* for England.

When he'd arrived in London, Oliver had taken a room at the Three Nuns Hotel in Aldgate, per the instructions of his German handler. When the Germans needed to contact him, a sealed, coded message arrived for him at the hotel reception desk. The first message he'd received had instructed him to recruit another journalist to partner with. The task having been accomplished, he now awaited further instructions.

A footman stepped onto the terrace and advised Drake of an urgent telephone call.

"If you'll excuse me," he said, leaving Ella and Oliver alone at the table.

"Say," Oliver said, leaning back in his chair. "Can you believe this place? It must be worth millions. If I were Drake, you wouldn't see me running around London chasing spies. I'd be here, doing this." He raised his wineglass and took a sip.

"I'll bet your family has an estate in Newport or some other elite enclave. Why not go there and drink wine all day?"

"You've clearly never met my family." He took another sip. "I'm just saying this place is nice is all."

"You don't have to pretend to be impressed for my benefit. I wasn't born into money, but this isn't the first estate I've ever visited."

"Wait a minute." Oliver leaned into the table, scrutinizing

her. "You're a millionaire, aren't you? That's right. I remember now. You inherited a bunch of oil wells or something." He leaned back, shaking his head.

"Copper mines."

"Why aren't you back at your mansion?"

"I don't have a mansion. I live in an apartment in New York."

"How modern of you. So, tell me. Who's running your copper mines while you're off playing spy, Agent Whiskers?"

Why had she used that name? "The mines are leased to another company."

"So, you just sit back and collect your cut?" He steepled his fingers. "Must be nice."

"There's more to it than that," she said, somewhat defensively. "It's not a trust fund. I have to approve all the sales. In writing."

"Wow. That must be a lot of signatures. I bet your hand really gets cramped." Oliver held up his empty glass. "Hey, pal," he called to the young footman standing watch over their table. "Mind topping this off?" He turned back to Ella. "So, how'd Drake convince you to do this? Are you two old friends?"

"Hardly. I only met him a few days ago. I'm doing it for the press credentials. What about you?"

"Oh, I don't know. Bertie made it sound like a lot of fun. Then there's the fact I'm getting paid by the Brits, the Germans and the *Journal.* That's a lot of cash. Well, it is for those of us who don't own copper mines."

She tried not to roll her eyes. Why did wealthy people make a habit of pretending small sums of money mattered? They were always bragging about bargains they'd secured while engaging in modest transactions—a hat they'd purchased for fifty percent off or a nickel they'd found on the sidewalk. Meanwhile, someone actually struggling to pay the bills would rather go bareheaded than admit they'd purchased a discounted hat.

Inspector Thomson had said money, blackmail and patriotism were the reasons people agreed to become spies. Maybe that was true as far as Germans spies were concerned. But if Oliver was any indication, British Intelligence was recruiting its agents from an entirely different pool of applicants, that of the wealthy and bored.

"Also, I'd never been to England before," Oliver continued. He waved a hand at the countryside. "I was curious to see if these sweeping meadows were as picturesque as Bertie and Jane Austen claimed."

"And?"

He leaned back in his chair, fixed his gaze on Ella, and smiled. "The view from here is certainly striking."

"How long have you been at the *Journal*?" she said, averting her eyes from his admittedly charming smile.

"Almost two years."

"Do you write under a different name?" She couldn't recall ever seeing his name in a byline.

"I take it you're not a baseball fan?"

She wasn't.

"I write a sports column. Well, I did before coming here."

"How'd you end up as the *Journal*'s war correspondent?"

"You mean why'd they send a lowly sportswriter to cover something of such importance?"

"Not at all," she lied.

"I was supposed to be writing a weekly column about American antics abroad. But then the war broke out." He shrugged. "Drake pulled a few strings. The rest is history."

"The *Journal* actually sent you to London to write about American antics abroad?" She laughed. "Why would anyone want to read about that?"

His smile faded. He straightened in his chair. "People don't only want to read about the horrible injustices in the world, you know. There are plenty of other articles in the paper that are just as important."

"I didn't say there weren't. I just think a column about American antics abroad is silly is all."

"That's the whole point. Some people pick up a paper because they want to smile. They want to laugh. They want to read something that makes them forget about their crummy lives for a minute or so."

"I just meant—"

"You think the kind of stuff I write is silly. I heard you the first time." He turned away.

Across the great lawn, a flock of geese abandoned the pond with thrashing wings and indignant squawks. Oliver sat with his arms crossed, avoiding her gaze.

She wished he would stop brooding. She hadn't meant to offend him. She wasn't saying he was a bad writer. She had no idea what kind of a writer he was. She didn't read the sports section. Why would she? And an article about American antics abroad *was* a silly idea.

She considered apologizing, not because she was sorry, just to smooth things over. But before she had the chance, Drake stepped out onto the terrace and ushered them inside the house.

CHAPTER 13

It was their second day aboard the *Providence*. Thus far, their crew of four had not sighted a single battle cruiser. At times, it seemed as if they had the entire North Sea to themselves. If the weather kept up, and they remained on course, they would reach Rotterdam the following day.

The silver cigarette case containing the tracer bullets was in Jay's jacket pocket. But, not wanting to chance ruining the film, he had put the camera in his suitcase, which he'd placed in one of the watertight compartments below deck. When he'd opened the suitcase that morning, everything inside was slightly rearranged. It was possible this was merely a result of the rocking of the boat. Nothing was missing. Still, it was somewhat unsettling. He spent the morning wondering which of his fellow crew members might have rifled through his things.

As the day progressed, the suitcase slipped from his mind. There was a more important matter of concern. The *Providence* was sailing into a storm. By midday, the air was thick and heavy with the promise of rain. By sunset, the sky had turned an inky black. Soon after, nature launched its assault on the *Providence.* Rain pounded the deck, waves crashed against the hull, and wind whipped at the sails.

Connor and Fritz had the first shift. Jay's watch with Horst began at midnight. He attempted to rest, but the violent rocking of the boat made sleep an impossible feat. At around eleven, he finally gave up.

Donning an oilskin over his jacket, he ascended the stairs and lifted the hatch. The storm had grown powerful. He braced himself against the wind. A strong gust propelled the rain sideways, and droplets struck his face like sharp pebbles.

The deck was drenched both from the rain and the rough sea. Connor and Fritz had secured everything on deck. They were now in the process of adjusting the sails to heave-to, in order to slow the boat's speed and create leeway. As Fritz lashed the tiller, Jay helped Connor ease the mainsail.

By midnight, the rain had stopped, but there was still a strong wind.

"I can stay and help if you'd like," Connor said when Horst appeared to join Jay for their shift. "Until the wind dies down?"

"Get some rest. If we need help, I'll wake you."

An uneventful hour passed. Jay went below to fetch a thermos of coffee. He was only gone a few minutes, but by the time he got back, the rain was coming down hard.

He crossed the deck to adjust the mizzen. Tucking the thermos of coffee under his arm, he knelt to retie the rope. At the thud of footsteps, he glanced over his shoulder.

Horst loomed over him, shouting over the rain, "Where did you hide the bullets?"

It took a moment for Jay to register that Horst was speaking English. He rose to face him. "Your English is very good."

"Never mind that." Horst brushed rain from his face with the back of his hand. "Tell me where the bullets are."

A flash of lightning lit the sky, followed by a crack of thunder.

"The tracers. Where are they?" Horst's eyes bulged.

"I don't know what you're talking about." Jay hadn't mentioned the tracer bullets to anyone.

"Don't play stupid," Horst jeered, taking a step closer.

Reaching inside his oilskin, he extracted a Mauser pistol and pointed it at Jay. "Hand them over. Now."

Still holding the thermos of coffee, Jay raised his hands and took a step back. "They're down below, in my suitcase."

"You're lying. Give them to me."

"Put down the gun, Horst." He tried to speak in a calming tone, but he had to shout to be heard over the rain. "If you put the gun away, I'll give them to you."

Lightning flashed in the distance. A blast sounded. There was a hot flash of pain in his left arm, just below the shoulder. Thunder rumbled as he dropped the thermos and let out a cry. He fell to his knees, blood seeping through his serge jacket onto the oilskin.

"Give me the tracers." Horst moved toward Jay, still aiming the gun at him. But before he reached him, a huge wave crashed over the rail onto the deck, causing him to lose his footing. As Horst fell backward, the gun slipped out of his hand.

Ignoring the pain in his arm, Jay dove for the pistol. After righting himself, Horst too lunged for the weapon. But before either reached it, the bow of the ship rose with the sea, and the gun slid down the deck to the stern.

Jay scrambled to his feet, but after two steps Horst was upon him. He thrashed uselessly as Horst pushed him against the mast and started choking him. Jay's arm throbbed as he struggled for breath.

A figure rushed toward them—Connor. He was yelling, but he was hard to hear over the howling wind and rain. He shouted for Horst to stop. But the German only tightened his grip. Jay was about to lose consciousness. Then there was a loud thump and Horst's grip released. Jay slumped to the deck as Horst stumbled aside.

"Teddy! Are you okay? Teddy, answer me." Connor crouched over him, the thermos of coffee in one hand.

Jay nodded. He sat up and scanned the deck for Horst. He was staggering toward the rail, a trickle of blood dripping down his temple from where Connor had hit him with the thermos.

Using Connor's arm for support, Jay attempted to stand. He was almost upright when the ship leaned sharply starboard. Both men fell to the deck. They clung to the mast as a huge wave washed over them. The strong surge of water overtook Horst, sending him over the rail into the thrashing sea.

"Man overboard!" Jay croaked. His injured throat ached. It was painful to speak. "Connor, throw him the life buoy."

Connor rushed to the railing, gripping it tightly. "He's gone. I don't see him." He turned back to Jay, eyes wide. "Jesus, I killed him."

"A wave got him," Jay yelled, clutching his wounded arm. "You had nothing to do with it." He sat on the drenched deck, unable to stand.

Connor staggered back to Jay, somewhat in shock. "His blood's all over you. Jesus Christ. I killed him."

"The blood's mine. He shot me." The left sleeve of Jay's oilskin was dark red.

"What? Why?" Connor knelt to look at Jay's arm.

"He wanted something I have." Jay's vision tunneled.

Connor helped Jay to stand. "Let's get you inside."

"We need the gun. It slid back—"

"Forget the gun. You're seriously wounded."

"We need it. Fritz might be armed."

Having found the gun wedged under the rail at the back of the boat, they descended below deck. Apparently, neither the forceful rocking of the boat nor the gunshot had disturbed Fritz's slumber. He was fast asleep.

"Let's take a look at your arm before we wake him."

While Connor retrieved the medical kit, Jay slid the case containing the tracers out of his jacket and slipped it into the pocket of his pants. He winced as he struggled out of the oilskin.

He was lucky. The bullet had only grazed the side of his upper arm. It was bleeding, but not uncontrollably. Jay steeled himself as Connor cleaned the wound, then wrapped his arm tightly with a bandage.

When they stepped into the sleeping compartment to inform Fritz of Horst's demise, Connor stood behind Jay in the shadows. He held the Mauser pistol in his hands, ready to take aim and shoot if Fritz attempted to attack Jay.

After yelling Fritz's name multiple times to wake the snoring man, Jay informed Fritz in German that Horst had fallen overboard in the storm. They had done their best to find him, but he was immediately lost. He didn't mention being shot and strangled or Connor's use of the thermos.

Jay had anticipated that upon hearing the news Fritz would jump out of his bunk and insist they continue searching the water for Horst. Instead, when Jay finished speaking, Fritz muttered something unintelligible, rolled over, and settled back to sleep.

Connor and Jay exchanged a look.

"Fritz, did you hear me?" Jay asked loudly in German. "Horst fell overboard and drowned." He shook the sleeping man's shoulder to make sure he was awake.

"Good riddance," Fritz grumbled in German, not bothering to turn over. "He cheated at cards." A moment later, he resumed snoring.

The rain had stopped, and the sea was much calmer. Although he'd been up most of the night, Connor insisted on finishing the watch with Jay.

"What did Horst want from you? If you don't mind me asking."

Jay could have lied, but he found he didn't want to. As the clouds cleared and the stars came out, he told Connor everything. After all his pretending, it felt good to be honest with someone. He told him about the tracer bullets, Martin Winter, the Eastman gang, Cody and Ella Kaye.

"What do you think Horst planned to do with the tracers?" Connor asked when Jay had finished.

Jay shrugged. He didn't know. Maybe Horst had hoped to claim the fifteen thousand dollars he'd been promised for the tracers. Or maybe he'd planned to sell the technology to someone willing to pay more.

What Jay wanted to know was how Horst had known he had the tracers in the first place. He had assumed Winter had sent the message to Connor to intercept Teddy Belmont, but what if it had come from Horst or someone else entirely? Other than Winter, who knew about the tracers? Did Horst have an accomplice waiting for him in Rotterdam?

Jay looked up at the sky. The clouds had begun to clear. In their place stars had appeared.

"You don't have to get off the boat in Rotterdam, you know, if you're concerned. You could come back to Ireland with me and figure things out there. I wouldn't tell anyone about any of this."

Jay appreciated the offer, but he'd come this far. He needed to see this through.

"I just wish I knew more about Horst," Jay said.

"Well, we know he cheats at cards." Connor grinned. "What about his duffel? Have you checked that?"

Jay sprinted below, retrieved the duffel, and emptied its contents onto the small table in the galley. In addition to several items of clothing, the bag contained a leather wallet, cartridges for the Mauser pistol, and a red notebook.

Jay opened the wallet first. It contained five English pounds, one hundred and eighty French francs, and seventy-five Dutch guilders. All in all, it came out to about seventy-five US dollars. It was no fortune, but it was enough for a hotel room and third-class passage back to New York from Rotterdam after he handed over the tracers.

Jay picked up the notebook. When he fanned through the pages a photograph flew out. It fluttered to the floor, landing facedown. He flipped it over to examine it, and his mouth fell open. The picture was of two smiling men standing on the deck of a yacht—Dan Cody and himself.

CHAPTER 14

The feast laid out on the sideboard suggested twelve or more guests would be breakfasting. But Ella and Oliver were the only two seated at the long oak table in the elegant dining room. Drake had been called back to London the night before and had yet to return.

It was their third day at Ashenden. After exchanging morning pleasantries, Oliver took up a newspaper, and Ella turned her attention to the letter the footman had given her, forwarded from the Savoy.

Dear Ella,

Please accept my sincere apologies for not contacting you sooner. I only just this morning received the message you sent from Scotland Yard. Upon reading of your distressing situation, I immediately visited the police station.

I was greatly relieved to learn that the misunderstanding had been resolved in your favor. I look forward to hearing more about your strange misadventure.

You will be pleased to learn that you were right, at least in part. Teddy Belmont isn't the perfect gentleman I thought him to be. In the very least, he is guilty of inexcusable rudeness. We had plans to meet in London, but without leaving a note or forwarding address, he checked out of his hotel and left the city. I know not the reason for his hasty departure, nor do I care. I only mention this to you in hopes we can put our silly quarrel over him behind us.

Father and I leave for Boston tomorrow. Despite the cancellation of the conference, I find my trip to London was not entirely in vain. I met a lovely group of Americans involved with the newly formed Belgian Relief Committee. In joining their efforts, I return home eager to encourage American support for the cause. How horrid it must be to have one's home and life destroyed by an invading army.

Father is insisting we leave for dinner now. Do write and let me know when you plan to return to New York.

-Millie

Ella folded the letter and replaced it in the envelope. She was pleased Millie had forgiven her. She would have to remember to make a donation to Millie's Belgian Relief charity.

She wished she could tell Millie what she had learned about Teddy Belmont—that he was possibly Jay Gatsby and probably a German spy. Of course, now that she worked for the Security Service, she couldn't tell any of that to anyone.

She supposed she could tell Oliver, but he'd probably just make fun of her for getting arrested by Scotland Yard. She couldn't picture him taking any of it seriously. Everything seemed a joke to him. It was beginning to make more sense why he'd been sent abroad to write a column about American antics. If he ran out of source material, he could write about himself.

She hadn't brought up the column again after offending him. And they hadn't quarreled since. It seemed their partnership wasn't doomed after all. His take on journalism clearly wasn't as serious-minded as hers, but maybe that didn't matter. Oliver was easy to get along with. And thus far, he'd refrained from boasting of his social standing, which was a pleasant surprise. There'd been no mention of his society acquaintances, club memberships, or any other ostentatious intimations.

After breakfast, Drake having still not returned, they went for a walk around the grounds. After crossing the wide stretch of lawn, they entered a formal garden. A maze of boxed hedges showcased an assortment of fragrant August blooms. In the center of the garden stood a large fountain encircled by marble statues.

"Did you know Bertie's in line to be an earl one day?" Oliver said as they rounded the fountain, apropos of nothing. "The Earl of Doncaster."

Ella snorted.

"What? He is."

"And?" So much for Oliver not bragging about his social standing.

"And nothing. I'm making conversation."

"Conversation that implies you hobnob with British nobility. Am I supposed to be impressed?"

"That wasn't my intention. But since you mention it, are you impressed?"

"No. But I suppose an association with old-world aristocracy would impress your crowd."

"What do you mean, my crowd?"

"You know what I mean. You and your blue-blooded friends from the ship."

"What do they have to do with any of this?"

"They're your crowd."

"What crowd?"

"The trust fund crowd."

Oliver stopped walking and turned to her. "Is that what you think?" He grinned and shook his head. "I hate to break it to you, but the only thing I inherited from my parents was my ravishing good looks."

"But I thought—"

"That I was incredibly handsome *and* a millionaire? Afraid not. You're right about those kids on the ship, though. One of them was an Astor."

They resumed walking down the gravel path.

"How do you know them?"

"I met them on the boat. They were a friendly bunch. Even told me their real names."

"Very funny."

"You should try it one day," Oliver said.

"What?"

"Being friendly. It's a lot more fun than skulking around the deck with a scowl on your face."

"I didn't skulk around scowling."

"Sure you did. Say, that reminds me. What were you doing out on the deck that last night on the ship? When I saw you in the lobby, you looked like you'd been wrestling a tiger."

She sighed. She might as well tell him. "Did you meet a man named Teddy Belmont?"

"Younger guy with a mustache?"

She nodded.

"Sure. I played shuffleboard with him one day. He seemed like a nice enough fellow. What about him?"

"I had just come from his room."

Oliver raised his eyebrows. "Well, well, Miss Whiskers."

"It wasn't anything untoward. Well, not in the way you're suggesting."

He gazed at her quizzically.

"I broke into his room while he was at dinner."

"What are you, some sort of kleptomaniac?"

"I didn't steal anything. Teddy Belmont isn't who he said he was. I was looking for proof."

"You still haven't answered my question. How does wrestling a tiger factor into all of this?"

"My dress got caught on the window when I was climbing out."

Oliver gave an amused grin. "So, what'd you find?"

"Nothing. But my suspicions were correct. It turns out Teddy Belmont's a German spy. Or, at least, Scotland Yard seems to think so."

As they ambled across the property, she told him everything—how she first suspected Teddy Belmont was a confidence man, then Jay Gatsby. By the time she finished answering Oliver's seemingly endless supply of questions, they'd traversed the entire estate. Now they were back on the terrace at the house, seated on a stone bench overlooking the great lawn.

"What do you think?" Ella asked. "Do you think there's a chance Teddy Belmont is Jay Gatsby?"

Oliver fogged the lenses of his glasses with his breath. He removed a handkerchief from his pocket and rubbed each lens in turn. "Honestly?" He held the glasses up to the light for inspection. "I think it's highly unlikely. The odds are probably a billion to one."

"Really?" She wasn't sure why, but this disappointed her.

Oliver narrowed his eyes. "Maybe some unconscious part of you wants Teddy Belmont to be this Gatsby guy. So, when you looked at him, that's who you saw."

"Thanks for the analysis, Dr. Freud."

"You don't think this Gatsby had anything to do with Dan Cody's death, do you?"

She hadn't intended to talk about Cody's death, but Oliver had somehow coaxed it out of her.

"Didn't you say he was the one who found the body?"

"Yes, but—"

"What if Cody was murdered?" Oliver said, seemingly intrigued by the possibility.

An engine sputtered in the distance.

"That must be Drake's car," Ella said, grateful for the interruption. She started for the house. She didn't want to talk about the night Cody died. Not now. Not ever.

Their training resumed shortly after Drake's arrival. The two reporters sat opposite one another at a small wooden table in the library. Between them lay a stack of papers and a box of sharpened pencils, which they were to utilize to practice coding and decoding messages.

A chalkboard had been brought into the room. On it, a jumble of letters and numbers were etched. Drake stood beside it, hands clasped behind his back.

"As you know, most of our information exchanges will be in person."

One of the typists at the *Journal*'s London office worked for the Security Service. All communications between the reporters and the Security Service were to go through her.

"As such," Drake continued, "most of what you are learning today will be of little or no use."

"Well," Oliver said, leaning back in his chair, "that certainly inspires me to pay close attention."

Drake smiled thinly. "If, however, you are unable to deliver a message in person, all information relayed to us must be coded. Assume everything written in a letter or transmitted via telegram will be intercepted and read by an enemy agent."

Oliver stifled a yawn. "That seems a trifle paranoid."

"Not at all. Most of the German spies arrested by us were caught because of intercepted mail."

"How'd you intercept it?" Ella asked.

"Through the post office."

Oliver sat up, his interest now piqued. "Are you saying the post office reads everyone's mail?"

Drake gave a slight nod.

Ella was taken aback by this revelation. "What about people's privacy?"

"The nation's safety is our priority."

"Is it legal?" Oliver asked.

"Everything we're doing is entirely legal under the Defense of the Realm Act. Well, as far as screening and censoring the mail."

A telephone rang in the other room, and Drake excused himself. Ella began jotting down the code on the blackboard.

Oliver got up from the table and turned his attention to the bookshelves. "You think Drake reads any of these books, or they're just for show?"

"Shouldn't you be writing this down?"

"What's the point? He said we'll never have to use this stuff."

Ignoring him, Ella focused on the board. She, for one, intended to be prepared if they needed to communicate with the Security Service in writing.

When Drake returned a few minutes later his face was animated. "A message arrived for Oliver at the hotel," he said. "The service took the liberty of decoding it. Your German handler wants to meet with you both tomorrow."

Ella put down the pencil. "What about the rest of our training?" It was only their third day, and they'd barely covered anything. She wasn't ready to meet with their German handler. They hadn't even gone over her purported reasons for being a German sympathizer.

"I'm afraid that will have to wait until after the meeting. You'll leave for London as soon as you're packed. The driver will drop you both back at your respective hotels. If the Germans have someone watching you, they'll expect you to depart from there."

"Where are we meeting him?" Ella asked.

"In Rotterdam. Your boat leaves tonight."

CHAPTER 15

Sitting at the back of the tug, Jay watched the *Providence* disappear into the North Sea. He was wearing one of Teddy Belmont's suits, having discarded Morgan Billingsworth Jr.'s bloodied sailing costume into the sea. As the tug navigated the choppy grey water of the river Nieuwe Mass, Jay retrieved Horst's red notebook from his overstuffed suitcase. In addition to his own belongings, the suitcase contained Horst's Mauser pistol, wallet, and the picture of Cody and himself. Also inside was a bag of safety pins. Connor had given them to Jay as a souvenir, something to remember their adventure, in case the bullet wound in his left arm wasn't reminder enough.

Jay flipped through the pages of the notebook, most of which were blank. Those that weren't contained an assortment of names and addresses. As far as Jay could tell, there were only two entries located in Rotterdam. One was the Maas hotel. The other looked to be a residence.

Jay didn't recognize any of the names written in the notebook, except for one. Toward the end, on a page of its own, was written, "Teddy Belmont." Below the name followed a perfect description of Jay in his disguise—black hair, mustache, one hundred eighty centimeters in height, twenty-four years of age, grey or brown tweed suit, small leather valise.

Who had provided Horst with this description of Teddy Belmont? Hardly anyone in New York had seen him like this. He had dyed his hair a few days before departing for England, but he hadn't gone anywhere dressed as Teddy Belmont until the morning he boarded the *Oceanic.*

A horrible thought crept into his mind. What if the Eastman gang was after the tracers? If they had somehow managed to learn about them and how valuable they were, they wouldn't blush at hiring someone to kill Jay to obtain them. But the Eastman gang wasn't an international crime ring with ties to German spies. They weren't capable of orchestrating something like this. Or were they?

By the time they reached Rotterdam, it was late afternoon. Ships from all over the world were moored on both banks of the wide river. The harbor bustled with activity. Dockworkers unloaded a seemingly endless supply of crates, which were then hoisted onto horse-drawn carts and driven to nearby warehouses.

Jay kept his head down as he made his way through the lively city lacerated with canals. There were ships everywhere. An assortment of boats floated beside electric trams, men on bicycles, and pushcarts of fresh-caught herring.

The German consulate was only a short walk from where Jay had disembarked. But he'd decided to wait and go in the morning. Thanks to Horst's wallet, he had ample money for a hotel. And he could use a good night's sleep before confronting whatever adversary might be awaiting him there. Besides, there were a few errands he needed to complete before the shops closed.

He located a pharmacy and purchased clean bandages for his arm. Afterward, he visited a second-hand clothing store and exchanged Teddy Belmont's belongings for a different suit and a leather cross-body bag. Finally, he found a barber shop. When he emerged half an hour later, he was a clean-shaven, close-cropped blond in a beige suit. Anyone going off the description in Horst's notebook would have a hard time identifying him as Teddy Belmont. Or so he hoped.

He checked into a cheap, dingy hotel, intending to book the room under a false name. But when the clerk asked for identification, he was forced to sign the hotel register as Teddy Belmont. Having been awake for close to thirty-six hours, Jay was too tired to argue.

When he stepped out of the hotel lobby the following morning, there was a chill in the air. He thrust his hands deep in his pockets and bent into the wind as he walked the four blocks to the office of the German Consul. A strong gust of wind lifted his hat. When he caught it with his left hand, he winced at the flash of pain in his upper arm.

The bleeding had stopped. His wound was healing as well as could be expected. But it was still painful.

The office of the Imperial German Consul was housed in an ornate, castle-like building on the north bank of the river in the city center. The ten-story façade, known as the Witte Huis, was something of a tourist attraction. For a small fee, visitors could take the elevator up to the roof terrace to enjoy unobstructed views of the city. A separate elevator on the west side of the building was reserved for tenants and their patrons. Jay rode this elevator up to the eighth floor. Midway down the hall he found the German Consul's office.

The waiting room was empty save for a clerk sitting at a desk in the corner. He was a slender man with pince-nez perched precariously atop the bridge of his nose.

"Please, sign the register if you will," he said, indicating the leather-bound book on the edge of the desk.

Taking up the pen, Jay started to write "Teddy Belmont," but after inscribing the top of the *T* he paused. He'd used the name at the hotel, but no one knew to look for him there. This was different. He formed the aborted *T* into a *J* and signed the register James Gatz.

"How can I help you today, Mr. Gatz?" The clerk smiled a thin smile.

"I was told to come here from London," Jay said vaguely, not wanting to give anything away.

The man stared at him, a blank expression on his face.

"I sailed here on the *Providence*."

This clearly meant nothing to the clerk, either.

"Is Martin Winter here?" Jay ventured.

The clerk furrowed his brow. "I'm not familiar with anyone by that name." He flipped through the registrar. "No. No Martin Winter."

"Did anyone leave a message here for me?"

"For a Mr. Gatz?"

Jay nodded.

"No."

There was no one else in the room. Nevertheless, Jay leaned forward and lowered his voice. "What about for Teddy Belmont?"

"No."

"Morgan Billings—"

"Perhaps I should say I have no messages for anyone."

"Is there someone else I could speak to? The Consul?" Jay gestured to the closed door leading further into the office.

"Consul Gneist is in Berlin on urgent business. I am the only one here today."

Jay frowned. Muffled voices could be heard in the adjoining room.

"I'm the only one here from the consulate," he clarified.

"Other German officials utilize the office on occasion when conducting business in Rotterdam."

"When will Consul Gneist be back?"

"In five days."

"You're certain there's no message from Martin Winter?"

"I am."

Jay stretched out his hands, then balled them back into fists. He wanted to shout at the frustrating man with his weaselly little eyes. The man was wrong. There had to be a message here for him. There just had to.

"Perhaps your message is at the German consulate in Amsterdam? Or the Hague?" he added unhelpfully.

"No. It's supposed to be here. I did some work for Herr Winter, you see. I was supposed to be paid for the work in London, but then the war broke out, and I received a message to come here, to Rotterdam, to the German consulate."

"And what was this work?"

Jay hesitated. "It was of a clandestine nature."

"Ah." The clerk nodded knowingly. "Say no more."

"So, you *can* help me?"

"Unfortunately, no. I, myself, am not involved in such matters. But, just to confirm, you are American, correct, Mr. Gatz?"

"Yes. Is there a way to get in touch with Consul Gneist?"

"I'm afraid not, not until he returns. But Rotterdam is a wonderful city. Much to see. Lots to do. Might I suggest the Museum of—"

"If Herr Gneist contacts the office, can you ask him about Martin Winter? I'm staying at the Hôtel Van Dam on Hoogstaat. You can reach me there." Jay paused. The clerk didn't seem to be writing any of this down. "Please, it's important."

Back in the dim lobby of his hotel, Jay approached the

reception desk. "Room fifteen," he said, gesturing to the cubby on the wall marked as such.

"Ah, yes." The greasy man behind the desk gave a lopsided smile. "Your friend took the key. He's waiting for you in the room."

Jay's shoulders tightened, causing his arm to throb. An image of Horst pointing the gun at him flashed through his mind. He tried to not to panic. Maybe Martin Winter was in his room.

"Did he leave a name?"

The man shook his head, a bored expression on his face.

"Is it always hotel policy to admit nameless strangers into your guests' rooms?"

"No, I—"

"What did he look like?"

"About your size. Perhaps a little older."

"German?"

"No. Not German. British."

Jay didn't know who this could be, and he wasn't about to find out. He had the tracers, the camera and the Mauser with him in his bag. There was no reason to risk it. He reached into his pocket and handed the man a few bills.

"I was never here. Understood?"

Outside, Jay hurried down the busy street. He didn't have a destination in mind—he just wanted to get away from the hotel. He wandered through unfamiliar streets, the city a blur of activity and noise. Along the river, dockworkers heaved sacks of grain. A tug honked. Seagulls squawked.

With the money from Horst's wallet, he could afford to stay in Rotterdam for five days and wait for Consul Gneist to return. But that was it. If the consul didn't have any further information for Jay, he'd be out of money. And then what?

He crossed a bridge and passed between market stalls

crammed with people. He'd never felt so alone.

"*Hoeveel kost dat?*" a woman asked a vendor.

Jay ambled past a row of shops running along a canal. An electric tram whizzed by. Another screeched to a halt. Where was Winter?

"*Vergeven*," someone shouted.

A pack of bicycles whooshed by, bells dinging. Jay walked faster and faster, as though trying to outrun his multiplying doubts. Had something happened to Winter? Had Horst gotten to him? He passed a church, a row of houses, a square.

He collapsed onto an empty bench under one of the elm trees dotting the pavement along a canal. He hunched over, holding his face in his hands, taking ragged breaths. What was he going to do?

A cloud of cigar smoke drifted in his direction. Someone took the seat next to him on the bench. Jay turned his head slightly, peering through his fingers.

An unfamiliar middle-aged man in an expensive suit sat beside him, puffing at a cigar. The man gazed out at the water. Jay sat up and did the same. They sat in silence for a time, watching the boats drift by.

Eventually, the man put out his cigar and faced Jay. "My name is Hilmar Dierks," he said, in a low gravelly voice that sounded German. "I have a proposition for you. A way to make some money."

Jay leaned away from the man. "Say, I'm not—"

The man laughed. "Not that kind of a proposition. This will interest you."

"No thanks." Jay rose from the bench and turned to leave.

"I have information to share with you, Herr Gatz."

Jay froze at the mention of his name.

"You don't know who the man in your hotel room is, do you?"

Jay turned to look at the man on the bench but didn't answer.

"Well"—Hilmar Dierks smiled—"I do."

CHAPTER 16

They took the overnight ferry and arrived at the Hook of Holland early the next morning. A chorus of horns sounded from the steady stream of ships passing into the canal. As the boat docked, Ella gazed longingly at the dry land. She wanted nothing more than to disembark this horrendous vessel.

For some reason, the entire ship smelled of spoiled seafood. And the sailing had been far from smooth. She'd spent the night clinging to the iron bed frame bolted to the wall of her abysmal cabin as the furious waters of the North Sea flung the ship every which way. She'd felt like a piece of ice trapped inside a cocktail shaker at Rector's on a Saturday night.

If the Germans expected her to make this ferry crossing to Rotterdam frequently, she was going to quit. The prospect of this becoming a routine voyage was too awful to contemplate. She probably should have taken into account the fact that England was an island before agreeing to any of this.

Having shoved her way to the front of the crowd, Ella was the first passenger on the gangway. Taking in her tousled appearance, for once Oliver had the good sense not to crack a joke. They walked the short distance to the station in silence.

On the train Ella took a seat next to an open window. As they sped past banks fringed with waving reeds and willows, she breathed in the briny air. Eventually, her stomach settled.

Oliver was seated across from her reading the paper. There was no one else in earshot. But Ella instinctively leaned closer and lowered her voice.

"When do you think we'll get to follow the British Army?"

Oliver looked up from the paper, feigning surprise. "She's alive."

Ella ignored this. "Next month?"

He shrugged. "Depends how long Drake wants us to stay in London working for the Germans. I'd say at least a few weeks."

"What if the war's over by then?"

"That would be a good thing. Wouldn't it?"

"Well, sure. That's not what I meant."

Oliver narrowed his eyes, examining her. "You really want to be a war correspondent, don't you?"

"Every reporter does. Don't you?"

"I can't say I'm all that excited about it."

"Why on earth not?" Was this another one of his jokes?

"I guess I'm not eager to watch a bunch of men get blown to pieces."

"But it's a chance to witness history in the making. To observe the honor, bravery and self-sacrifice that is war. Just because it's unpleasant—"

"Unpleasant? War is a hell of a lot worse than unpleasant. It's a living nightmare."

"Then why'd you agree to it?"

"I didn't. Not exactly. Drake signed me up without asking."

"You still could have said no."

"I thought about it. But then I got a telegram from the fellow who was supposed to cover the war for the *Journal* thanking me for taking his place. He's got a wife and five kids. I don't have anyone depending on me to come home. Maybe it's for the best. I'm much more expendable."

"Well, that's a grim way to look at it."

Oliver sighed. "I know it's an important assignment. And I'm going to give it my all. But, like my own funeral, I can't say I'm looking forward it."

A stout well-dressed man of about forty, by the name of Fritz Schnitzer, was waiting for them on the crowded platform. Ella had barely stepped off the train when he rushed toward her, shouting her name. Apparently he recognized her from back when her picture graced the front page.

"Welcome to Rotterdam." Schnitzer shook her hand, smiling with genuine enthusiasm. "We are honored to have you working with us, Frau Kaye. You too, Herr Engel," he added quickly.

Schnitzer found a porter and made arrangements for their luggage in fluent Dutch. Then he led them to a nearby restaurant. They took a table on the second floor near the window with a view of the adjacent canal.

Eschewing the offered menu, Schnitzer ordered an extensive array of local delicacies for the table. He was more than familiar with the cuisine, having lived in Rotterdam for over a decade. He'd spent the past ten years running a successful wholesale coffee business with his brother. But when war broke out, the siblings had put the venture aside and returned to Germany to offer their services to the Fatherland.

Schnitzer's English was far from perfect, and Oliver had to translate a portion of the exchange. The conversation turned to journalism. Schnitzer was himself a former reporter, having worked for a Berlin newspaper some years back. Schnitzer was now stationed in Berlin, working for a division of the German intelligence department. He had returned to Rotterdam solely to meet with them. Since the Netherlands was neutral, he explained, the city was a popular meeting place for spies.

"How often will we be meeting here?" Ella grimaced at the untouched herring sandwich on her plate.

"Not often," he replied, a smile forming on his face, "because of the exciting news I bring for you both." He clasped his hands.

Ella straightened, her interest piqued.

"There has been a change of plans." He leaned back and looked at them in turn, his eyebrows raised. "I cannot go into the details here. For now, just know that you will not be taking the ferry back to England on Saturday as planned."

Well, that was a relief. Ella could use a few more days in Rotterdam before having to get back on that awful boat.

"Come," Schnitzer said, rising from the table. "Let us go somewhere more private to discuss this further."

"I don't suppose we could stop by our hotel first?" Ella asked as they followed Schnitzer out of the restaurant onto the street.

"My apologies, Frau Kaye, but that will not be possible." Schnitzer paused on the walkway outside the restaurant and frowned. "I have not engaged a hotel room for you here, as we will not be staying in Rotterdam overnight."

"Oh?" She hadn't even considered this possibility. "Where are we going?"

"To Germany." He smiled. "Our train leaves late this afternoon."

As they followed Schnitzer down the street, Ella and Oliver exchanged a tentative glance. Why were they going to Germany? There had been no prior mention of any such trip.

She didn't think they'd been found out as double agents. Schnitzer was being too friendly for that. Still, the fact they were taking an unplanned trip to Germany was worrisome in itself. They needed to figure out a way to get in touch with Drake and let him know of the change in plans before they left Rotterdam. Once in Germany, it would be near impossible to get a message to England.

Rotterdam's bustling city center was carved in two by the river Nieuwe Maas. On the south bank, ships crowded the old medieval harbor. Teams of dockworkers loaded and unloaded a seemingly infinite stream of goods. On the northern bank of the wide river, rising above all the commotion, was a ten-story white building. The Witte Huis, as it was called, was diminutive compared to the lofty skyscrapers of Manhattan, but according to Schnitzer it was the tallest building in Rotterdam.

They ascended the elevator to the eighth floor, then followed Schnitzer down the hall to a door marked "Office of the German Consulate General." Beyond the door lay a small reception area where a bespectacled clerk sat behind a desk. Schnitzer nodded to the man before guiding them through another door leading to a large well-appointed sitting room. On the far wall, soaring windows revealed an expansive view of the city and its grand network of canals.

Once they were seated, a butler appeared with a silver tray of coffee.

"It was a fortuitous accident that your name came across my desk, Frau Kaye," Schnitzer said. Oliver translated. "How is the coffee? Do you like it? It is a coffee of fine quality."

Ella found it bitter but kept this to herself.

"As I was saying, a list of agents intended for my brother, Ludwig, was sent to me by mistake. Ludwig works in a different department of German intelligence, you see."

Ella forced a smile, attempting to conceal her impatience as she waited for Oliver to translate. It was taking forever. And who knew if his translation was even accurate. She had no idea how proficient he was in German.

"When I read Ella Kaye had been recruited as an agent, I immediately recognized a huge mistake was being made," he said in English.

Ella's smile faded. "There is no mistake, Herr Schnitzer."

"Frau Kaye supports the German cause with great pride," Oliver added. "Of that, I can assure you. Why, just this morning on the train she was telling me how much she admires the Kaiser."

Ella shot him a look. That didn't sound very believable.

"Is that so?" Schnitzer seemed uninterested. "Herr Engel, I'll admit, your name was not familiar to me. But my colleague knew all about you."

They sat in uncomfortable silence. Ella swallowed, forcing herself to look Schnitzer in the eye.

"Ella Kaye!" he yelled, slapping his thigh.

She startled, fumbling the cup and saucer in her hand, coffee spilling in her lap.

"You are a world-renowned journalist! You should be writing of Germany's great victories! Not passing back scraps of information from England."

Ella put the cup and saucer down, smiling with relief.

He turned to Oliver. "And you! You are also very famous in America. I am told you write a funny baseball column."

"That's right."

Schnitzer walked over to the desk in the corner of the room. He picked up a stack of newspapers and spread them out on the coffee table.

"Every single one of these newspapers is filled with lies about Germany and the war." He shook his head with disgust. "I have been tasked with countering the misinformation circulating in the foreign press," Schnitzer explained as he paced around the room.

"This is difficult, as our officers are hesitant to allow foreign reporters to interview them. They fear the reporters might be spies." He paused. "Which, in your case, I suppose is true."

Oliver let out a strange and unconvincing laugh.

"Joking aside, you are foreign journalists we can trust. We trust you, and the world trusts you." He walked over to the large window overlooking the city. "We therefore invite you to travel to Germany so you may tell the world the truth of Germany's strength and power."

Oliver cleared his throat. "Well, that certainly sounds swell. But we should probably check in with the London office of the *Journal* first. I'm sure our editor will want to—"

"That has already been taken care of," Schnitzer said, pleased with himself. "Herr Hearst himself has approved the journey, and I have already arranged a series of exclusive interviews with key military personnel." Schnitzer consulted his watch. "Now, we shall walk back to the station. Our train to Düsseldorf leaves in one hour."

CHAPTER 17

Eyes narrowed, Jay examined the well-dressed middle-aged man sitting on the bench facing the canal. Aside from the fact he knew Jay's name and the hotel where he was staying, there was nothing particularly menacing about Hilmar Dierks. In fact, his tranquil demeanor and unhurried manner of speaking was almost soothing amid the frenetic discord of Rotterdam. But after Horst, Jay wasn't giving anyone the benefit of the doubt.

"Please." Dierks gestured to the side of the bench where Jay had been sitting.

Jay hesitated. Dierks might have a pistol tucked away in his jacket pocket. But even if he did, he wouldn't shoot him here. There were too many witnesses in this busy stretch of town. Jay took the seat beside him and stared out at the string of small boats floating down the canal.

"Erich from the consulate called me as soon as you left," Dierks explained. "He said you might be the sort of person interested in taking on some work for me. When I went to your hotel to leave a message for you, I was just in time to see Inspector Frost harassing the clerk for the key to what I suspected was your room."

Jay's shoulders tensed. Who was Inspector Frost? Were the Rotterdam police looking for him?

"I didn't think you'd be so foolish as to go up to your room with him there, but I waited in the lobby just in case. Then, I followed you here."

"Who's Inspector Frost?"

"He works for Scotland Yard."

Jay frowned. He'd thought he'd made it out of England without coming under suspicion. "What's he doing in Rotterdam?"

Dierks smiled slyly. "Hunting for German spies, of course."

Ella Kaye must have reported him. Had they connected Teddy Belmont with the missing tracer bullets? "How did he know where to find me?"

Dierks waved a hand. "Frost's underlings check all the hotel registers. Whenever they spot a name from their list of suspected spies, he pays the guest a visit."

Jay's eyes grew wide. Whatever dangers he faced in Rotterdam, he had at least thought he was safe from Scotland Yard.

"Don't worry. Inspector Frost and his men are like flies. They are irritating, but they do not bite. Not here in Rotterdam, anyway. Unless you return to England, they have no authority to arrest anyone. But Inspector Frost may have tried to convince you otherwise."

"I won't be going back to England."

"No. You shouldn't, not if you're on Inspector Frost's list. But there are other places you could go to collect information that would be of use to us."

Jay ignored this last statement. He still hadn't been paid for his initial spying endeavor; he wasn't about to sign up for another.

Dierks rose from the bench. "Come, let me buy you lunch. By the time we are finished, Inspector Frost will have grown bored with sitting in your room."

They found a café and sat outside at one of the tables overlooking the canal. After engaging in a few minutes of polite conversation, Jay asked the question he'd been wanting to ask since Dierks had revealed he knew Jay's name.

"Do you know a man by the name of Martin Winter? I'm trying to find out if he's here in Rotterdam."

Dierks seemed to have expected the question. "Erich said you mentioned someone by that name." He touched his fingers to his chin as though stroking a phantom beard. "I do not know a Martin Winter. But there are over sixty-five million Germans in our great empire. I cannot be expected to know everyone." He grinned. "He works for German intelligence?"

"I believe so."

"Do you know what division he's in?"

"He didn't say."

"That may have helped to locate him, but no matter," Dierks said.

"I should have asked." How had he not thought to ask more questions of Winter? Had he really believed there was no chance things might not go as planned?

"No. It was appropriate not to ask. Ours is a world of secrets. My guess is he works with Nachrichten-Abteilung im Admiralstab, as they handle most of our British networks. Tell me, when did you last see Herr Winter?"

"A few weeks ago, in New York. He left a week before I did, for Berlin." Winter had departed somewhat abruptly on urgent business. He had mentioned something about finalizing a large shipment. Perhaps he'd been referring to the rifles.

"How long did he plan to be in Berlin?"

"I don't know." Jay had been so focused on memorizing the details of his cover story and learning everything else he needed to know to steal the tracers that he hadn't concerned himself with Winter's future whereabouts. Not that Winter would have told him. Winter had never offered up his permanent address. At the time, Jay had assumed this was a precaution intended to further conceal the identity of Winter's employer. But if that was true, why had Winter told him he was traveling to Berlin?

"Herr Winter instructed you to meet him in Rotterdam?"

"Not exactly. I was supposed to meet his associate in London, you see. But he was arrested. Or, at least, I think that's what happened."

"Yes. Quite a few of our men were."

Jay didn't want to reveal too much. He particularly didn't want to bring up anything relating to the tracers or Horst. He chose his words carefully. "In London, there was a message saying I should go to the consulate in Rotterdam. I assumed the message was from Winter. But now, I'm not so sure."

Dierks considered this. "As far as I know, no one by the name of Martin Winter is in Rotterdam. Are there any other names he might be using? An alias perhaps?"

Jay shook his head.

"Well, if he's working for naval intelligence, someone in Berlin should be able to tell us where we he can be contacted. Unless, of course, he's on a covert assignment. In that case, it may be difficult to locate him."

"What about Consul Gneist?"

"My guess is he knows as much as I do about this. He's a diligent man. If he had a message for you, he would have told Erich."

Jay waited for the server to remove their plates before speaking. "What type of work would I be doing for you?" He wasn't eager to take on another job spying, but he figured there was no harm in asking.

"You have an American passport, yes?"

He nodded. It was in Teddy Belmont's name, but as long as he wasn't going back to England, he supposed that didn't matter.

"I need someone to act as a courier between various points in Belgium. As an American, this would be easy for you. Would you be willing to travel to Belgium?"

"I don't know. Maybe." He had no desire to travel to yet another foreign country. But he didn't want to alienate the only person who might be able to locate Winter.

"Think about it." Dierks reached into his pocket and handed Jay his card. "You can call me at this number. In the meantime, I'll see if I can locate Herr Winter."

A large crowd, including several uniformed members of the Rotterdam police, was gathered outside the Hôtel Van Dam. One of the officers stood at the lobby door, blocking the entry. An ambulance was parked on the street.

Jay spotted the hotel's young bellman among the onlookers. "What happened?"

"A man was shot and killed," the bellman said with the bright enthusiasm of a child who's just learned the circus is in town. "The bullet went straight through his heart. It killed him on the spot."

"Killed who?"

"The thief who broke into the room. He had a gun on him. But so did the British detective."

Inspector Frost. When the name burst into Jay's mind his skin prickled. Someone must have come looking for the tracer bullets.

"Which room?" he asked, though he already knew the answer.

"Fifteen."

Jay pulled his hat down, covering his face. They'd want to

question the man who'd rented the room. He crept away from the crowd before anyone could identify him.

He hurried down the busy street, past a row of shops, glancing over his shoulder. Inspector Frost had taken of care *that* would-be assassin, but what if there were more? Any one of the dozens of people walking beside him on the sidewalk could be after the tracers.

He needed to get out of Rotterdam. Maybe working in Belgium for Dierks wasn't such a bad idea after all. A man brushed past him, knocking into his shoulder. Pain radiated down his arm. He needed to buy more bandages. The ones he'd purchased before were still in the hotel room.

When he walked into the pharmacy, the jangle of the bells attached to the door startled him so much, he almost shrieked.

He needed to calm down. Aside from the man at the register, he was alone in the small shop. He was safe, for now.

Back on the street, bandages in hand, he tried to collect his thoughts. Inspector Frost and the thief who'd broken into his room had both been looking for Teddy Belmont. Now, so would the Rotterdam police. He needed a new identity. At the top of a stone footbridge stretching over a canal he paused and pretended to admire the view. He removed Teddy Belmont's passport from the bag slung over his shoulder and casually dropped it into the water.

Unlike its German counterpart, the waiting room of the US consulate was packed with people. Jay signed the register and prepared himself for a long wait. Almost every seat in the room was taken by a seemingly agitated American, most of whom had luggage with them. One woman had a steamer trunk twice her size. How had she had managed to get it up the stairs?

From the bits of conversation he overheard, it seemed everyone in the waiting room but him wanted the same thing—to get back to America. Unable to book passage home on their own, they now hoped the consulate might act as a travel agency. Would his desire to travel to war-torn Belgium sound suspect by comparison?

Beads of sweat trickled down his neck as he attempted to concoct a compelling cover story in the stuffy room. He'd say the sister of a good friend was trapped in Belgium. He was going there to rescue her. That sounded believable, didn't it? He spent the next hour nervously picking at the skin around his nails until his fingers were raw, convinced he'd soon be the subject of intense scrutiny. But it turned out the opposite was true.

When Jay revealed to the vice-consul he had come for a passport in order to travel to Belgium, the exhausted man gave a relieved, almost grateful smile. He could not conjure a steamer out of thin air to transport everyone else in the waiting room back to America. But this he could do.

The man was so thrilled to be presented with a task he could actually accomplish, he didn't give it a second thought. Even the fact that Jay had no proof of identity, save for a silver cigarette case with his initials, was brushed aside. Ten minutes later, Jay walked out of the consulate with a smile on his face and a passport for James Gatz in hand.

CHAPTER 18

The Palast-Hôtel Breidenbacher Hof on Alléestraße in the city center was one of the finest hotels in Düsseldorf. The large windows of Ella's expansive corner room showcased views of the Rhine River to the west and the Hof-Garten to the north. Aside from a smattering of men in the blue-green uniforms of the Imperial Army, there were few indications the bustling city below belonged to a nation at war.

For a brief moment, gazing out at the view, she imagined spending the day walking around, exploring the city at her leisure. The thought, of course, was ludicrous. There wasn't time for any of that. They were leaving the hotel now to interview their first officer.

Besides, Schnitzer had no intention of letting the two reporters wander off on their own. They were not to leave the hotel unaccompanied. They weren't being treated like prisoners, not exactly, more like the children of excessively protective parents.

Outside the lobby, a German Army staff vehicle was waiting for them. Behind the wheel sat a uniformed soldier. Unteroffizier Peters, as he was introduced, was to be their chauffer and military liaison for the duration of their visit.

Peters's English was impeccable, which was a relief. Not that he spoke much. His economy with words was almost startling. Even Oliver, who could get a stone wall to talk, eventually gave up trying to engage Peters in conversation.

After a twenty-minute drive they arrived at a military checkpoint. Behind it stood an enormous curved metal shed large enough to house a football stadium. Two armed soldiers in German Army uniforms approached the car. Peters spoke to them in German, and Schnitzer handed over his identification card and a stack of papers. After inspecting the documents, the soldiers allowed them through the barricade.

A dozen more armed soldiers stood guard outside the entrance to the cavernous structure. The hangar, Schnitzer explained, was originally constructed by the German Airship Travel Corporation, Deutsche Luftschifffahrts-Aktiengesellschaft, DELAG for short, for commercial use. But, having been appropriated by the government at the start of the war, it was now being utilized by the Imperial German Army. Inside was the army's latest acquisition, a brand-new Zeppelin Z IX.

Recently built by the Zeppelin Works in Friedrichshafen, the cigar-shaped airship stood twenty meters high and over one hundred meters in length. Its huge metal frame, which contained over twenty-eight thousand cubic meters of hydrogen gas, was covered in a shiny silver fabric. The zeppelin was fully inflated, held in place by thick cables attached to cranes. It was further tethered to the ground by a series of ropes.

Clinging to the base of the large balloon, hovering inches above the ground, were two crew cabins, one at each end. The passenger cabins aboard commercial zeppelins were enclosed seating areas akin to train cars. But the crew cabins on the army's zeppelin resembled the large wooden lifeboats found on ocean liners. The cabin nearest the bow had a glass windshield in front of the steering apparatus, but otherwise the cabins were entirely open to the air.

Ella pictured herself floating in the air, dangling precariously below the massive oblong balloon, and shuddered. The idea of having to fly in such a thing seemed like something straight out of a nightmare. Not only did the zeppelin's boatlike cabins summon notions of seasickness, Ella was terrified of heights.

The twenty-man crew, wearing matching belted uniforms and high leather boots, stood in a line before them. When the captain approached, the line of men saluted in unison, raising their arms and clicking their heels together. Hauptmann Dietrich Vogel was a trim man with a thick peppered mustache. He was the man they had come to interview.

Ella was relieved to learn he also spoke English. She listened carefully as he explained how having only arrived three days ago, the airship, regrettably, had yet to see battle. Its crew had, however, taken it on a series of successful test flights. Another was scheduled for today.

"We would be honored," Hauptmann Vogel said in his heavily accented English, "if you would join us on the flight."

They couldn't possibly expect them to go up in this sausage-shaped balloon boat. Without meaning to, Ella began slowly backing away from the zeppelin. It wasn't until she slammed into Oliver that she realized she was moving.

He whispered into her ear. "I thought the unflappable Ella Kaye was willing to face any danger for a story. You aren't afraid, are you?"

"Of course not," she whispered back with false bravado. She stepped forward. "Thank you, Hauptmann Vogel, we'd be delighted. I've never been on a zeppelin before, but I adore hot-air ballooning."

She'd never been hot-air ballooning. She was supposed to go up in one for a story a few years back, but after ascending a few feet in that wobbly wicker basket, she'd screamed until they let her out.

"I can't wait to get up there," Oliver said. "My pal Ber—" He cleared his throat. "My friend Dieter went up on one of these a couple years ago. He said it was a lot of fun."

"You'll be happy you brought your camera, Herr Engel. The view from a thousand meters above is spectacular."

They joined Hauptmann Vogel in the small forward gondola slung under the hull, which served as the command center. It reminded Ella of the wheelhouse on a ship.

As they made their vertiginous ascent, Ella gripped the bottom of her seat. A safety belt was fastened tight across her lap, but it felt like the strong wind might carry her out of the airship at any minute.

She tried to put on a brave face. Teeth clenched tightly, grimacing, she wasn't doing a very good job of it. Oliver, seated to her right, looked equally ill at ease. His arms were wrapped tightly around his chest, ostensibly to protect the camera slung around his neck. But the terrified expression on his face suggested he was hugging himself for comfort.

Hauptmann Vogel roamed the cabin confidently, hands clasped behind his back, shouting commands to the officers manning the two nautical-style steering wheels. When he needed to communicate with the men in the rear engine gondola, he spoke into a long tube that carried his voice back to them.

Hauptmann Vogel positioned himself to Ella's left, one arm resting casually on the outward rail, the other holding a pair of binoculars to his face. Wind thrashed at his uniform. It seemed a miracle his officer's cap didn't take flight.

"Thrilling, isn't it!" he shouted. His voice was barely audible over the incessant drone of the zeppelin's propeller engines.

Ella gave a weak smile. Then, despite her racing pulse, she unbuckled her safety belt and forced herself to stand. The cool beads of sweat forming on her temple evaporated instantly in the strong wind.

She peered over the ledge. She had to admit, the view was spectacular. The Rhine River looked like a thin serpent snaking through the city.

"Everything looks so small," she marveled.

Oliver, also having summoned his courage, joined them. He peered over the side. "Are those tiny dots people?"

"Yes," Hauptmann Vogel confirmed. "They look like tiny insects you could crush with your fingertips. Do they not?"

"Not the first thing that came to my mind." Oliver nudged Ella with his elbow. "But sure, why not?"

"You need not be nervous, Frau Kaye."

Ella realized she was gripping the ledge so tightly her knuckles were white. "Me?" She released her grip, letting her arms fall to her sides. "I'm not at all nervous."

"Only those below us should be afraid," Hauptmann Vogel said, with a dramatic sweep of his arm. "The powerful zeppelin, floating over cities and dropping its bombs, is meant to inspire fear and terror in our enemies. This is what we Germans call Schrecklichkeit." He paused, giving Ella a menacing scowl, as though to make sure she fully grasped the word's intended effect.

Thinking she should probably write this down, she reached inside her jacket and removed the field notepad she'd purchased in London. But the pages flapped so violently in the wind, she abandoned the effort.

"Schrecklichkeit," she repeated instead, vaguely attempting to commit the term to memory. She'd ask Oliver to spell it for her later.

"Up here, we are very safe." Hauptmann Vogel gestured to the terrain. "There are no mountains or tall trees. And, as we are still in Germany, there is no danger of enemy troops firing artillery at us."

"Can a bullet easily puncture a zeppelin?" Ella tilted back her head, considering the massive oblong balloon causing them to float. If so, that wasn't very reassuring. They weren't in enemy territory, but what if something else punctured it, like the beak of a bird? How long would it take before they plummeted to the ground?

"You must understand, Frau Kaye, the zeppelin isn't one big balloon, easily popped. Inside the aluminum frame, there are nineteen separate cells of hydrogen. Even if one or two were to rupture, the other cells would easily compensate. A bullet is no threat to us. Only large artillery shells are cause for concern."

Oliver shouted over the buzz of the rear propeller engines. It sounded like they were being chased by an angry swarm of bees. "What are the cells made out of?"

"It is the same material used for sausage casings—cow intestines. It takes over two hundred fifty thousand cows to make the airbags for one zeppelin."

Oliver whistled. "If you make many more of these, there won't be anything left for schnitzel."

"That is a sacrifice the German people may soon face," Hauptmann Vogel responded solemnly.

"How fast are we going?" Ella asked.

"Approximately sixty kilometers per hour. But with a more favorable wind, the Z IX can fly up to one hundred kilometers per hour. However, the more weight we carry, the slower our speed. For this reason, we are pleased that a lighter new bomb manufactured by Krupp has been acquired for our use. Soon, we will be able to carry enough bombs to obliterate an entire city." He turned to gauge the reporters' reaction.

"That's wonderful," Oliver said, prodding her again.

Ella gave an unconvincing smile. If Schnitzer was expecting them to write a flattering article about this guy, he was in for a big disappointment.

"How do these new bombs work?" Ella asked, thinking this was the sort of thing British intelligence would want to know about. "Is there a special apparatus utilized to shoot the, or rather . . ." She searched her mind for the correct terminology. "Launch them?"

"We pick them up and drop them over the side."

"I see."

"The bombs were initially intended as mortar shells for ground use. However, their lightweight casing was so thin, the force of launching them caused them to explode prematurely."

Oliver glanced around, as if to make sure there weren't any of these new bombs aboard. "Is it safe to carry that much explosive material? Isn't hydrogen flammable?"

"Hydrogen is extremely flammable. But,"—Hauptmann Vogel held up his index finger—"without oxygen, a spark cannot ignite. The zeppelin cells contain pure hydrogen, so as long as the cells are intact, there is nothing to worry about."

Hauptmann Vogel clasped his hands behind his back, turned, and gazed out. "There will be explosions, but they will be far below us." He turned and smiled at the two reporters. "With our new bombs, the Schrecklichkeit we inflict on our enemies will be relentless. Villages all over Belgium, France and England will burn."

When they arrived back at the hotel, they learned the two officers of the Imperial Army Schnitzer had arranged for them to interview that afternoon had departed on urgent war business. As such, Ella and Oliver had no further obligations until the following morning. Schnitzer had other business to attend to, but Peters, their military liaison, would be on hand in the lobby should they need any assistance.

Having been under constant surveillance by Schnitzer, they hadn't had an opportunity to speak in private since the train to Rotterdam. Under the pretense of exchanging notes for the zeppelin article, Ella and Oliver agreed to meet in the hotel café in one hour. But when they did, Peters followed them into the restaurant and took a seat at an adjacent table. And since the café was otherwise empty, Peters could hear every word they said.

"Say, Peters," Oliver said. "I don't suppose you could get us a newspaper?"

"Certainly. Which one? *Norddeutsche Allgemeine Zeitung*? *Berliner Tageblatt*? *Vossische Zeitung*?"

"Any of those will do. Thanks a million."

As soon as Peters was out of earshot, Ella said, "Do you think Drake has any idea where we are?"

"The London office of the *Journal* must know we're here. That means Drake does too." Oliver spooned sugar into the cup of coffee on the table in front of him. "Not that it really matters. Drake can't get us out of Germany."

"Well, we can't stay here for the rest of the war."

"Relax. We've only been here a day. Eventually they'll run out of officers for us to interview. In the meantime, why not try and enjoy ourselves?" He poured milk into his cup and stirred. "This hotel's a hell of a lot nicer than the Three Nuns in London. That's for sure. That place is a real dump. Say, how come you get to stay at the Savoy?"

"Because I'm paying for it myself."

"That's right. I keep forgetting you're a millionaire. We've been friends for over a week, and I haven't received a single lavish gift from you. What gives?"

"How inconsiderate of me," she said dryly. "I assumed your pal Bertie the Earl had already gifted you everything you desired."

"I said he's in *line* to be an earl."

"Right. Well, when we get back to England, why don't you stay at his family castle if you're so dissatisfied with your accommodations?"

"Can't." Oliver shrugged. "Their castle's in Scotland. I'm better off staying here."

"Well, I'm eager to—"

"Peters," Oliver called out, cutting her off.

"The *Berliner Tageblatt* was all I could find." The young soldier approached the table and handed the newspaper to Oliver.

"That'll do just fine. Thank you, Peters."

"I'm eager to report from the front line, is all," Ella said. It didn't matter if Peters overheard this part of the conversation. He would assume she was referring to the front line of the German army.

"As am I," Oliver said. "Why, I'm eager as all hell to get to the front line." He wasn't, of course. He'd made that much clear. "But Schnitzer's not a magician. The German army isn't allowing reporters on the battlefield. That's why we're interviewing the officers here, in Germany, while we stay at this very nice hotel."

Ella rolled her eyes. She gestured to the newspaper. "What's going on with the war? What does it say?"

Oliver skimmed the paper, sipping his coffee. "It seems Germany's captured a fair number of Belgian towns. But the articles don't go into much detail." He stifled a yawn.

"That's why they need reporters on the front line. The articles written by the war department are boring." She splayed her hands triumphantly. "People will grow weary with the war if there isn't anything decent to read about it. They'll clamor for peace."

"Wouldn't that be a shame," Oliver said wryly.

"Please, excuse me." Peters rose from his table. "There is something I must attend to. When I return, per Herr Schnitzer's instructions, I will accompany you on a tour of the city."

"It is Herr Schnitzer's desire that you enjoy Düsseldorf's fine examples of architecture, impressive collections of art, as well as its immaculately manicured gardens," Peters said, kicking off what proved to be an incredibly dull tour.

Eventually they found themselves walking along one of the tree-lined paths of the Hof-Garten, Peters following a short distance behind. The sun had yet to set, but it was getting late. Rather than return to the hotel for dinner, at Peters's suggestion, they went to one of the park's large outdoor cafés.

The Hofgartenhäuschen's hundred or so tables were crowded with local patrons enjoying the warm summer evening. There was a large fountain in the center. Off to the side, a colorful three-piece band played German folk songs.

Ella and Oliver found a small unoccupied table away from the crowd. Having run into some acquaintances, Peters had disappeared into the throng with a promise to find them after their meal.

Raising a gargantuan stein of beer, Oliver proposed a toast. "To health, happiness, and Schrecklichkeit."

"Shhh." Ella laughed. "You're going to get us into trouble."

"Me? You're the one who asked Hauptmann Vogel how to destroy a zeppelin. It sounded as though British Military Intelligence had sent you here with a list of questions."

"Schnitzer said I could ask anything."

"You asked if a bullet could take down a zeppelin."

"I was genuinely curious to know."

"You should be more careful in the next interview. Drake wouldn't approve."

"Drake will be absolutely thrilled."

"I doubt that. None of it has to do with counterespionage or his department."

Ella glanced around, making sure Peters hadn't crept up behind them. "So what? This information could help England to win the war."

"Not if you get us caught before we tell anyone." Oliver lowered his voice. "Besides, you're sticking your neck out for nothing. The *Security* Service doesn't handle that sort of information. The *Secret* Service handles foreign intelligence gathering. And it's an entirely separate department."

"How do you know?"

"Bertie told me."

"How would he know?"

Oliver leaned in conspiratorially. "Because Bertie works for the Secret Service."

"Is that so?" Oliver had made it sound as though the Englishman's daily agenda consisted of a series of never-ending cocktail parties. "I assumed he was in America as Britain's social attaché."

"Bertie's been all over the world on missions for the Secret Service."

"Well, I'm not sure how long that job's going to last. It

sounds like your friend Bertie isn't very good at keeping secrets."

"He wouldn't share this stuff with just anyone. Bertie and I are old pals."

"If you say so."

"My point is, we're supposed to be collecting information about the German spy network, not zeppelin technology. Gathering foreign intelligence abroad is Secret Service territory."

Ella gestured to the nearby table where a loud group of Germans were singing, steins raised in the air. "If I'm not mistaken, you and I are very much abroad. If Drake isn't interested, then he'll pass the information along to the Secret Service."

"I doubt it. According to Bertie, the two departments are very distinct. And they don't exactly get along. Apparently, the head of the Secret Service doesn't see eye to eye with the head of the Security Service."

"And who is that?"

"Bertie wouldn't tell me. But he signs his name *C* in green ink."

Ella stifled a laugh. "I think Bertie's pulling your leg."

"It's true."

"All right—who's the head of the Security Service? No wait. Let me guess. It's a mysterious man who signs his name *M* in red ink."

"Close. He goes by *K*."

"Ha."

Oliver held up a hand. "It's true. I swear."

The band, which had been on a break, started up again, this time playing a polka. The dance floor began to fill. Couples whirled in circles with their arms linked.

Oliver stood and offered her his hand. "Shall we dance?"

"I don't know how to do that dance."

"Neither do I. We'll make up our own version. Look." He pointed into the crowd. "Even Peters is dancing, and he's sulkier than you."

Ella made a face.

"Come on, who knows what terror cruise Schnitzer has planned for us for tomorrow. Let's enjoy ourselves while we can."

She reluctantly followed him to the dance floor. They spun in circles along with the crowd. Peters wasn't the only uniformed man dancing. Most of the young men were outfitted similarly. In a matter of days, they would be on the battlefield. But tonight, the war was far from their minds. The soldiers laughed and twirled with youthful exuberance, unaware or unconcerned this dance might be their last.

CHAPTER 19

It was Jay's third day in Rotterdam. He peered out the smudged window of his dismal hotel room and sighed. The sky was a dreary grey. It had been raining all morning. And there was still no word of or from Martin Winter.

Dierks seemed to believe he would eventually turn up. But Jay didn't share in his optimism. Winter wouldn't abandon him like this. It was entirely out of character. He would have at least sent Jay some sort of a message by now.

Had Horst had gotten to Winter? Was Martin Winter dead? He banished the thought from his mind. Wherever Winter was, Jay needed to make a move. He was running out of money, and it was probably only a matter of time before someone else looking for the tracers came after him here.

Jay couldn't imagine Winter advising him to sit around Rotterdam waiting for him to show up. Winter would tell him to keep going, to move on. That had always been Winter's advice.

It wasn't that Winter had disapproved of the fact Jay worked for Cody on the *Tuolomee*. Winter was Cody's friend, after all. But, assuming the role of a wise uncle, Winter had cautioned Jay that the longer he stayed aboard Cody's yacht, the less opportunity he would have to learn the ways and means of other industries. Sailing around the world was an exciting adventure right now, but what about ten years from now?

"Time won't stand still while you're on this ship," he'd said. "Don't expect to disembark and join the ranks of your peers. You'll have to start at the bottom with men ten or fifteen years your junior. And they'll be quicker and hungrier than you."

Jay's bag sat atop the flimsy table in the corner of the room. It was already packed. He slung it over his shoulder and headed out the door. He was going to accept Dierks's offer.

The job paid sixty dollars a week. This wasn't anything near what Winter had promised him for the tracers. But Dierks wasn't asking him to steal anything. He only wanted Jay to act as a courier. Based on his stints as Teddy Belmont and Morgan Billingsworth Jr., Jay assumed that before traveling to Belgium, he would need to commit another lengthy backstory to memory. But Dierks was surprisingly casual when Jay inquired about his supposed reasons for heading to Belgium.

"Say whatever you like. There are all sorts of Americans in Belgium right now. You can be a reporter, a tourist, a missionary—anything, really. All that matters is that you're American."

Jay found this hard to believe. He thought his Americanism would render him conspicuous. Why would a US citizen choose to visit a country being invaded by the German Army? But Dierks was right. Belgium was swarming with Americans.

Many claimed to be news correspondents, but few actually were. Most were better described as voyeurs who'd come for a front-row seat to the spectacle of war. They seemed to think the bombardment of Belgium was a sporting event akin to the World Series.

There was no deficit of American businessmen in Belgium either. The war made them uneasy, but they were determined to peddle their merchandise in spite of the unrest. Jay was tempted to assume this role, but the only thing he had with him he could pretend to sell were the safety pins Connor had given him as a parting gift.

Safety pins were arguably something a war-torn country might find useful, but if anyone placed a large order, he would have no way to fill it. Jay wasn't sure how long he was going to be in Belgium. He didn't want disgruntled customers chasing him down.

After much deliberation, he decided to pretend he was the agent of an American charity organization. He'd been sent to Belgium to determine how the charity's funds should be allocated to assist civilian victims of war. This, he hoped, would provide enough of an explanation as to why he was traveling haphazardly through Belgium, should anyone ask.

Jay's first assignment as a courier for German Military Intelligence was to deliver a set of letters to an address in Brussels. After which, he'd been instructed to engage a room at the Palace Hotel, where he would await further instructions. Jay didn't know what the sealed letters contained, nor did he want to. Whatever German plots or intrigues the documents contained were of no concern to him. He was doing this job strictly for the paycheck while he waited for Dierks to locate Winter.

Brussels, with its broad tree-lined avenues, picturesque parks, and abundance of outdoor cafes, was said to resemble a miniature Paris. Having never stepped foot in France, the comparison meant little to Jay. But he liked it here. It was a placid and orderly city with none of the jarring chaos of Rotterdam. Even on the verge of a German invasion, its inhabitants maintained a sense of refined composure.

By the time Jay arrived, the Belgian Army and the national government had relocated to Antwerp. The Belgian fortresses along the Meuse River at Namur were on the verge of collapse. When they fell, German troops would be in Brussels in a matter of days. The city was to be peacefully surrendered. Resigned to their fate, all the citizens could do now was wait.

Having delivered the letters and secured a room at the Palace Hotel, Jay too was waiting. He had yet to receive further instructions. Not that he minded the delay. His expansive room overlooking the Place Rogier was a far cry from his seedy accommodations in Rotterdam. Besides, he could use the extra time to get his bearings.

American or not, it seemed traveling throughout Belgium wasn't going to be quite as simple as Dierks had implied. Jay had arrived by rail earlier that day on one of the last commercial trips into town. The trains were now being used exclusively for military purposes. He attempted to hire a car, but there were none to be hired. Apparently the Belgian Army had requisitioned anything with wheels. Even bicycles were hard to come by.

Of the many Americans staying at Jay's hotel, only one was in possession of an automobile. Robert Washington was a salesman for the Imperial American Tobacco Company. And his car wasn't just any car. It was a 1913 two-seater Mercer Raceabout, one of the fastest automobiles on the road.

Robert himself had the athletic build and confident swagger of a college football star. Like Jay, he was new to Belgium. He'd arrived with his impressive vehicle less than a week ago.

After discovering Jay spoke German—Robert did not—the cigarette salesman invited Jay to join him for dinner. He hoped Jay might teach him a few phrases in case he ran into

German soldiers on a sales call. Having nothing better to do, Jay agreed.

It was a warm summer night. They took an outside table at one of the bustling cafés on the Rue Royale. As soon as they sat down, the waiter presented them with a complimentary bottle of champagne, which he placed in a bucket of ice. The proprietor, he explained, was determined to empty his wine cellar before the Germans arrived. He would rather pour the wine down a drain than relinquish it to their soon-to-be captors.

Jay had accepted Robert's invitation with no expectation other than the benefit of a free meal. But as dinner progressed he found he was enjoying himself. Robert was easy to talk to. Not that Jay had said all that much. The less he spoke, the fewer lies he'd have to tell.

Robert was originally from Chicago, or so he claimed. His accent didn't sound anything like any other Midwesterner Jay had ever met. But that was probably a result of his cosmopolitan lifestyle.

Robert's job as a cigarette salesman had taken him all over the world. He'd lived in Paris, Madrid, and St. Petersburg. He'd even done a stint in Tsingtao, China. During his time there, he'd travelled to Japan as well as the Philippines.

Jay yearned to tell Robert about his years spent sailing around the world with Dan Cody. He wanted Robert to know he too had traveled to exotic locales. But he wasn't sure that was the kind of life that led one to become a charity worker. So, he mentioned none of it.

Before coming here, Robert had spent the last two years working in New York. So had Jay. But the glamorous version of Manhattan Robert described was so foreign to Jay it might have been a city on the other side of the globe.

When he wasn't in his plush office on State Street in Lower

Manhattan, Robert spent his days zipping around town in his roadster, golfing and lunching with clients. His nights were filled with cocktail parties, Broadway shows, and expensive dinners charged to the company account.

Jay envied Robert's life. Everything about it sounded grand. He wished he'd gone into sales. He wished he'd gone into *something*. Martin Winter had been right about that. Instead of wasting all that time sailing around the world, Jay should have been working, building a career like Robert.

"Say," Jay said, "why'd you get transferred to Belgium?"

They'd almost finished the bottle of champagne. And despite his earlier resolution, Jay found himself in a talkative mood.

"Well, I suppose it's because I speak French."

"No, I mean, what with the war and all. You must have done something to get such a lousy posting."

Robert pointed a finger at him. "That's where you're wrong, Gatz. I wanted to come. I work on commission, you see. When the world's going up in flames, everybody wants a smoke." He reached into his jacket pocket, extracted a packet of cigarettes, and offered one to Jay.

"No thanks. I don't smoke."

Robert put the packet back in his pocket. "Me neither. It's a filthy habit." He winked. "Don't tell any of my customers."

"So, business is good?"

"Sure is. I've already got a few big orders up in Antwerp. I'm heading there tomorrow, in fact."

"You don't say? That's a funny coincidence. I was thinking of going to Antwerp in the next few days myself." A sealed envelope had arrived at the hotel earlier that evening with instructions to take it to Antwerp.

"You're welcome to join me. I wouldn't mind the company."

"Really?" Jay couldn't tell if the invitation was genuine.

"Why, sure." Robert grinned. "That'll save me having to learn any German. I'll have a live translator with me."

Seeing as this was likely his only chance at a ride, Jay readily agreed. Not only did he have the envelope to deliver, he wanted to send a telegram to Dierks to ask if he had located Winter. In anticipation of the impending arrival of the German Army, all telephone and telegraph cables connecting Brussels to the rest of the world had been severed. Communication-wise, Brussels was as cut off from the rest of the world as a remote island in the Pacific.

They met in the plaza outside the hotel early the next morning. Antwerp was a fifty-kilometer drive north. The German First Army was still at least a two-day march away in the east. It was highly unlikely they would come across any German troops along the way. But Robert Washington wasn't taking any chances.

Affixed to the hood of his car was an enormous American flag. Two smaller flags were attached to each side. Anyone they encountered along the way, German or otherwise, would have no doubt as to the nationality of those riding in Robert's automobile.

Jay walked around the vehicle, inspecting the conspicuously draped displays of red, white, and blue. "Wow. Three flags. That's a lot."

It was such an exaggerated pageant of patriotism, it almost seemed suspicious.

"Nothing wrong with letting everyone know we're proud Americans."

"Well, sure, but—"

"That reminds me." Robert dug into his pants pocket.

For a second Jay thought he might pull out chewing gum

and insist they chew it to further emphasize their Americanism. Instead, he took out two small embroidered American flag patches.

"I don't suppose you've got a needle and thread on you. I was thinking we should affix these to our lapels."

Jay shook his head.

"You may think I'm overdoing this, but trust me. The last thing you want is for a German to mistake you as British, or vice versa. Unless you wanna get shot."

Jay nodded with a grimace. He certainly had no desire to relive that excruciating experience. His arm began to throb as though in accord.

He opened his bag and rummaged through it until he found the bag of safety pins. "Will these do?"

"Say, they're perfect! You're a regular Boy Scout, Gatz."

They only planned to spend one night in Antwerp, but Jay had all his belongings with him. If Dierks had managed to locate Winter, he wouldn't be returning to Brussels. There was ample room in the car for everything. Robert's two-seat roadster was equipped with an oversized storage compartment in back, which he used to transport cases of cigarettes.

They had just reached the outskirts of Brussels when the car was stopped by two sentries dressed in the navy blue tunics of the Belgian Army. Their passports were examined with the utmost scrutiny. But it wasn't until Robert handed them an official-looking piece of paper with a seal that they were allowed through the checkpoint.

"What was that you showed them?"

"It's a pass allowing me in and out of the city. I'm sure the mayor would gladly issue you one, being as you're here to help with Belgian relief."

Jay wasn't so sure about that. But without a pass like that, getting around Belgium on his own would be near impossible.

A few miles later, they approached a small slow-moving group of shabbily dressed peasants.

"I wonder where they're from," Robert said as he pulled to the side of the road.

"Why are you stopping?"

"What do you mean?" Robert furrowed his brow. "They're Belgian refugees. From the looks of them, they're clearly in need of relief. Don't you want to talk to them?"

"Of course. It's just—well, my French is really bad." He didn't know any French other than *bonjour* and *merci*. Even if he could have communicated with them in their language, what was he supposed to say?

"Don't worry. I'll do the talking. There's a jug of water and some bread in the back of the car. Grab them, will you?"

Robert jumped out and jogged over to the weary group. Jay sat there, somewhat stunned. He felt like an idiot. He was supposed to be the representative of a Belgian relief charity, but a cigarette salesman knew more about providing charitable relief than he did. He hadn't even thought to stop and give the poor people water.

It had been a mistake to say he worked for a relief organization. He had no idea what he was doing. Every decision that had led him here had been a mistake. He was tired of pretending to be someone other than himself. Everything about this charade was so consuming, he could no longer see what was happening right in front of his eyes.

He gazed at the group on the side of the road. The bedraggled quintet was clearly in need of assistance. They had left their homes with nothing but the clothes on their backs and a rickety wagon heaped with their effects—pots, blankets, a lamp. The youngest, a girl of about five, was dressed in a nightgown. She stared down at her worn boots, desperately clutching a rag doll.

He got water and bread from the storage compartment. He reached into his bag for Horst's notebook, thinking he should pretend to take notes for his nonexistent charity, but thought better of it. What was he doing? These were real people in need of assistance, and he was going to provide them with a false hope of getting it.

He left the notebook in his bag. Instead, he took out his wallet and removed half the bills. His relief organization may not exist, but that didn't mean he couldn't help.

CHAPTER 20

The next morning Ella and Oliver set off for Essen with Peters at the wheel. There, they would spend the day learning about Germany's new heavy artillery. Schnitzer wasn't joining them on the excursion. But during breakfast he had emphasized the importance of the visit to the two reporters.

Schnitzer was convinced this new weaponry was so impressive it would persuade President Wilson to align the United States with Germany. But Ella didn't think Wilson would be stirred by armaments. Were Teddy Roosevelt still president, this may have been the case. But Wilson was no gunslinging Rough Rider. He was an academic. Before entering politics, he'd served as the president of Princeton University. Besides, Wilson didn't want to take sides. He wanted America to stay out of Europe's war.

As they approached Essen, a dark veil of clouds hung in the air. It looked as though a thunderstorm was imminent, but the black sky had nothing to do with the weather. The shroud of soot was comprised of the plumes of smoke rising from the stacks of eighty factories, all owned by Krupp.

Everything in the city of Essen belonged to Krupp. The company maintained its own police force, fire department, and hospital. Krupp even owned the homes on the outskirts of town where most of their employees lived free of charge.

Ella raised her handkerchief to her nose. The amalgamated odor of sulphur and other noxious chemicals was revolting. Free housing was probably the only way to convince anyone to work here. Ella couldn't imagine living in this toxic stench.

Apparently, neither could the Krupps. Rumor had it, it was the putrid air that had precipitated their recent departure from Villa Hügel—the family's two-hundred-sixty-nine-room estate in Essen. They had escaped to a recently vacated castle in the Austrian Alps. Schloss Blühnbach, with its fresh alpine air, had belonged to Archduke Franz Ferdinand, heir to the Austrian throne. But thanks to his recent assassination, the estate had been theirs to acquire. And thanks to the war his untimely death had triggered, the Krupps stood to double their fortune.

The large Krupp symbol—three overlapping metal rings—was prominently displayed above the entrance to the chief administration building. Although recently erected, the large crenelated structure resembled a medieval castle. The stone walls, which had originally been white, were now black as night, coated in layer after layer of soot.

Inside, the walls of the cavernous marble reception hall were decorated with a series of German flags. A trim, efficient-looking man by the name of Herr Hügenberg was to be their guide for the day. His voice echoed in the large room as he launched into a detailed history of Krupp.

Herr Hügenberg had a rapid, almost convulsive way of speaking. He spoke without hesitation, as though he had a loaded, never-ending magazine of thoughts in his head. When he was finished he clapped his hands together with a loud thwack.

"Follow closely behind me at all times, please." With an

abrupt turn, he marched out the door.

They were led into one of the many indistinguishable grey buildings. Inside, massive shells well over a foot tall were being forged by teams of intently focused men.

"Here we have the shells used by the Minenwerfer-Gerät," Herr Hügenberg explained. "With this mighty machine, shells can be launched up to ten kilometers. It is with the M-Gerät, or Big Bertha as we affectionately call it in honor of Frau Krupp, that now, as we speak, the German Army reduces the forts of Liège to rubble." A proud grin spread across his face. "Do you have any questions?"

Ella was about to ask about the shells Hauptmann Vogel had mentioned, the ones being converted to aerial bombs, when a series of large crates lining the wall caught her attention. She stared at them, confused. Not trusting her eyes, she moved closer to confirm what she had read. On the crates, block letters spelled out three words: *Platacobre Copper Mines.*

The crates were from Cody's—or rather her—copper mine. How had these gotten here? Cody wouldn't have sold copper to Krupp. And she certainly hadn't approved the sale. Was United Copper Works selling copper under the table?

Oliver tugged at her arm, pulling her back toward Herr Hügenberg.

"Is everything all right, Frau Kaye?" Herr Hügenberg asked, clearly annoyed by the interruption. "Shall I continue?"

"Please."

He went on describing the process of making shells. The metals were heated and melted in enormous cauldrons. Then they were poured into cast-iron molds in the shape of the conical shells. Once cooled, the shells were removed and filled with explosives.

She tried to listen to Herr Hügenberg, but her eyes wandered back to the crates. If United Copper Works was violating their contract, she would have her attorney put an end to it as soon as possible. But there were already hundreds of crates lining the wall. How long had this been going on?

Back at the Palast-Hôtel Breidenbacher Hof that night, they dined with Schnitzer in the hotel's formal restaurant. The room was packed with patrons, an equal mix of German officers and well-dressed civilians. A crystal chandelier sparkled in the center of the high ceiling.

Since this was a farewell meal, Schnitzer had ordered a bottle of champagne. Tomorrow, he would depart for Berlin. Peters, who was also at the table, would remain with the two reporters, continuing to act as their driver and military liaison.

"And now for the big surprise," Schnitzer said after the waiter had poured them each a glass of champagne. "Tomorrow, you travel to Belgium, where I have arranged for you to join a division of the German Third Army."

Apparently, Schnitzer *was* something of a magician. In less than a day's time he had managed to get the Imperial Army to make an exception to their no-reporters policy.

"Herr Schnitzer, that's wonderful news," Ella said with genuine enthusiasm. "Thank you for arranging this."

"Thank Peters, it was his idea."

Having overhead their conversation at the café yesterday, Peters had relayed their eagerness to report on the fighting itself to Schnitzer. Peters would accompany them to Belgium, coordinating interviews and facilitating their observation of the army.

"I look forward to reading your vivid reports from the battlefield, which are sure to captivate readers and maintain interest in the war," Schnitzer said, parroting what Ella had said yesterday.

"What wonderful news," Oliver said in an unconvincing monotone voice. He downed his entire glass of champagne, then signaled to the waiter for more.

Ella couldn't comprehend his lack of enthusiasm. Every reporter dreamed of being a war correspondent. It was the most exciting, not to mention most important, assignment there was. The disappointment on Oliver's face suggested he had just been assigned the dull task of interviewing the winner of a pie-eating contest.

Ella was thrilled. She couldn't stop smiling. The situation wasn't entirely ideal. She would have preferred to accompany the British Army into battle, of course. But, ultimately, did it matter? In their capacity as journalists, at least, they were there as neutral observers. Regardless of which army they followed, what they wrote would be the unbiased truth.

They didn't linger over dinner. The articles they were working on needed to be finished before they left for Belgium in the morning. Oliver was tackling the Krupp article. Ella was writing the zeppelin article. Or, rather, she was attempting to write it. She had been sitting at the typewriter Herr Schnitzer had sent up for close to an hour, but the page was still blank.

Usually, Ella couldn't stop herself typing. The hardest part was editing down an article's length. Now, she found herself at a loss for words, which was silly, considering it probably didn't matter what she wrote.

Toward the end of dinner Schnitzer had informed them that instead of submitting the articles directly to the *Journal*, as was the usual custom, they would first be reviewed by the German Press Bureau. Schnitzer's department would remove any sensitive information and revise any inaccuracies before forwarding their work to the *Journal*. Ella found the news incredibly disturbing. How much of what she wrote would they change? Would this ultimately be a German propaganda piece written by the German Press Bureau with her name slapped on it?

That wasn't all that was bothering her. She'd seen dozens of crates of copper from her mine at Krupp. She'd never approved any such sale. United Copper Works, the company leasing Platacobre, must be selling copper under the table. That was the only explanation.

Perhaps she'd been too trusting. Back when the lease was signed, Martin Winter had worked for United Copper Works. Under his watch, something like this would never have happened. But he hadn't worked there for years.

She needed to put a stop to this. But how was she supposed to do that if they were leaving for Belgium tomorrow? Her train of thought was interrupted by a series of loud knocks.

"It's Oliver," he called through the door. "I'm going downstairs to the bar. Wanna join me?"

"I'm still writing."

"Aw, come on. Just one drink," he slurred. It seemed he'd already had a couple. "This is our last night in the civilized world. Tomorrow—"

She opened the door.

"Tomorrow," he repeated with a dramatic sweep of his arm, "we journey into the heart of darkness."

"Shouldn't you be writing the Krupp article?"

"Already did. Wanna read it? After all, it's gonna have your name on it too."

With everything else, she'd almost forgotten they were sharing the byline.

"I'll go get it. I'll bring some scotch too. We can have a drink while you look it over."

She glanced back at the blank sheet of paper in the typewriter. "I'll come to your room. Give me a few minutes."

His room was a few doors down the hall. It was practically indistinguishable from her own. Even the typewriter on the desk was identical. Except next to it sat bottle of scotch and a neat stack of typed pages.

Oliver poured two fingers of scotch into a glass and held it out to her.

"No thanks."

He shrugged, took a sip, then handed her the stack of papers.

She took a seat in the armchair by the window. Outside, city lights twinkled in the night. As she read, Oliver paced around the room, his hands shoved in his pockets.

"Well?" Oliver asked, studying her face.

"It's incredibly well written." It was. Reading it, she felt as though she were back on the tour. He'd even managed to insert a touch of humor into the piece that somehow didn't feel out of place. She'd had no idea Oliver was such a talented writer.

"Really?" He looked at her closely, as though trying to discern if she was lying. "You're sure it lives up to your exacting standards?"

"Yes," she said with a hint of irritation. She'd said it was good. What did he want, a round of applause? She handed him back the papers. "I'll have that drink now."

"How's the zeppelin article coming?" he asked, fetching another glass.

"Almost done," she lied. "It's hard to choose which of Hauptmann Vogel's inspiring quotes to use."

He handed her a glass. Then he crossed to the window and opened it. The clamor of traffic and conversation from the street below drifted into the room along with a cool breeze.

"What's with the gloomy face?" he asked, taking the seat

beside her. "I thought you couldn't wait to be a war correspondent."

She swirled the scotch in her glass, then looked up at him. "Do you remember the crates of copper we saw at Krupp? The ones that said Platacobre?"

He nodded.

"Platacobre is the copper mine I own."

"It is?"

She sighed. "I don't know how, but apparently I've been supplying copper to Krupp to make German shells."

"Well, look on the bright side. Now that we're following the Germans into battle instead of the British, at least you won't get blown up by your own copper."

"Thanks. That's a real comfort." She downed half the scotch in a single gulp and tried not to make a face. "What do you think Drake will make of the fact we're following the German Army?"

"He's a smart guy. He'll figure it out."

"But what if Schnitzer's department changes our articles? What's Drake going to think when he reads pro-German propaganda with our names on it? What if he thinks we've switched sides?"

"He won't. Besides, that's the least of our worries."

"You think the Germans suspect we're working for the British?"

He shook his head. "What we should be worried about is that we're heading into a war zone. The spy stuff doesn't matter anymore. As long as we keep our opinions to ourselves, and don't do anything incredibly stupid, we're safe. Well, safe from being found out as spies. We could still get blown up by the British."

"What do you think I should do about Krupp and the copper?"

"Nothing. What can you do?"

"I could send a telegram to my attorney asking him to put an end to it."

"Absolutely not. That falls under the incredibly stupid category."

"It does not."

"Sure it does. It's the sort of thing that would make them suspect we're not on Germany's side. You can contact your attorney when we get back to England."

She sighed. "I should have sold the mine a long time ago."

"Why didn't you?"

"I don't know." She'd come close once but had felt guilty selling it.

"Can I ask you something?" Behind his gold-rimmed glasses, Oliver's eyes shone in the dim light. "What happened to him—to Cody, I mean? How did he die? You said it was an accident, but what kind of an accident?"

She thought for a long moment. "No one knows exactly what happened. He was alone on his yacht. He'd given the crew the night off. When they found him, he'd been dead for a couple hours. He . . ." She trailed off.

"Say, we don't have to talk about it if you don't want."

"The autopsy showed a high blood-alcohol level, which"—she exhaled sharply—"was nothing new. They also found traces of arsenic in his system."

"Arsenic? That doesn't sound like an accident."

"Arsenic accumulates in the body. It was probably from all the time he spent in mines. But it was impossible to tell. The official cause of death was heart failure."

"What do you think? Do you think it was an accident?"

She finished what was in the glass and placed it on the small table next to the chair. "I think he killed himself."

CHAPTER 21

They were back on the road, driving to Antwerp in Robert's American-flag-adorned car. It was approaching midday and having no roof, the car provided no protection from the scorching sun. Jay's sweat-drenched shirt clung to his chest in the humid breeze.

He glanced over his shoulder hoping to catch a final glimpse of the family of refugees, but they had disappeared into the distance. When he turned back around, Robert was staring at him. Jay wished he would look at the road instead. He was driving extremely fast.

"Don't look so upset, Gatz. They'll be fine." Robert squinted at the road ahead, then turned back to Jay. "Those were the first refugees you've seen, weren't they?"

Jay nodded, unsure what to say.

"I thought as much. Listen, you can't go giving all of them money like that. It was kind of you, but unless you came over here with a million bucks, it's not sustainable."

"They . . . I had to do something." He stared straight ahead. He could feel Robert's eyes on him, scrutinizing him for what seemed like a very long time.

"You're not really a charity worker, are you?"

Jay stiffened. "Of course I am. What do you mean?"

"What I mean is this isn't your real vocation, is it?"

Jay swallowed.

"You signed up for this because you thought it would be fun and exciting to travel to Europe. Am I right?"

"I—"

"But now you're over here and see all the poor people devastated by the war, and it's a different story."

"Well—"

"Hey, I get it. It's okay. Don't look so petrified. All I'm saying is, just because you came here for the wrong reasons doesn't mean you can't do some good." Robert was still staring at him. "Take me for example. I came over here to make money selling smokes to a war-torn population. That's certainly not noble, but I help when I can. You see—"

"Stop!" Jay yelled.

"Let me finish—"

"Stop the car!"

Robert slammed on the brakes, and the car screeched to a halt. Less than three feet away from the hood stood two Belgian soldiers. Their rifles were pointed directly at them.

After shouting what sounded like a series of French expletives, the officer on the left shook his head at the American flag stuck to the front of the car and switched to English.

"When you see Belgian uniforms in the road, you stop immediately. Do you understand?"

"Yessir," Robert answered. "Understood."

The angry soldier took a step closer to the car. With the tip of his rifle, he touched a barely visible line of wire strung tightly across the road between two poles.

"Always stop," the soldier continued. "Unless, of course, you wish to decapitate yourselves."

Jay instinctively brought a hand to his throat. Had Robert waited a second or two longer to brake, the chin level cable would have sliced neatly through their necks.

Even after Robert issued a series of profuse apologies, the guards were reluctant to allow them past the checkpoint. But after he gave each of them a free carton of cigarettes they acquiesced.

After two additional checkpoints—fortified by actual forts rather than wire strung across the road—they reached the final gatekeepers of Antwerp. These sentries guarded an opening in the newly constructed electric barbed wire fence. Beyond the fence, piles of rubble stretched for miles.

It looked as though a thousand bulldozers had descended upon the city outskirts. According to Robert, the destruction before them was self-inflicted by the Belgians, a gallant sacrifice to save the city of Antwerp. Engineers had demolished millions of dollars of real estate. And sappers had cut down a forest's worth of trees to create a clear line of vision. Not so much as a shrub remained, and not a single German soldier could approach Antwerp without being seen.

"If you head back this way without me," Robert said as they drove through the leveled ruins of what had once been an affluent suburb, "be sure the guards give you new directions. This route may be clear today, but it's temporary. They move the mines around regularly. And don't even think about trying to get past that fence without permission. It's wired with more voltage than the electric chair at Sing Sing."

Antwerp proper remained unscathed. Its ancient stone façades retained all their medieval splendor. They navigated through a labyrinth of winding cobblestone streets before emerging onto a wide modern boulevard bustling with activity.

The city possessed none of the resigned tranquility of Brussels. There was an almost palpable frenetic energy coursing through the streets. Everything seemed to be moving at an accelerated pace. Cars raced through the avenues, barely pausing at intersections. Pedestrians hurried down the sidewalks with purposeful strides.

Only the huddles of displaced refugees were stagnant. They had abandoned their homes and livelihoods in haste. Now that they were here, there was nothing more to rush toward. They wandered around the city in a torpid stupor like a cluster of lost sheep.

Belgium's newfound capital was teeming with all manner of evacuees. Those with the wherewithal to engage a room had done so. As a result, accommodations were scarce. They drove to the Grand-Hôtel on Rue Gérard, where they'd intended to stay, only to find it was occupied in its entirety by the government officials from Brussels.

They managed to secure one of the few unoccupied rooms in all of Antwerp, a double at the nearby Hôtel St. Antoine on Place Verte. Members of the foreign diplomatic corps inhabited most of the hotel's other rooms, and a cacophony of dialects reverberated through the lobby. It was all a little disorienting, and Jay wasn't thrilled to have a roommate. But their room on the tenth floor was spacious. And Robert would be out most of the time on sales calls.

Since charity workers didn't typically sport bullet wounds, Jay waited until Robert left the room before changing the bandage on his arm. Robert didn't seem the type to go snooping through other people's luggage, but Jay wasn't taking any chances. He removed the Mauser pistol from his bag and shoved it under his mattress.

His bandage changed, contraband concealed, Jay set out to send Dierks a telegram. In the plaza outside the hotel, hundreds of refugees were lined up outside the colossal gothic cathedral on the other side of the square. High above the throng, in the spired tower, armed Belgian soldiers kept watch over the city.

It was a short walk to the telegraph office. But when he arrived, the two policemen guarding the entrance wouldn't let him in the building. He had his passport with him, but apparently one needed "papers" to enter the telegraph bureau.

Upon seeing his frustration, a well-dressed elderly Belgian woman with a slightly hunched back shuffled toward him.

"You mustn't take it personally. They're only doing their jobs." She lowered her voice conspiratorially and raised her painted eyebrows. "Antwerp is crawling with German spies, you see."

Jay cleared his throat. "Is that so?" He gave a nervous smile. "I'll keep that in mind."

Now, it seemed everywhere he looked, people were staring at him, eying him with suspicion. He had intended to deliver the envelope from Brussels after visiting the telegraph office. But he wasn't sure if he needed "papers" to wander around the city. So, he hurried back to the hotel.

It was a good thing he did. It turned out foreigners did need a pass to move freely about the city. Fortunately, with Robert's help, Jay was able to obtain a *permis de séjour* later that afternoon. But by the time he did, the telegraph office was closed for the day.

Robert himself had managed to obtain the much-prized *laissez-passer*, as he had in Brussels. It not only allowed him to remain in the city, it gave him permission to come and go as he pleased. Robert didn't share how he had managed to secure this coveted pass. But Jay suspected it involved a sizeable endowment of cigarettes.

The palm-filled courtyard of the Hôtel St. Antoine was packed with men and women in dinner dress juxtaposed with military officers in an assortment of Belgian, French and British uniforms. Aside from all the insignia, nothing about the jovial ambiance suggested several battles were being fought mere miles away from the city.

Robert was sitting with a group of British diplomats at a table next to the gurgling fountain. The men's loud voices and high spirits suggested they had all been drinking for some time. Given the fact he was working as a German spy, Jay didn't think it wise to hobnob with the veritable enemy. But before he could slink away, Robert spotted him.

"Why, here's my savior now," he called out, motioning for Jay to join the group. "Gentlemen, may I present the man who literally saved my neck, Mr. James Gatz."

"I didn't have much choice," Jay said, taking a seat in the empty chair next to Robert. "My neck was on the line too."

The men at the table laughed, and Jay relaxed.

Robert raised a hand to get the waiter's attention. "Drinks are on me, Gatz. What'll it be?"

"Whatever you're having."

"Gatz is here on behalf of the American Belgian Relief Charity."

"Ah, yes," one of the British men said knowingly. "You're one of Hoover's boys, then."

"Well, actually—"

"Interesting chap. Met him in London earlier this summer. Apparently he's managed to convince a host of Americans to stay abroad and work for his relief committee."

Jay had no idea who Hoover was or what the man was talking about. But he couldn't get a word in edgewise.

"You're a Rhodes Scholar, then," the man continued. It wasn't a question. "Can't say I blame you for wanting to come to Belgium. Oxford must be near abandoned, what with all the boys joining up to fight the good fight."

"I'm an Oxford man myself," one of the other men put in. "Trinity College."

"Oh, well, I'm not—"

"Here you are, sir," a waiter said, handing Jay a small stemmed glass containing a honey-colored aperitif.

Jay sniffed the aromatic liqueur warily. Robert certainly had a sophisticated palate for a cigarette salesman hailing from the Midwest. Jay'd have preferred a beer. He'd expected a beer. Wasn't that what Belgium was known for?

"It's jolly good of you Americans to step in and help with Belgian aid," the British diplomat resumed. "We've enough on our plate as it is. But don't you worry. This war will be over soon enough. You'll be back at Oxford before you know it."

Jay looked at Robert, hoping he might help clear up the misconception that he was an Oxford Rhodes Scholar working for a relief committee run by some man named Hoover. But Robert only shrugged, as if to say it wasn't worth correcting the man. So, Jay stopped trying.

Armed with his passport and *permis de séjour*, Jay set out the following morning to send a telegram to Dierks. It was a pleasant, breezy day. The sky was the infinite blue of endless possibilities. It was at odds with the disenchanted crowd trudging through the plaza. The number of refugees seemed to have doubled overnight. German howitzers boomed in the distance.

The telegram sent, Jay made his way across town to deliver the envelope. He turned down a narrow cobblestone street. The address was in the center of a row of houses. Aside from a maid sweeping a door stoop, there was no one else on the street. Ordinarily, nothing about the tranquil scene before him would be cause for alarm, but the emptiness and silence reminded him of Caledonian Road.

What if this address had also been compromised? What if the police were watching it now, as they had been in London? Was that really a maid? Or did she work for Belgian Intelligence?

Instead of sliding the envelope through the slot on the front door, Jay walked right past the address and circled the block. When he approached the house a second time, the maid on the other side of the street stopped sweeping.

"*Vous êtes perdus*?" she called to him.

Ignoring her, he fumbled in his jacket pocket, retrieved the envelope, and thrust it through the mail slot. Then he raced down the street and hurried back to his hotel.

He spent the rest of the morning pacing his hotel room wondering whether he'd been reported to the Belgian authorities by a woman who may or may not have been posing as a maid. Working as an undercover courier was a thousand times more stressful than he'd anticipated. Every so often he stopped at the window and gazed gloomily at the ever-expanding crowd of refugees he was purportedly here to help with a pang of guilt.

The door to the hotel room flew open.

"There you are," Robert said, entering the room. "What are you doing this afternoon?"

"I don't have any plans."

"Wanna come with me on a sales call? I could use your help if I run into any Germans. What do you say? I'll buy you lunch."

Seeing as he had nothing to do, other than wallow in remorse and wait to see if he'd be arrested, Jay agreed. On their way out of the city, Robert made a stop on the Rue de l'Esplanade. He'd promised a friend he'd deliver a letter to her sister.

Jay waited in the car while Robert went to the door. An

attractive woman answered. They exchanged a few words, then she handed Robert an envelope.

Witnessing the transaction, Jay felt like a complete fool. There was no reason for anyone to think delivering a letter was suspicious. Unless, of course, you raced down the street like a terrified rabbit after doing so. He was overthinking all of this. In the future, he resolved to act more like a normal person going about their business, like Robert.

The town of Pertés was located twenty kilometers southeast of Antwerp. After a series of sentry stops, they reached a stretch of open road.

"See that?" Robert took one hand off the wheel and pointed at the horizon. Pillars of smoke rose in the distance. "They say the Germans might reach Pertés as soon as tomorrow."

"What happens when they do?" Jay asked. "As far as selling cigarettes, I mean. Will you still be allowed to enter the city on business?"

"Eventually. Or so I hope. But I wouldn't want to be there when the Germans arrive. From what I've heard, they've adopted a 'shoot first, ask questions later' policy."

Jay squeezed his eyes shut. He should have stayed in Antwerp. So what if some maid had seen him deliver a letter? By coming with Robert, he had potentially put himself in real danger. What if the car broke down, or something else caused them to get stuck in Pertés? Jay didn't want to get caught in the crossfire. It wasn't as though he had some sort of secret agent badge he could flash to the Germans to let them know he was on their side.

The streets of Pertés were eerily vacant. There wasn't a person or animal in sight. It looked as though the plague had descended upon the town. The townspeople must have also heard the news the Germans would be arriving soon.

"The café I'm delivering the cigarettes to isn't half-bad. We'll eat lunch there before heading back to Antwerp. I just need to drop this letter off first."

Robert stopped the car in front of a small white house on the stretch of town along the train tracks. "This will only take a minute."

It took twenty. And when Robert finally emerged from the house, it was to coax Jay out of the car. They'd eat at the café in town some other time. Today, Madame Lejeune insisted they join her family for lunch.

The dining table, laid with a tablecloth of crocheted silk, took up most of the small room. Neither Madame Lejeune, her two young daughters, nor her elderly father-in-law spoke a word of English. But that didn't stop them from giving Jay the third degree with regard to his charity.

With Robert acting as translator, Jay fumbled his way through the interrogation. He tried to recall what he'd told Robert, so as not to contradict himself. He'd given some spiel about the charity the night he and Robert first met. But his memory of the evening was hazy from all the champagne.

"How do you know Robert, Madame Lejeune?" Jay asked, trying to change the subject.

"It's a long story," Robert said, thwarting his effort. "I'll tell you on the ride back."

The meal seemed to last forever. And Robert still had cigarettes to deliver in town. If they stayed here much longer, by the time they got home the telegraph bureau would be closed. Just as they were about to leave, there was a loud clap of thunder followed by a torrential downpour of rain. Robert had parked the car in the barn. It was dry for now. But, given the automobile had no roof, once they started driving, that wouldn't matter much.

Jay didn't mind getting wet, not if it meant getting out of

here. But Robert agreed with Madame Lejeune that they should stay until the weather cleared. Not for the first time, Jay wished he were back in Antwerp.

His regret at having accompanied Robert increased exponentially when a young man burst through the front door shouting, "*Les Allemands sont arrives*!"

Upon hearing the Germans had arrived, Madame Lejeune threw up the kitchen rug, revealing a trap door.

"She wants us to hide in the cellar," Robert said.

They'd already spent half the day stuck in the Lejeunes' house—Jay wasn't keen to spend the remainder trapped in their cellar.

"Maybe we should make a run for the car," Jay suggested.

Robert shook his head. "It's too late for that. The boy says the German soldiers are rounding up all the men in town between the ages of fifteen and sixty."

"I'll talk to them. I can explain we're American."

"Trust me, it's better if we stay here. As soon as the Germans are done inspecting the house and the coast is clear, we'll leave. I promise."

Jay didn't have much choice in the matter. He couldn't get anywhere without Robert and his car. He followed him down the ladder into the small dank space. The trap door shut with a thump. And, crouching in the darkness, they waited.

CHAPTER 22

Ella lay awake in the four-poster bed as dawn filtered into her hotel room. She had barely slept. She couldn't stop thinking about the crates she'd seen at Krupp. Copper from Platacobre was being used to make weapons. She couldn't just ignore this and go to Belgium.

Later that morning, she took the stairs down to the first floor and slipped out the back of the hotel. Satisfied she wasn't being followed, she walked the three blocks to the telegraph office. There she sent a telegram to her attorney, asking him to put an end to any under-the-table sale of copper from Platacobre to Krupp.

Two hours later, they boarded a train bound for Aachen. The cars were filled with German soldiers heading off to battle, but Peters and the two reporters had a compartment to themselves. The whistle blew. Puffs of steam billowed into the sky as the train chugged down the track.

They were heading to the front line. It was really happening. She was finally going to be a war correspondent. She was going to bear witness to history in the making. To behold men inspired by the noblest of intentions: courage, pride of country, and loyalty.

She would be front-page news again. She wondered what picture of her the *Journal* would use for their column. Perhaps she and Oliver should take a photograph together with the fighting in the background.

When Peters went to the dining car, they were left alone in the compartment. Oliver put down the paper he'd been reading.

"I saw you out my window this morning." His voice was sterner than usual. "Where'd you go?"

Ella stared at her lap. She felt like a schoolgirl who'd been caught cheating on an exam. "I sent a telegram to my attorney."

"About Krupp?"

She nodded.

"Damn it, Ella." He managed to keep his voice down, but he was angry. "I thought we agreed that was a bad idea. Are you trying to get us caught?"

"Calm down," she whispered. "It's not like I sent a message to the British Security Service. It was a telegram to my personal attorney in New York."

"About Krupp, Germany's largest weapons manufacturer. If they censor everything here like they do in England, your telegram's going to raise a giant red flag. You know what they do to enemy spies, don't you?"

"Don't be so dramatic. It was a telegram sent in the ordinary course of business. Unlike you, my sole enterprise in life isn't having fun. I have other obligations."

"Obligations," he scoffed. "You don't give a damn about obligations. You just do whatever you want whenever you feel like it without a second thought. You don't care who gets hurt as long as you get what you want."

"Of course I care." She gaped at him incredulously.

"Don't send any more telegrams."

"Don't tell me what to do." She turned away from him and fixed her gaze out the window.

Four hours later, they were driving through the Belgian countryside. Thus far, the landscape bore no evidence of the war. Fields of wheat, illuminated by the midday sun, rippled in the wind like the waves of a golden ocean. But in the distance, giant columns of smoke rose into the sky.

Peters was at the wheel of the German army vehicle he'd been issued for their transportation. The two reporters sat side by side in the back seat. They still weren't speaking to one another.

Ella had no intention of breaking the silence anytime soon. She stared out the window determinedly. They passed a whitewashed farmhouse with a cobalt blue advertisement painted on its side, one of many dotting this region of the Belgian countryside. The word "*chocolat*" curved elegantly over a little girl seated alone at a small table crowded with an assortment of chocolates.

Oliver had completely overreacted about the telegram. And what he'd said about her, that she only cared about herself, was completely inaccurate, not to mention incredibly rude. Ella cared about all sorts of people other than herself. That was why she was an investigative journalist. Because she cared. Unlike *some* people, when she researched a story, it didn't involve sitting in a baseball stand eating peanuts and cracking jokes.

She'd endured prolonged discomfort so her articles might improve the lives of strangers. She'd spent weeks working at a shirt factory, toiling twelve hours a day in crowded, filthy conditions in the sweltering heat in order to bring attention to the abhorrent working conditions in factories. After all the public outcry her article generated, laws requiring better working conditions at factories had been proposed.

And that was only one example. Thanks to another one

of Ella's stories, an insane asylum had been shuttered for the mistreatment of its female wards. Sure, those articles had made her famous, but that wasn't why she'd written them. She'd written them to help others.

Oliver didn't know what he was talking about. Despite being inanely large, his glasses clearly weren't doing him much good, seeing as he was blind to the truth. She cared if others got hurt. Of course she did. She stared out the window watching the countryside fly by, her arms crossed tightly.

"How long will we be with the army?" Oliver asked sometime later.

Ella perked up at the question. In all her excitement, she'd neglected to ask Schnitzer this.

Peters responded in his usual bland, matter-of-fact tone. "Until we reach France."

"How long will that take?"

"The projected estimate is three weeks."

"Three weeks!" Oliver cried, his face aghast. Then he slumped into the seat melodramatically.

Ella shot him a look.

"Why, that's barely any time at all," he amended.

"What if the army doesn't make it to France by then?" she asked.

"You will remain with the division until they do. Unless . . ." Peters didn't finish the thought.

"Unless what?" Oliver asked.

"Unless you get killed first."

They soon had their first glimpse of the German Army. Peters had intentionally taken a different route than the regiment in order to overshoot the march. Perched atop a hill, they could now observe the parade from start to finish.

The sheer number of soldiers was overwhelming. From afar, the unending column of green-grey uniforms marching in unison looked more like a thick fog rolling down the road than a collection of men. In front, seated atop majestic horses, were the Uhlans. Their lance tips glinted in the sunlight. Their pendants fluttered in the wind.

Next came an unending river of infantry. Countless men donning spiked helmets marched in time, stepping and swinging their arms in unison. A series of canvas-topped ambulances painted with red crosses followed. Then came the artillery. Teams of thirty horses pulled each gigantic siege gun.

After driving alongside the parade for close to an hour, they parted company with the battalion. They would rejoin them at camp later this evening. But now they were going to tour one of the towns already captured by the Germans. Afterward, they were invited to dine with a group of high-ranking German officers.

After a few miles the road cut into a forest. The light faded, the sun obscured by the thick branches of ancient trees.

"What's so special about this town?" Oliver asked Peters.

"There was a civilian uprising there yesterday."

"And Schnitzer wants us to write about it?" That seemed opposite the sort of thing the Germans would want to advertise. Doing so might encourage others to resist the German army.

"The uprising was efficiently quelled," Peters explained. "The town is now firmly under German control. You are to write about that."

Having just witnessed the size and strength of the German army, Ella wasn't sure if attempting a civilian uprising was an incredibly brave or foolhardy notion. She felt the same way about King Albert's insistence Belgium battle the Germans rather than allow them to pass through the country to

France without a fight. In principle, it was a noble and courageous decision. But how much of Belgium would be destroyed as a result? How many Belgians would lose their lives in a war that, aside from their nation's geological location between Germany and France, didn't concern them?

The trees fell away, and the town came into view. Whatever Ella had expected to see, it wasn't this. A blanket of smoke hovered over the town—an impenetrable cloud of darkness masking the otherwise clear blue sky. The houses lining both sides of the street had been reduced to piles of rubble, most of which were still smoldering. Machine guns rattled in the distance, punctuated every so often with a loud boom. Dynamite was being employed to destroy some of the larger structures, including the church on the other side of town.

Out of the car, they stood on the street taking in the carnage before them. Ella clutched Oliver's arm to steady herself, their earlier quarrel forgotten. The air smelled of smoke and rotting flesh. Flies buzzed above the dozens of corpses strewn about the street. These were not fallen soldiers but civilians, men and women alike. A few faced up, blank eyes staring at the dark sky. But most had been shot in the back. Dispersed amid the detritus covering the road were the remnants of their former lives—scattered clothing, broken plates, wooden shoes.

Further down the street, soldiers were still in the process of scouring the homes for valuables. The procedure was systematically repeated house by house. After the looting was complete, the structure was doused with gasoline and set aflame.

In the epicenter of the apocalypse was an elegant carved mahogany table that had been dragged into the middle of the street. Seated at the table were two men in decorated uniforms. Seemingly amused by the horrific tableau before them, each held a cigar in one hand and a bottle of wine in the other.

Peters was trying his best to appear unfazed, but his eyes were wild. He gestured to the men at the table. "Would you like to meet the officers in charge?"

Ella stared at Peters incredulously. Had he really just asked if she wanted to meet these monsters? If anything, she wanted to rip the cigars out of their grotesque mouths and slap them each in the face.

"No thanks," Oliver said.

"Very well, then," Peters said, steeling himself. "Stay here while I speak to them." He marched over to the table, navigating around the thin corpse of an old man.

To their left was an alley. Four German soldiers, guns slung over their shoulders, swaggered down it in their direction. One of the soldiers shouted something in German, pointing an accusatory finger at them.

Ella gripped Oliver's arm. Did the soldiers think they were Belgians? Peters was only a few meters away, but at that distance there was nothing he could do to stop anything.

"It's okay," Oliver said. "They just want me to take a picture."

The soldier had been pointing at the camera hanging around Oliver's neck. Posing in front of a smoldering façade, they held up their rifles. Big lascivious grins were stretched across their young faces.

Down the street, an animated soldier emerged from one of the yet-to-be-burned houses. He yelled something to the officers seated at the table.

"He said they found someone inside," Oliver whispered into her ear.

A terrified boy, no older than twelve, was prodded out the house, a rifle at his back. He was barefoot.

Ella took an instinctive step toward the boy, but Oliver put a hand on her shoulder, pulling her back.

The soldier holding the rifle said something, which prompted the other men to laugh.

One of the officers at the table motioned for the boy to come forward. When he didn't move, the soldier jabbed him in the back with the rifle, causing him to stumble toward the table.

The officer who had beckoned the boy to come forth puffed at his cigar. Then he pulled out a pistol and shot the boy twice in the chest.

Back in the car, they rode in a different kind of silence than before. Ella kept waiting for Oliver to say something along of the lines of, *I told you so. War isn't noble or exciting. It's death and despair.* But he didn't say anything.

The massacre they'd just witnessed wasn't war. It was murder, a killing with malice aforethought, a depraved indifference to human life. Were the commanding officers they were on their way to meet aware of what was happening in that town? They couldn't be.

Ella wasn't sure she believed this, but she spent the rest of the ride attempting to convince herself it was true. Otherwise, she didn't think she'd be able to stomach being in their presence, much less dine with them.

Half an hour later, they arrived at the château the commanding officers had appropriated for their own use as a private hotel. Château de Prucet was a diminutive limestone castle in the middle of a small lake. Its circular shape and unadorned stone façade caused it to resemble a medieval tower. A narrow stone bridge, some twenty meters long, connected the castle to land.

They crossed on foot and entered through a large stone

archway. Based on the exterior, Ella expected to find something akin to a dungeon inside. Instead, the high paneled walls, wooden chevron floors, and baroque furnishings reminded her of a well-appointed Parisian apartment.

The owner, an elderly aristocratic Belgian woman, was visibly displeased by the presence of her uninvited German guests. The unchanging expression on Madame de Nicolaÿ's face was one of utter disgust. Having been forced to play hostess, she greeted the reporters impassively before showing them to the dining room.

There was a celebratory air in the elegant room. Three German officers, each with an abundance of medals decorating their uniforms, sat in a line on the far side of the oval table as though conducting a tribunal. Ella, Oliver and Peters took the seats across from them.

Wine flowed freely, further lifting the officers' already high spirits. As they rattled off the list of defeated Belgian towns for the reporters' benefit, they toasted one another. It was no wonder their hostess preferred to dine alone in her room.

All the officers spoke English, but Ella engaged little in the conversation. She should be asking questions. This wasn't just a meal; it was an interview. But images of the smoldering town they'd just visited kept flashing through her mind. And the jovial men seated across from her now seemed interchangeable with those at the table in the corpse-strewn street.

Oliver was forced to pick up the slack. His voice was strained, and his laugh was stilted, but the officers didn't seem to notice. With forged enthusiasm, he carried the conversation for both of them.

"How long do you think it will take the army to reach France?" Oliver asked. "Peters's guess was three weeks."

The senior officer of the group, Oberst Knauff, an older

man with a prominent jaw, replied. He described the projected timeline for the westward march into France in detail. When he finished he turned his attention to Ella.

"Is something wrong, Frau Kaye?"

"There was a boy." Her voice caught in her throat.

When she didn't continue, Peters explained what had happened in the town.

"The boy disobeyed orders to turn himself in," Oberst Knauff said to Ella. "There was nothing else to be done." He picked up his utensils and resumed eating.

"It was a mistake for Herr Schnitzer to send a woman to report on the war," the portly officer seated to Oberst Knauff's left said. "Women are not suited for such things."

"Ella's a top-notch journalist," Oliver said. "I think Herr Schnitzer made an excellent choice sending her."

Oberst Knauff smiled, dabbing at the corners of his mouth with his napkin. "Well then, Herr Engel, remind me never to rely on your judgment."

The other men at the table laughed.

"It is a fact of nature. The lesser sex is not equipped for violence. Isn't that right, Frau Kaye?"

Oberst Knauff's condescending tone and air of masculine superiority was nothing new. As a female reporter, she experienced such on a daily basis. But that didn't make it any less infuriating.

Chin tilted up, Ella replied in an even tone. "The fact I'm a woman has no bearing on my opinion of what I witnessed today." She fixed her gaze on Oberst Knauff. "It was a horrendous display of unnecessary cruelty. Not only did your soldiers shoot an innocent boy, they burned an entire town and murdered its unarmed inhabitants."

"But it *was* necessary." The officer to Oberst Knauff's right spoke with a slight lisp that made his words sound even more sinister. "They left us no choice but to punish them. One of the townspeople shot a German soldier."

"But why punish the entire town?"

"To set an example," he said without the slightest bit of remorse.

"What did you expect to see, Frau Kaye?" Oberst Knauff said with a patronizing grin. "War is violent. Glory has its price."

"I know war is violent," she spat back. "But what you're doing to the Belgian civilians isn't fair."

"Fair?" He laughed. "You Americans, always going on about justice, freedom, equality—but those are just words. Just because they are spoken doesn't mean they are true. You may not like what I have to say, Frau Kaye, but at least I am being honest with you."

By the time they rejoined the Third Army that night, most of the camp was already asleep. Ella lay awake on her cot in her small tent. It had begun to rain. The droplets pounding the canvas above her head thudded like muted gunshots. She was exhausted. But every time she closed her eyes, a violent picture show played in her mind.

She had dreamed of being a war correspondent for years. But in the space of one day that dream had transformed into a nightmare. War was not a series of honorable battles. It was cruelty and madness. Oliver was right.

Their fight earlier today felt like a lifetime ago. Maybe Oliver had been right then too. Maybe she shouldn't have sent the telegram to her attorney.

He was wrong about her only thinking about herself, though. She'd put her own safety in jeopardy to expose injustice and better the lives of others. She'd almost lost a finger while pretending to be a factory worker.

She hadn't done it for the headline. She'd done it to help those women, to shed light on the low wages and inhumane working conditions they faced. Reforms to the law had been proposed in the wake of her story. But had the laws ever been passed? Had she actually helped anyone?

And what had happened to the women at the asylum? It had been shut down after her story exposed the neglect and abuse the caretakers were inflicting on their charges. But where had those women gone when it closed? Were they receiving better treatment wherever they were now? She had no idea. She'd never followed up with any of them.

She lay there shivering and miserable, questioning everything. She didn't want to be here—alone in this stupid soggy tent. She wanted to talk to Oliver.

She slipped into her boots and threw on her rain jacket. As she lifted the flap of the tent, a shrill, piercing whine accosted her eardrums. There was a bright, blinding flash, then everything went dark.

CHAPTER 23

Jay sat on the damp floor of the small cellar under Madame Lejeune's house, Robert beside him. A thin stream of light filtered in from the air vent leading outside. Otherwise, it was completely dark.

At first, the only sounds were the muffled voices and footsteps of the family above and the patter of rain. Then came a low persistent thump, thump, thump, thump. It sounded like a thousand drums beating in time. The rhythmic thud grew louder. The walls of the cellar quivered.

Robert spoke in a whisper. "The German Army must be marching right past us, along the train tracks."

Hours passed as the endless parade trudged forth. At some point the soldiers would have to stop and make camp. Hopefully they would be past the town by then. Otherwise, it was unclear when Jay and Robert would be able to get to the car, which was parked in the barn, without being seen.

Eventually the marching petered out. But just when they thought it might be safe to emerge from the cellar, a commotion erupted overhead. Jay held his breath. The heavy boots of soldiers thudded on the floor above his head.

A garbled dispute broke out, half in German, half in French, all indistinguishable from Jay and Robert's subterranean position. The elderly father-in-law shouted something.

A gunshot exploded. Something hit the floor with a thud. There were screams and some sort of struggle. It sounded as though Madame Lejeune and her daughters were being dragged out of the house.

Jay looked at Robert, then pointed at the ceiling. Should they go up and try to do something to help? Robert shook his head, a pained expression on his face.

Jay knew he was right. They were unarmed. The only thing they would accomplish by revealing themselves was getting shot. Something dripped through the floorboards onto the sleeve of his jacket. He touched a finger to the sticky substance. It was blood. Bile rose up his throat, but he quelled the urge to be sick.

For a few moments the house was quiet. Then there was a crash of breaking glass. The sharp smell of gasoline commingled with that of burning wood. Smoke seeped down into the cellar. The Germans had set the house on fire.

"Help me. We've got to get out of here," Robert yelled, pressing up against the trapdoor. They pushed against the door with all their strength, but it was no use. It was locked from above.

The air in the cellar was thick with smoke now, making it difficult to breathe. They were both coughing uncontrollably. Jay crossed to the small vent to get a breath of fresh air. When he pressed his face against the grate, it gave slightly. Gripping the bars, he pushed and pulled, until it finally came free.

"Robert. Quick, help me with the bricks."

Together they pried the loose bricks free first. Then Robert rammed the others out with a tin milk pail. Until, finally, there was a space large enough to fit through. With a boost from Jay, Robert climbed out first. The smoke was unbearable as Jay reached his arms up through the gap. His hands landed on sodden earth.

Robert grabbed his forearms, attempting to pull him through the opening. But Jay's jacket caught on something.

"I'm stuck," he yelled. "Let go."

The heat from the flames was almost unbearable. Arms freed, Jay tore off the jacket. Flames singed his trousers as he clambered out the hole onto the soggy ground. He scrambled to his feet, covered in filth and mud.

"Come on," Robert yelled, waving an arm.

They sprinted to the barn. Thankfully, the roadster lay untouched, just as they'd left it. Jay swung the large wooden doors open, while Robert started the car.

Soon they were out of the barn, racing into the dark night. Ignoring the shouts of German soldiers, Robert accelerated. A barrage of bullets pierced the back of the car. But, otherwise, they escaped unscathed. Soon, they were out of Pertés, alone on the open road.

It wasn't until Jay was back at the hotel, cleaning up, that he realized what he had done. In his frantic attempt to escape the fire, he had abandoned his jacket on the cellar floor. In it were the tracer bullets and the camera.

Two torturous days later, Jay and Robert were still in Antwerp. And the tracers—assuming they hadn't exploded in the fire—were still in the cellar of Madame Lejeune's torched home in Pertés. Jay hadn't left the hotel since their return. The thought of having lost the tracers now after everything he'd been through was almost too much to bear.

His eyes were sunken and hollow from lack of sleep. He had no appetite, and he passed the time wandering the halls of the hotel like an aimless ghost.

Robert attributed Jay's malaise to their brush with death in Pertés. He wouldn't stop profusely apologizing for the incident. He was so remorseful, if Jay didn't know any better, he'd think Robert was the one to incinerate the house they'd been trapped under.

It was early afternoon, and the lobby was nearly empty. Jay found a seat by the window and stared out vacantly at nothing.

"James?" Robert said, brow furrowed, when he found him there some time later. "Everything okay?"

"What?" Jay said, his trance interrupted.

"Come have a drink with me in the courtyard. The fresh air will do you some good."

Outside, sitting at the table next to the burbling fountain, was one of the British diplomats—the one who had insisted Jay was one of "Hoover's boy" and an Oxford Rhodes Scholar. The man waved, beckoning them to join him at the table.

"Robert, I'm not in the mood to socialize."

"One drink. I think you'll want to hear this." Robert urged him forward. "James, you remember Niles Cartwright."

Jay reluctantly took a seat.

"I heard the two of you had quite an adventure the other day," the man said.

Jay nodded weakly.

"I told Niles what happened," Robert said, then interrupted himself to flag down a passing waiter. "We'll have two of the usual." He turned back to the table. "I told Niles about Pertés and how, I assume, you want to go back there to survey the damage. For your charity and whatnot."

Jay sat up. "I do," he said quickly. Why hadn't he thought of this? "But I'd need some sort of a German pass or something. Wouldn't I?"

"And that's the conundrum," Robert said. "To get a German pass you would need to speak to a German official. But to gain access to a German official, you would need a pass."

The waiter arrived with two small glasses of the same liqueur Robert had ordered the first time Jay had met the British diplomats.

"But Niles, here," Robert said with burgeoning enthusiasm, "figured out a way to circumvent that."

"How?"

"It's simple." Niles grinned, pleased with himself. "All you've got to do is get to Brussels before the Germans do."

The city was still under Belgian control, which meant Robert's *laissez-passer* would permit them to enter the city.

"And then, what?" Jay asked, somewhat dubious. "We just stay until the Germans arrive?" After Pertés, he wasn't sure that sounded like such a good idea.

"That's the plan," Robert said. Then, as if reading Jay's mind, he added, "It'll be nothing like Pertés. Both sides have agreed to a peaceful surrender."

As Jay gathered his belongings for the trip, the sack of safety pins Connor had given him seemed noticeably lighter. He held the bag up, examining it. It wasn't his imagination; almost half were missing. He hadn't taken the safety pins anywhere since checking into the hotel. Had someone stolen them?

Jay didn't need hundreds of safety pins. He wasn't entirely sure why he had even held on to them this long. But the fact they were missing was disturbing. It meant someone had gone through his luggage.

He slid his hand under the mattress, relieved to find the Mauser pistol still nestled in place. But when he emptied the contents of his bag onto the bed, he discovered the safety pins weren't the only thing missing. The red notebook he had taken from Horst was inexplicably absent.

They made it back to Brussels without incident. A day later, they watched the German army march into the city from the window of their hotel, where they remained until the peaceful surrender of Brussels was complete.

When they emerged from the Palace Hotel a few days later, they found the city entirely intact. The transfer had indeed been peaceful. No one had been harmed; nothing had been damaged. But in seventy-two hours, Brussels had undergone a complete transformation.

The once prevalent Belgian flag, with its vertical stripes of red, yellow, and black, had disappeared entirely from sight. The flag of Imperial Germany now flew from all the official buildings as well as the cathedral. The large square in front of the Gare du Nord train station was now being used as German army barracks. And a portion of the Hôtel de Ville, Brussels's city hall, had been converted into a dormitory for German soldiers.

It was all very civil. The Germans inhabiting the city seemed entirely at ease in their new home. Officers filled the tables of the outdoor cafés. And groups of soldiers strolled casually down the tree-lined boulevards, stopping in boutiques to purchase gifts to send back to Germany. It was hard to believe this was the same army that had set fire to Pertés. Had Jay not experienced the invasion personally, he would have found it hard to believe tales of such atrocities.

On their fourth day in Brussels, Jay and Robert approached the governor general in his new office at the Hôtel de Ville. The stout red-faced man sat behind an imposing desk with an enormous stack of papers piled atop of it. As Jay pled their case, the general seemed to be only half listening. Most of his attention was focused on the mountain of paperwork before him.

When Jay finished, the general considered the request for an instant. Then, without looking up, he answered, "Absolutely not."

Jay argued their case further to no avail. When it became clear the general wasn't going to change his mind, Jay asked for a private audience. The general acquiesced, and Robert left the room.

"There's another reason I require a pass," Jay said in German. "One that I hesitate to mention, even to a general such as yourself."

The general eyed him dubiously.

Jay lowered his voice. "I'm a German spy. Employed to deliver messages throughout Belgium."

The general scoffed. "Or so you say. How am I to know? Who hired you?"

"Herr Hilmar Dierks in Rotterdam."

"That name means nothing to me." The general continued sifting through the papers on his desk. "If someone from Berlin were to contact me on your behalf, that would be a different matter. But I cannot issue you a pass based on your word alone."

The general clearly wanted him to leave, but he couldn't give up. If he wanted to get the tracers back, he needed a pass. "Please, I have no way of getting in touch with Berlin." Not that he knew anyone in Berlin who could help. "And there's something else." He hesitated. But, deciding this might be his last chance to recover the tracers, he forged on. "I was hired to obtain weapons technology intended for the British Navy that will be of great use to the German Army."

At this, the general lowered the stack of papers. "By Herr Dierks in Rotterdam?"

"No." Jay looked him in the eye. "By Herr Winter in New York."

The general raised an eyebrow. "Martin Winter?"

"Yes!" A smile spread across Jay's lips. Upon hearing the name, he could have reached across the desk and kissed the general's plump, ruddy cheek. "You know him?"

"Oh, I know that scoundrel." The general laughed. "I see he's up to his old tricks again." He wagged a finger. "He could have gotten us both in a good deal of trouble. I was lucky to only get a slap on the wrist."

Jay forced a laugh. He had no idea what the general was talking about. "What happened?"

"They called it the Kornwalzer scandal." He groaned. "It was all over the papers. That's why everyone was so upset."

This meant nothing to Jay, but he nodded at the general sympathetically. "Remind me what happened?"

"Winter and a few others obtained classified information about German military technology. I'm not sure what else he did to get such information, but as it relates to me, it was more or less harmless." He smiled, remembering. "He took a group of army officers, including myself, out for an extravagant meal. He ordered bottle after bottle of champagne, wine, and schnapps. Then he introduced the subject of Germany's impressive weaponry." The general threw up a hand. "You know how men can be, boasting and bragging. For my part, I probably said too much."

This was the first Jay had heard of any of this. But it must have been some sort of internal squabble between the German Army and Navy. The general wouldn't be laughing it off if it were anything else. Did this mean Winter was already working for German Naval Intelligence a few years ago?

"Tell me," the general asked. "What is the weapons technology Martin Winter hired you to procure?"

Jay described the tracer bullets manufactured by ACC, which he'd stolen from Felton. He didn't mention the fact he was no longer in possession of the tracers.

"Well, that technology *will* be of great use."

"You wouldn't happen to know where Herr Winter is

now?" Jay asked.

The general shook his head. "I haven't seen him in over a year."

"Or know how I could get in touch with him?"

"I'm afraid not, but . . ." The general scribbled something on a sheet of paper, signed it, and stamped it with a seal. "You may have the pass you requested. When you find Herr Winter, send him my regards. Tell him there are no hard feelings."

"Thank you. I certainly will, General. And"—Jay knew he was pressing his luck but went ahead anyway—"might you make out a pass for Herr Washington, as well? I wouldn't want him to suspect anything."

The general considered this. Then, putting pen to paper, he issued another pass.

CHAPTER 24

Ella opened her eyes, unsure where she was or what was happening. It was night. She was lying on wet, trampled grass; raindrops fell on her face.

"Ella? Ella!"

The ground shook. Her eardrums vibrated, absorbing the recurring thunderous blasts of sound. Someone was calling her name.

"Ella, are you okay?" A tall figure knelt beside her. Concerned eyes peered through smudged glasses. "Are you hurt?" Oliver's hand hovered over her uncertainly.

"I'm fine." She sat up, grabbing his arm for support. She was dizzy. Her entire body ached, but she didn't think anything was broken.

Her tent was gone. The camp was in chaos. Cracks of gunfire sounded in the distance, accompanied by shrill whistles and loud booms. All around them German soldiers shouted, running in different directions.

"We're being shelled," Oliver said. "One of the soldiers said it was the British Army."

A bright flash of white illuminated the sky, accompanied by the ascending screech of fireworks. Acrid smoke swirled around them.

"Where's Peters?"

Oliver shook his head. "A shell . . ." His voice trailed off.

Her eyes darted around, surveying the pandemonium. Injured men screaming, their shattered silhouettes illuminated by the bright flash of explosions.

A pack of soldiers ran past. Ella called out to them. Oliver did the same in German. The men kept moving, ignoring them. She tried to think. Was there someone other than Peters they were supposed to report to?

"Come on." Oliver took hold of her arm, pulling her up. "We need to get somewhere safer."

A shell landed with a whine a few yards away, spewing dirt into the air and tearing the legs off one of the soldiers. Ella stared at the maimed limbs, unable to move.

"Let's go." Oliver grabbed her by the shoulders, steering her away from the carnage.

"Go where?"

Shells exploded all around them. The ground spurted up like a series of geysers.

"To Peters's car."

They raced through the ruins of the camp, past shredded tents and wounded men. They reached a stretch of woods. Ella's ankle twisted on a mound of damp pine needles. She fell to her knees but forced herself up and continued running.

Finally, the trees gave way to the large field where Peters had parked the car. When they'd arrived earlier that night, a score of German army vehicles had been parked here. Now, only Peters's car remained.

Oliver leaned against the hood of the car, trying to catch his breath. "You know how to drive, right?"

"Don't you?"

Oliver shook his head.

Ella had only driven a car twice in her life. It had been years since her last attempt, during which she'd hit a curb, severing a tire from its axel. But she was still vaguely aware of the different pedals and gears. And really, now wasn't the time to deliberate her proficiency. She slid into the driver's seat.

Oliver took the seat beside her. "We should try and find the road," he said, glancing around uselessly. It was too dark to see anything.

She put the car into gear and took a deep breath. Hands gripping the steering wheel, she pressed down on the gas pedal. The tires sunk into the soggy earth, spinning futilely.

"*Halt! Steigen aus dem Auto.*" Three German soldiers jogged toward them.

"They said to get out of the car," Oliver said.

A shell exploded with a bang, flinging pieces of earth onto the hood of the car.

"We can't stay here," Ella said. "We'll be killed."

The men were getting closer. One of the soldiers pointed a rifle at them. He was yelling something she couldn't understand. The car was still stuck in the mud. Panic creeping in, Ella shifted the gear into reverse. For whatever reason, this caused the tires to gain traction. The car lurched backward.

She didn't want to lose momentum. So, looking over her shoulder, squinting into the dark night, she kept driving. A series of bullets dinged the hood. Ignoring this and everything else, she maneuvered backward through the dark field, in what she hoped was the direction of the road.

They had been driving for close to an hour, making their way slowly down the unlit road. They had no idea where they were. The Belgians had removed all signs in order to confuse the German troops. Peters's map of Belgium was in the glove box, but since they didn't know where they had started from, it wasn't any help.

Ella was about to suggest they pull to the side of the road

and sleep in the car, when they came upon a small house. Despite the late hour, a light flickered in an upstairs window. They knocked on the front door. A middle-aged woman in a dressing gown opened it a crack and poked her head out. She looked them up and down, frowning at their disheveled appearance, and said something in Flemish, which neither Ella nor Oliver understood.

"We're American," Ella said. "Do you speak English?" When the woman didn't reply, she switched to French. "We're American journalists. We're looking for somewhere to spend the night. Are there any inns nearby?"

The woman replied in kind. "None where it is safe. Dinant on the west side of the river has several, but there is fighting there now." Ella guessed that was where they had come from.

"Would it be possible to lodge here? We would of course pay you."

"Tell her we're on Belgium's side—that we work for British Intelligence," Oliver said.

Ella wasn't sure they should be telling anyone this but went ahead and translated.

The woman's face lit up. She lifted the collar of her dressing gown to reveal two safety pins. "You know the safety pin man?"

"No." Ella frowned. Who was the safety pin man? "We work for the British Security Service."

The woman looked over her shoulder at some undisclosed person. "One moment please." She closed the door. They waited on the porch, listening to a muffled discussion in Flemish.

The door opened, and a large man with a bad leg limped out onto the porch. He pointed to their car, which was parked in front of the house.

"Why do you drive this German car?" he asked in French.

"We stole it."

The man smiled at this. He asked a few more questions before inviting them in to stay for the night. They were shown to an upstairs room barely bigger than a closet. Ella took the small iron bed, Oliver the floor.

Ella stared at the ceiling, trying make sense of everything she'd seen that day. It felt as though a veil had been lifted, that the orderly, civilized world she'd lived in her entire life was but an illusion. That theirs was a civilization teetering on the brink of chaos, a place where the rules of law and religion were easily cast aside.

Oliver sat on the floor beside her. "Are you all right?"

She hadn't realized she was crying.

"Hey. It's okay. We're safe."

"You were right," she managed to say between ragged breaths. "You were right about all of it. It's awful. We should never have come here." Ella wiped at her eyes. "I don't think I can stand another day of this."

"Then, we'll leave."

"How?"

Oliver waited for her sobs to subside before speaking. "We'll rejoin the battalion first thing in the morning. And we'll tell the commanding officer we want to go home. If he thinks we're cowards, so be it." He looked away. "I suppose we are, considering we stood there and watched them shoot a child."

"They would have shot us too."

"At least you said something to Oberst Knauff at dinner," Oliver said, running a hand through his hair. "I just sat there grinning and laughing like a chump."

"Nothing I said made any difference. And leaving doesn't make us cowards."

"If you say so."

"We're not supposed to be here. If anything, our presence here is doing more harm than good. Who knows what the German Press Bureau is sending to the *Journal* with our names on it? If we go home, at least we can share the truth of what we saw here with the world."

"You're right." Oliver let out a sigh. "It's just . . . Well, a part of me feels like we're giving up."

"Giving up on what?"

"I don't know. But Bertie wouldn't leave. Whatever God-forsaken hellhole he's in right now, I'll bet it's ten times more dangerous than it is here. But he wouldn't leave."

"Isn't Bertie in New York? Crime in the city isn't that bad," Ella said, attempting a joke.

"He left for Europe a few days before I did. Wherever he is, whatever he's been sent to do, I know he'll follow it through to the end."

"Our situation isn't anything like Bertie's. We aren't giving up in the middle of a mission. We don't have a mission, not in Belgium, anyway. And we aren't helping anyone by staying. Sometimes the bravest thing you can do is admit there's nothing else to be done."

"I guess." Oliver lay back down. "We should get some rest."

Ella stared up at the ceiling. Leaving Belgium was the right thing to do. There was nothing else to be done. It was for the best.

She wished she'd been brave enough admit there was nothing else to be done two years ago. If she'd acknowledged that her and Cody's relationship was beyond repair, maybe things would have turned out differently. Maybe he'd still be alive.

She should have ended things with Cody long before she did. But pride and pure stubbornness had prevented her from conceding that their once harmonious coupling had become as discordant as an untuned violin. She'd invested so much time and energy defending their relationship to the rest of the world, it had been difficult to admit to herself they were no longer suited for one another. Instead of ending things civilly, she'd allowed her grievances to pile up like a tower of blocks. Then in Boston, the night of the party, everything came crashing down.

She had been invited to give the commencement speech at Radcliff College. Afterward, an extravagant dinner honoring her and celebrating her achievements as a renowned female journalist was being held. With some hesitation, she'd invited Cody to attend the dinner some months earlier.

Cody had always enjoyed drinking. And, on occasion, he overindulged. But as time went on, the frequency with which he became intoxicated increased exponentially. The last few times Ella had seen him, by the end of each night, Cody was so inebriated he was incoherent. She'd worried his recent tendency to overindulge would distract from the evening. And, so, she had asked him not to drink that night.

Ella had never had a party thrown in her honor before. It was an important night for her. When Cody finally arrived at the dinner two hours late, stumbling drunk, she'd been furious.

She said cruel, unspeakable things to Cody that night. If she could take them back, she would. At the time, she hadn't known they'd be the last words she'd ever speak to him. Cody died a few hours later. He took his own life. But it was her words that prompted the act. She, alone, was to blame.

They woke early the next morning, hoping to locate and rejoin the battalion as soon as possible. They attempted to pay the owners of the house for their lodgings but were refused.

Instead, the couple asked a favor of them.

"Twenty kilometers down the road, a large oak stands alone off the side of the road. In its trunk, a discreet hollow exists where messages can be placed." Their host extracted a folded note from his jacket pocket. "Might you take this there?"

Ella didn't ask what was in the letter. But it clearly had something to do with the Belgian resistance. She turned to Oliver and translated. They agreed they would deliver it. In doing this, at least they would have done something, however small, to help the Belgians before they left.

But as Ella pulled the car onto the road, she was met with a rush of unease. She'd slipped the note between the pages of her notepad. It was now under her seat. It was just a piece of paper, but carrying it was dangerous. If the Germans caught them with it, it might as well be a bomb intended to blow up German troops.

"What if the Germans are watching the tree trunk?" she asked.

"Then we'll keep driving."

They never made it to the tree trunk. They had only driven about ten kilometers when the car began to sputter. Ella steered the car to the side of the road, where it slowed to a stop. They were out of petrol.

"I suppose a German patrol will pass by sooner or later," Oliver said, surveying the desolate surroundings. He held a hand above his glasses, shielding his eyes from the glare of the sun. Empty fields stretched in both directions.

As the minutes went by, Ella grew more and more anxious. "I think we should destroy the note."

"Might be too late for that," Oliver said, as a green army truck came into view.

The truck pulled up beside them. Two uniformed men

climbed out the back of the vehicle. The soldier in the passenger seat pointed a rifle at them. He yelled something in German.

"He said to get out of the car slowly," Oliver translated.

As they did, Oliver launched into German, purportedly explaining their situation. He was silenced when one of the approaching soldiers drew out a pistol and held it to his temple. The other soldier began searching the car.

"This vehicle is the property of the German Army," the soldier pointing the pistol said. "It was reported stolen last night. You are both under arrest."

"This is a misunderstanding," Oliver said. "We didn't steal it. We're reporters following the Third Army. The car was for our use."

The soldier lowered the gun and stepped in front of Ella. He was at least a foot taller than her. He picked at his teeth with his thumbnail as he looked down at her. The sour stench of his unwashed uniform made her gag. She wished he would take a step back.

The soldier searching the car shouted something, holding up the Burberry raincoat Ella had purchased in London.

"Are you British?" the tall soldier asked.

"American," she responded.

"He says everything in your car is from England. That you must be British spies."

The soldier searching the car held up Ella's leather notepad. The note the Belgians had entrusted them to deliver was inside. He handed it to the soldier holding the gun.

"Why do you have a British Army notebook?"

"I bought it in London before I came here. We're reporters. Those are just notes." Ella held her breath as he ran his thumb over the leather cover.

He undid the band and flipped the notebook open. He

flicked through a few more pages. Before reaching the folded note, he snapped it shut.

"We were with Oberst Knauff yesterday," Oliver said. "We dined with him and a few other German officers at the château, the one in the middle of the lake. If you take us there, he'll explain everything."

The soldier considered this. "Very well," he said, motioning with the gun. "Get in the back of the truck."

Ella held out her hand for the notepad. The soldier looked at her, then back at the small leather-bound book. He started to hand it to her, then, changing his mind, tossed it back into the car.

CHAPTER 25

Early the following morning Jay and Robert returned to Antwerp. They had kept their room at the Hôtel St. Antoine. When they arrived, a letter was waiting for Jay at the front desk. His instructions were to deliver it to an address in the nearby city of Malines.

Robert—grateful for Jay's help obtaining his German travel pass—drove him there that very afternoon. Jay delivered the letter without any fanfare, and Robert didn't suspect a thing. Why should he? Since the German invasion, the Belgian postal service couldn't be counted on to deliver mail. Hand-delivering correspondence wasn't strange at all.

The task complete, they were now driving to Pertés. It had been over a week since their narrow escape from Madame Lejeune's cellar. Since then, fighting in the vicinity had ceased. And the city of Pertés was now firmly under German control. At least, what was left of it was.

"Good God," Robert said, as the city came into view.

Madame Lejeune's house wasn't the only one that had been burned. Half the structures in town were now charred heaps of ruin, some still smoldering. Those still standing had smashed doors and broken windows. Many of the exterior walls were perforated with bullet holes, splattered red with blood.

Only a few homes were left unscathed. On those the words, "*Güte leuite. Nicht zu plündern.*"—Good people. Do not plunder—were scrawled on the front door.

"I'm not sure you being here alone is such a great idea, Gatz," Robert said, casting a wary gaze at the quartet of German soldiers approaching the car. "Maybe we should come back another time."

Robert had a sale to make in a nearby town that afternoon. Jay wasn't thrilled to be touring this hellscape by himself. But if Robert accompanied him, he couldn't dig through whatever remained of the Lejeune cellar.

"I'll be fine." Jay stepped out of the car.

"You're sure?"

"Yep." In an attempt to appear casually indifferent to the apocalyptic scene before him, Jay shoved his hands in his pockets, rocked back on his heels, and grinned.

"In that case, would you mind taking some photographs?" Robert reached into his jacket pocket and pulled out a small camera. It was similar to the one Jay had lost with his jacket.

"What for?"

"Evidence it's not my fault we lost the Pertés account. My boss can be a real jerk." He handed the camera to Jay. "Take the whole roll, why don't you? You can send some of the pictures back to your charity."

Robert waited to make sure the pass the governor general had issued proved sufficient. It did, and the soldiers invited Jay to roam Pertés at his leisure.

As he made his way through town he snapped photos of the devastation. The story of a debauched orgy of destruction was written everywhere. The sidewalks were strewn with empty wine bottles. Furniture had been tossed into the streets—emptied dresser drawers, bayonetted mattresses, three-legged chairs.

Jay wondered if Robert really needed photographic evidence or if he had loaned him the camera solely so he could take pictures for his purported charity. He hoped that wasn't the case. Jay didn't want any of these pictures. They would only serve as reminders that not only was he not going to help the Belgians obtain relief, his *actual* employer was responsible for their predicament.

He wondered if the messages he'd delivered on behalf of the Germans had contributed to the ruin before him. Even if there wasn't blood on his hands now, there would be when he gave the Germans the tracers. He pushed away the thought.

Other than those four German soldiers, he hadn't seen a single person since arriving. Where was everyone? It seemed the entire town had fled—or tried to. No corpses remained, but there were bullet holes and bloodstains everywhere.

The grass along the train tracks where the army had marched looked as though it had been trampled by a thousand galloping horses. And the adjacent string of homes looked like they'd been charred to cinders by a thunder of dragons. Jay was beginning to worry he might not recognize the Lejeune house. But he soon spotted the barn where they had parked the car. It stood intact just as they had left it.

The Lejeune home was another matter entirely. Its brick frame still stood, but the front door was gone. In its place stood a gaping hole that resembled a giant mouth stretched into a scream. Inside, piles of scorched rubble and broken glass littered the floor. Somewhere, underneath all the wreckage, lay the trapdoor to the cellar.

He retrieved a shovel and rake from the barn and set to work. Eventually he located the trap door, but when he opened it he discovered a portion of the cellar had caved in. It wasn't where he believed his jacket to be, but it made going down there to retrieve it out of the question. He didn't want to risk being buried alive.

Lying on his stomach, he lowered the rake into the cellar. Slowly and methodically, he dragged it along the floor, scouring for his jacket. Holding the rake with his left hand, he used his right arm to clear away the adjacent pile of debris to adjust his position on the floor. When he realized what he'd just shoved aside, he let go of the rake with a shriek. It dropped to the cellar floor with a clank. On the floor beside him was a charred human arm.

He scrambled to his feet and hurried out of the house. He shuddered vigorously, like a dog shaking water off its coat, brushing at the soot covering his suit. The scorched appendage he'd just encountered must have belonged to Madame Lejeune's father-in-law.

Bile crawled up his throat. He bent forward and wretched onto the ground. What was he doing? Was he really going to sell more weapons to the monsters who had done this?

He shook away the thought. He couldn't think about it that way. He'd already stolen the tracers. The crime had already been committed. And he needed the money. His life depended on it. If Winter didn't show up in the next couple of days, he'd go see the governor general again. He'd find someone else in the German Army to sell the tracers to. Then he'd get the hell out of Belgium.

But first, he needed to the retrieve the tracers from the cellar. As soon as he did, he'd head straight to the church to inquire about Madame Lejeune's whereabouts. Further down the tracks near the center of town a church tower rose into the sky. If the priest was still here, he must have some idea where the citizens of Pertés had sought refuge.

He found a length of rope and used it to retrieve the rake. Then, steeling himself, he shoveled everything, including the arm, away from the area adjacent to the trapdoor. Back on his stomach, he resumed combing the cellar floor. Finally, he snagged the jacket with an elated gasp.

He lifted it through the trapdoor, and with abundant relief, he found the case of tracer bullets nestled safely inside the pocket. The camera was missing, but at this point that hardly seemed to matter.

The cigarette case pressed against his chest, he followed the tracks until he reached the church. The Église Sainte-Agathe, with its gothic pointed arches and ribbed vaults, was situated at the far end of a small plaza. On each side of the entrance stood a German soldier.

When he approached, they informed him that no one, including the priest, was allowed inside the church. When he asked why, the younger of the two soldiers gestured to the church tower. Reaching one hundred and sixty meters into the sky, it was the optimal height for a lookout or sniper hide. The task of destroying the tower deemed too cumbersome, they had been ordered to remain in Pertés to guard the entrance, which was located inside the church.

Jay supposed this meant the priest, like his parishioners, had also fled town. He was therefore surprised to find the black-robed clergyman shuffling through the remains of a neighborhood on the other side of town. The slight man's black-cassocked back was hunched with age. Wispy tufts of white hair peeked out from the biretta atop his head.

The priest was alone, save for a murder of crows pecking through the rubbish-strewn street. Absorbed in muttering the Latin words of a prayer, the priest didn't register Jay's approach.

"Excuse me, Father?"

The priest turned to him and repeated the prayer in English. "Say not thou vengeance I shall seek. Wait thou, for the

Lord shall avenge thee."

Jay waited for the man to acknowledge him, but the priest stared blankly at him, then recited the prayer again. His voice was now a low whisper. "Wait thou, for the Lord shall avenge thee."

Jay cleared his throat. "Say, do you mind if I ask you a few questions? I'm looking for someone."

"Do you understand the prayer, my child? Do you comprehend the words' meaning?"

Jay thought for a moment. "That God will punish the Germans for what they've done to the town?"

"No." The priest shook his head gravely. "It is *we*, the Belgians, who are being punished. God avenges the innocents slaughtered on King Leopold's behalf." The clergyman's voice grew louder. "The innocent people of the Congo murdered and maimed for their ivory and rubber."

"Oh. I see." Jay didn't want to be rude, but his patience was wearing thin. "Listen, I was really hoping you could help me, Father. I'm looking for a woman and her daughters. Her name is Madame Lejeune."

The priest seemed not to have heard him. "I was there in the mission. I saw it with my own eyes. They shot them, then cut off their hands and collected them, baskets upon baskets overflowing with these trophies of flesh."

One of the crows cawed. The others responded, and they all took flight. As they ascended into the sky the priest began uttering the prayer again.

Jay didn't attempt to question the man again. Wherever Madame Lejeune and her daughters were, one thing was certain. If they were alive, they weren't in Pertés.

When they arrived back at the Hôtel Saint Antoine later that day, a telegram was waiting for Jay. Declining the invitation to join Robert and the British legation for drinks in the courtyard, he retreated to an empty corner of the lobby and tore into the thin envelope. The telegram was from Dierks.

As he read the message, the trickle of hope he'd held on to for weeks swelled like a stream turned mighty river. A wide grin spread across his face. Dierks had located Winter. Jay should expect a telegram from Winter himself shortly.

He wanted to shout with joy. He wanted to hug someone. Instead, he smoothed his jacket and adopted a neutral expression. He tore up the telegram and tossed the pieces in a waste bin. And, resisting the urge to skip up the stairs like an elated schoolboy, Jay slowly ascended to their room on the tenth floor.

It was past midnight. On the other side of the room, Robert was deep in slumber. But Jay was too excited to sleep. Winter was alive. And in the pocket of the jacket on the bed beside him were the tracers he'd retrieved this afternoon. Everything was finally coming together. This nightmare would soon be over.

Jay couldn't wait to leave Belgium and get on with his life in New York. After paying off the Eastman gang, he'd have a little over a thousand dollars left. It wasn't a fortune, but it was enough to start a new life. Maybe Robert could get him a job selling cigarettes in New York. Or maybe he'd take the money and move somewhere else entirely.

Maybe he'd take a cue from Teddy Belmont and move to San Francisco. Most of the city had been destroyed in the 1906 earthquake and subsequent fires. But that was almost ten years ago. Surely, most of it had been rebuilt by now.

He'd seen pictures of San Francisco in the aftermath of the earthquake. The city and its buildings were larger, but the destruction catalogued in those photographs was eerily similar to what he'd seen earlier today. He wondered how long it would take to rebuild Pertés and all the other cities demolished by the German Army.

Maybe he wouldn't go to San Francisco after all. He didn't need any reminders of his time working for the Germans and this horrific war. The priest's words echoed in his head. *Wait thou, for the Lord shall avenge thee.* But the haunting prayer was soon interrupted by a curious noise coming from outside. Jay sat up.

What started as a faint hum became a steady rumble. Clutching his jacket, he got out of bed and went to the window. He pushed aside the curtains just in time to see an orange ball of flame plummet from the sky with a thunderous boom. The walls of the hotel trembled.

Robert leaped out of bed. "What the bloody hell was that?" He'd been spending so much time with the members of the British delegation housed at the hotel, he was starting to pick up their accent.

Eyes wide, Jay offered a confused shrug. He had no idea what was happening. It looked as though fire was raining from the heavens. Maybe the priest was right. Maybe God *was* punishing the Belgians. This time he was forgoing his German intermediaries and personally launching the attack.

Jay raised the window, leaned out the frame, and looked up. An enormous cigar-shaped balloon hovered in the sky. "It's a zeppelin."

Robert joined him at the window. They stared in awe as another burst of light streamed down. It hit the building directly across the street with a shattering crash. Rubble flew in all directions. The floor and walls of their room shook as though a subway train was racing directly beneath them.

"Come on, let's go," Robert said.

"Where?"

"Anywhere but here. If they drop a bomb on the hotel, the top floor's a rotten place to be."

Jay reached for his suitcase.

"No time to dress. Just put your shoes on."

Jay slipped into his shoes and slid his jacket—containing the tracers—on over his pajamas. Downstairs, the lobby teemed with an international assortment of dazed and scantily clad diplomats. No one seemed to know where to go or what to do. Why should they? None of them had ever experienced an air raid before, this being one of the first to ever occur.

Many of the hotel patrons, including Robert, had the notion it was safer outside on the street. Jay wasn't sure he agreed with this sentiment. But having no alternative plan, he followed Robert out of the hotel.

Out on the street, the crash of explosions grew fainter with each blast as the zeppelin glided out of Antwerp. They made their way to the Rue de Bourse, where the bomb had hit one of the buildings across the street from the hotel. It looked as though an angry giant had slammed a heavy fist down upon the structure. The three upper stories of the tall baroque apartment building were gone, collapsed in their entirety. Flames poured out the shattered windows of the remaining floors.

Those residents who had made it out of the building huddled in the middle of the street. Some were sobbing. Others silently gaped in horror at the blazing wreckage.

A pleading cry for help came from somewhere within the building. The crowd murmured, but no one responded. If they recognized the despairing woman's voice, they gave no sign.

"I'm going in to see if I can help." Without looking back,

Robert dashed up the stairs into the apartment building. Less than a minute later he emerged and shouted. "James, I need your help." Then he darted back into the building.

Jay stood paralyzed in the street. Part of him wanted to follow Robert and help, but he wasn't sure it was such a good idea. Actually, he was certain it was a terrible idea. What if the rest of the building collapsed while they were in there?

Another desperate scream resounded from the ruined building. Followed by Robert's voice. "James, help!"

Leaving his common sense on the street, Jay sprinted into the building. Inside, the dusty smoke was so thick, he had to cover his mouth with his arm in order to breathe.

"Robert! Robert!" Jay called out his name repeatedly. He got no response. "Hello? Anyone?" He bounded up the stairs. As he did, a woman and her two small boys came barreling down toward him.

"Do you need help getting down?" Jay asked.

The woman said something in French he didn't understand and pointed up the stairs before turning her attention back to getting her children out of the building.

Jay continued to the second floor. There was a loud crash from above. It sounded as though another part of the building had collapsed.

At the top of the stairs Jay continued yelling Robert's name between coughs. But there was no reply. And there was no getting to the third floor. The stairs leading up to it were now a pile of rubble. Had Robert been on the stairs when they collapsed?

"Robert!" he yelled one last time. He could barely breathe. He couldn't stay here, or he'd be killed too.

A door flew open, and Robert emerged from one of the apartments. "James!" he said, with a look of surprise.

On Robert's arm was an ancient man. He looked about

two hundred years old and was moving at the pace of a geriatric tortoise.

"Help me carry him down the stairs, will you?"

Coughing and wheezing, they carried the old man down the two flights of stairs and out of the building. There, he was reunited with the woman and boys Jay had passed on the stairs.

Fire trucks arrived, their sirens wailing in the cool night. Jay and Robert stood on the street, catching their breath, watching the firefighters battle the blaze.

"Thanks for helping me out in there," Robert said. "It would have been a struggle getting that man down the stairs alone. For a minute I thought you weren't coming."

"Couldn't you hear me in there?" Jay asked. "I must have called your name a hundred times."

"It's funny. I did hear you. But, what with all the excitement, I didn't realize it was me you were calling."

"Did you think I'd raced into a burning building to help out a different Robert?"

"Of course not." He laughed. "The thing is, I don't usually go by the name Robert."

Jay stiffened. Was Robert Washington someone other than who he claimed to be?

Jay turned to look him in the eye. "Who are you, then?"

Robert waved a hand and offered a reassuring grin. "It's nothing like that. Everyone at home uses my nickname, is all."

Jay relaxed. Robert wasn't hiding anything from him. Just because Jay had secrets to hide didn't mean anyone else did. "So . . . what should I call you? Bobby? Rob?"

"Call me Bertie."

CHAPTER 26

Handcuffed in the back of the German Army truck, neither Ella nor Oliver spoke as they drove the twenty or so kilometers to Château de Prucet. When they arrived, morning mist lingered over the lake, causing the château to resemble a tower rising above the clouds. Oberst Knauff was crossing the narrow footbridge, at the end of which a car idled, waiting to deliver him to the battlefield.

He greeted the reporters with a dismissive nod, seemingly in a hurry. But upon learning they had been detained for stealing a Germany Army vehicle, his departure was suddenly no longer a matter of urgency. After speaking with the soldier who had arrested them, Oberst Knauff walked around to the back of the truck. His mouth upturned in a half smile, he regarded Ella as though she were an insect stranded on its back, and he was a child contemplating what fun to have with the stick held in his hand.

Oberst Knauff confirmed to the soldiers that Ella and Oliver were indeed American reporters assigned to follow the Third Army. But he suggested an investigation be made into their sudden departure from the camp before allowing them to rejoin the regimen. While the investigation was carried out, the reporters were to remain at the château, locked in separate rooms, held as quasi prisoners.

They followed Madame de Nicolaÿ's servant up three flights of stairs. The soldier assigned to guard them trailed behind with a rifle pointed at their backs. Ella feared their makeshift cells would be something akin to dark broom closets. Instead, she was led into a well-appointed guest room. The iron bars outside the window were the only feature remotely prisonlike.

She passed the day pacing the room, occasionally pausing to gaze out at the tall pines encircling the lake. Too nervous to eat, she ignored the trays of food brought at mealtimes. She was fairly certain their departure from camp would be excused. But the folded note concealed in her leather notepad intended for the Belgian resistance was another matter entirely.

Why had they agreed to take the note? They had decided they were going to leave Belgium. Once out of Belgium, they could tell the world about the German Army's disgraceful behavior. That was how they could help the Belgians, not by delivering some note. Now, they might never make it out of Belgium.

Later that evening, long after the officers had returned from the day's battle, the two reporters were escorted downstairs to the parlor. The dissonant chords of a Wagner opera resonated from the gramophone in the corner of the room. Oberst Knauff sat in an armchair in front of the unlit fireplace, drinking cognac and smoking a cigar. As they stood before him, he seemed in an excellent mood.

"Any word on when we get to rejoin the army?" Oliver asked. "It's a nice enough tower, but I'm starting to feel like Rapunzel." His smile was almost convincing.

"Surely the details of our departure from the battalion have been confirmed by now," Ella said with what she hoped was the impatience of the falsely accused.

Oberst Knauff informed them that the details of their departure had indeed checked out. However, for reasons he didn't share, they were still under investigation. As such, they were to remain at the château until further inquiries were complete.

"I learned today," he said with a hint of a smile, "that you are not just reporters. You were originally recruited as spies for Germany."

"That's right," Oliver said. "We were originally stationed in England, but Herr Schnitzer thought we might better serve the German cause in our capacity as journalists."

Knauff considered this. "I find this strange, Frau Kaye. Why would someone with so much sympathy for the Belgians agree to be a German spy?"

"My sympathy extends to all civilians affected by war, regardless of their nationality."

Oberst Knauff puffed at his cigar, considering this, then waved a hand, dismissing them.

Back in her room, Ella stood at the window staring through the iron bars at the moonlit lake below. Had Oberst Knauff mentioned her Belgian sympathies because they had discovered the message in her notepad, or was that a reference to her outburst during dinner the other night?

Perhaps it was wishful thinking, but Ella was inclined to think it the latter. If they had found the message intended for the Belgian resistance, surely that was evidence enough to try them as spies. The fact that further inquiries were being made suggested they hadn't found it, didn't it?

There was a knock at the door. Ella stiffened.

"It is Gabrielle, mademoiselle."

Ella relaxed when the servant girl stepped into the room

alone, closing the door behind her. In her hand was a book. On the cover was a drawing of a man in a top hat squinting through a monocle. Ella furrowed her brow. It was a copy of the novel *Arsène Lupin, Gentleman-Burglar* in French.

"It's from Madame de Nicolaÿ's library. She thought you might like something to read, to occupy the time."

"Oh," Ella said, a little taken aback by the unexpected gesture. "Thank you. That's very kind of her."

When Ella reached for the book, Gabrielle held on to it and leaned forward to whisper in her ear. "There is paper and a pen inside. Tomorrow our groceries are delivered. If you want to send a letter, the man who comes can be trusted." She released the book to Ella and took a step back.

Ella considered the girl, unsure if she could trust her. This might be a trap laid by Oberst Knauff.

"I don't know anyone in Belgium to send a letter to," Ella finally said. Trap or no trap, it was the truth. The only members of the resistance they'd encountered were the elderly couple who'd asked them to deliver the incriminating letter.

The next morning, just as Gabrielle had said, a man arrived on a horse-drawn cart and unloaded crates of groceries. Ella wondered if she should have penned something. Maybe it wasn't too late. She could write to the American consulate in Belgium. Although, when she'd been arrested as a spy in London, the American consulate there hadn't been much help.

Still, there had to be someone who could help them. There must be some way to get a message to Major Drake. Perhaps Gabrielle's contacts could get a message to the British consulate in Antwerp. They'd know how to contact the British Security Service. If not, they could forward the message to Scotland Yard or even to Ashenden. Eventually the letter would find its way to Drake. But by then it would probably be too late. By then, their fate would have been decided, one way or another.

Trays of food came and went. Days passed. Each morning Ella watched the officers parade across the misty lake to the idling cars that would deliver them to the battlefield. By mid-morning, the fog having cleared, the pair of swans which inhabited the lake appeared. They glided contentedly, unperturbed by the distant booms of cannonry, until the sun dipped behind the pines and the officers returned.

She still regretted agreeing to deliver the note. But with each passing day, it seemed more and more likely the Germans hadn't discovered it after all. Surely, carrying correspondence on behalf of the Belgian resistance was a punishable offense. If they'd found it in her notepad, they would have already charged them as spies. Perhaps Oberst Knauff was prolonging their time here as punishment for the insolent remarks she'd made about German atrocities during dinner.

It wasn't until the evening of their fourth day at the château that they were again summoned to the parlor. Judging from the doomed expression on his face, Oliver didn't share her optimism that the Germans hadn't discovered the letter. And, based on the rifle being employed to usher them down the stairs, neither did the guard.

Tonight, the gramophone played no record. The room was silent save for the occasional crackle of wood in the lit fireplace. Oberst Knauff offered them a seat, which Ella took to be a good sign. He was probably about to offer up an insincere apology for detaining them here.

Only, he didn't look like a man about to admit fault. He looked like someone sitting on an exciting secret. He crossed the room to the carved Louis XV writing desk. Retrieving a small key from his pocket, he unlocked the drawer and extracted a single sheet of paper. He gave a curt smile, then translated the document for their benefit.

"By order of the general officer commanding occupied Belgium, based on evidence supporting the charge hereafter stated, Ella Kaye and Oliver Engel are to be tried by general court-martial for acting against Germany as enemy spies."

He turned to the guard. "Take them back to their rooms."

They were roused from their beds before dawn, blindfolded, handcuffed, and loaded into a German Army truck. After an hour's drive, they stopped somewhere in the Liège province, in the German-occupied town where their trial was to be held.

Unlike the previous town they'd visited, this one hadn't been burned to the ground. The courthouse, at least, was still intact, as this was where the two reporters found themselves when their blindfolds were finally removed.

They were seated on opposite sides of a small courtroom. A series of German flags were draped along the walls. An armed guard stood behind each of them. The room was otherwise empty.

Eventually, they were joined by the prosecutor, a thin, wiry man with a complexion as cratered as the moon. Sometime after that, the officer presiding over the tribunal took his place at the bench at the front of the room.

Ella had never witnessed a military tribunal before. She had expected a panel of German officers would decide their fate. Instead, the verdict would be rendered by a single major, whose most distinguishing attribute was the haste with which he conducted the proceeding. It was clear he did not think the trial a valuable use of his time.

They were each given an opportunity to make a statement. But they were not allowed to hear what the other had to say. As such, they were led out of the room in turn.

Ella plead her innocence vaguely. She wasn't a spy. This was all a misunderstanding. She was loyal to Germany. Given she didn't know what evidence they had against them, there wasn't much else she could say. It was still possible they hadn't discovered the letter intended for the Belgian resistance. Or so she hoped.

This hope was soon dashed. The letter was the prosecutor's first piece of evidence supporting the allegation the two reporters were spies. The contents of the message were thoroughly damning, noting troop movements and the names of commanding German officers, Oberst Knauff among them.

"How long have you been working with the Belgian resistance?" the prosecutor asked Ella.

"I'm not working with them."

"Herr Engel said it was he who agreed to carry the message. That you knew nothing about it. Is this true?"

Ella turned to look at Oliver, confused.

"That's right," Oliver said. "I already told you, she didn't know anything about it."

"Why then, Frau Kaye, did we find the letter in your notebook?"

"I put it there," Oliver insisted.

"Herr Engel, the question is not directed at you." He turned back to Ella. "What was a message intended for the Belgian resistance doing in your notebook?"

She swallowed. "I didn't know what the message said. Neither did Oliver—Herr Engel. We didn't read it."

"Why not?" he asked Ella.

"It's not my habit to read other people's letters. We had no idea what the letter said. I swear."

"Let's move on," the major said impatiently. "Have you any other proof they acted against Germany?"

"Yes, Major. In fact, I only discovered that letter last night when going through Frau Kaye's notebook in preparation for the trial."

"Let's see it, then."

The prosecutor picked up a thin piece of paper from the table. He brandished it with a victorious smile. "*This* is a telegram posted by Frau Kaye from Düsseldorf to her attorney in New York."

Ella felt sick.

"It instructs her attorney to cease sale and shipment of copper from Platacobre, a Montana copper mine which Frau Kaye owns."

"Get to the point, please."

"Krupp obtains a large amount of copper from Platacobre. This telegram clearly demonstrates it was Frau Kaye's intention to disrupt the sale of copper to Krupp, thereby depriving Germany's most important weapons manufacturer of a vital resource."

"I was merely asserting my contractual rights. I'm happy to sell copper to Krupp or any other German company, but I was neither notified of the sale, nor was I paid for it."

"Ah, but Frau Kaye," the prosecutor said, "we contacted Krupp to clarify the context of your telegram. According to them, their acquisition of copper from Platacobre was entirely legal under the existing contract."

"They're lying."

The major ignored her. "Did you obtain a written statement from Krupp stating the sale was legal?"

"We have a representative from Krupp who will testify to the matter," the prosecutor said. "He should be arriving shortly with a copy of the contract."

The major consulted his watch and shook his head. "Type a statement for the witness to sign when he arrives."

The major gathered his things, preparing to leave. "Even

without the Krupp testimony, it is my opinion that there is enough evidence to render a verdict at this time. Please rise."

When she stood, Ella stumbled backward into the guard. The room seemed to be moving, rocking as though she were on a ship. And when the major spoke he sounded very far away.

"The German Army and German State, under the Kaiser's supreme command, hereby find Ella Kaye and Oliver Engel both guilty of espionage, the punishment for which is death by firing squad. The prisoners shall be transported to the prison immediately, where they will be held until they are shot tomorrow morning at dawn."

CHAPTER 27

Jay sat at the small table by the window in their room at the Hôtel St. Antoine, flipping through Horst's red notebook. It was late afternoon. Ten stories below, the courtyard was beginning to fill with diplomats toasting the day's end. Somewhere in the distance heavy artillery boomed.

The notebook had magically reappeared in his bag yesterday. Jay was pretty sure Robert—or rather, Bertie—had taken and returned it. Ordinarily he would have confronted him about the matter, but he needed a ride to Brussels. Getting there was all that mattered.

Earlier that morning, Jay had received a telegram. Unable to restrain himself, he'd opened it in the lobby. It was from his Aunt Mary—a rambling dissertation of her future travel plans. He clutched the telegram to his chest and sprinted up the stairs to his room, where he'd waited impatiently for Bertie to leave on his sales call.

Jay didn't have an Aunt Mary. The message was from Martin Winter. As soon as he was alone, he set to deciphering it. On a blank sheet of paper he ripped out from Horst's notebook, he inscribed the third letter of each word and every other number included in the telegram.

The decrypted message read, "*Wednesday, 10 a.m. 18 Rue*

Saint Anne, Brussels. Leave now."

Giddy with excitement, Jay read the message at least twenty times before destroying it. Tomorrow was Wednesday. In less than twenty-four hours, this horrendous adventure would come to an end, and he would finally be paid for the tracers. All he had to do was get to Brussels.

He assumed the part about leaving now was meant to suggest he should travel before the nighttime curfew went into effect. Pass or no pass, civilians weren't allowed on the roads after dark. If guards from either side discovered you out past curfew, there was a good chance you would be shot.

Whether he could leave for Brussels immediately would depend on Bertie's schedule. Jay wasn't overly concerned. The meeting wasn't until 10 a.m. If Bertie couldn't take him today, they'd still have time to drive to Brussels in the morning.

Jay was still sitting at the table when Bertie entered their room a few minutes later.

He gestured to the red notebook. "Say, what's that for, anyway?"

Jay shifted in his chair. Bertie really had some nerve. "It's just a notebook. Why were you looking through my things?"

"I wasn't. It was on the floor." Bertie shrugged. "I was curious is all. What are all those addresses for?"

"I don't know anything about them. I picked up the notebook in a secondhand shop."

"Is that so?"

"I noticed some of my safety pins are missing. Was that you too?"

Bertie scoffed. "Don't be absurd. What would I want with those? Maybe it was the woman who cleans the room. I can ask her for you, if you like."

"Forget it. Say, I don't suppose you could give me a lift to

Brussels today? I've got an important meeting there tomorrow morning."

Before Bertie could respond, the door to their room flew open. A young out-of-breath Belgian boy burst in and ran up to Bertie.

"Are you the safety pin man?" he asked with wide eyes.

Bertie nodded. He flipped up the lapel of his jacket, revealing two safety pins. The boy turned up his shirt collar, revealing the same.

"Seriously?" Jay threw his hands up. Not only had Bertie stolen his safety pins, apparently he was handing them out all over town.

The boy dug a small folded piece of paper out of his trouser pocket and handed it to Bertie. Before he had time to thank him, the boy ran out the room.

After reading the note, Bertie cursed. He crumpled the paper into a tight ball and tossed it into the large ashtray on the table. He struck a match, setting the paper ablaze. Then he set to pacing the room, muttering something under his breath.

Jay leaned back in his chair, distancing himself from the conflagration. He had never seen Bertie this distraught. Something truly terrible must have happened.

"Is everything all right?"

"No, it's not. Not at all." Bertie ran a hand through his hair.

"Is there anything I can do to help?"

Bertie took the seat opposite Jay and leaned his forearms on the table. "Can you keep a secret?"

"Sure."

"You swear on whatever you find sacred?"

Jay raised his right hand and placed his left across his chest atop the pocket containing the silver cigarette case. "I swear."

"My friend was arrested by the Germans as a spy."

"Here? In Belgium?"

Bertie nodded, then looked away.

"What friend? What happened?"

Bertie let out a long sigh. "I haven't been entirely honest with you, Gatz. I'm involved in something, well . . ." His voice trailed off. "You see, I'm not really a cigarette salesman." Something about Bertie's voice was off.

"You're not?"

"And I'm not American." Bertie's voice was entirely different now. "I work for the British Secret Service. I'm sorry I lied, but it couldn't be avoided. And you're right." He flipped up his lapel. "I did take your safety pins. Sorry about that. I'm happy to pay for them." He shrugged. "They've become a sort of symbol of the Belgian resistance. Helps us to know who we can trust."

Jay sat there, taking it all in.

"The name's Scott." Bertie extended his hand to Jay as if it were their first time meeting. "Bertram Scott."

Bertie was a British spy. He supposed it made sense. It explained all the time he spent with the British legation and his seemingly endless supply of petrol.

"I'm sorry for all the lies, old sport, but they're part of the job."

Jay focused his attention on the blackened ashtray. Did Bertie suspect *he* was a spy? Was that why he'd taken the notebook and rummaged through his belongings?

Bertie stared out the window, tapping his fingers on the table. "Damn it!" He slammed his fist on the table, causing the ashtray and Jay to jump. "This is all my fault. It was my idea. I have to do something." He got up and resumed pacing the room. "The note said they're executing them tomorrow morning. I have to get them out. He's—well, he's the kind of chap that always has my back, and now— I can't just leave him there." He stopped walking and turned to Jay. "You understand? I'm sure you've got a pal like that."

Jay nodded and gave a tight smile. He didn't have anything close to a pal like that. The closest thing he had to a friend right now was Bertie—and they'd both been lying to each other this whole time. He supposed Martin Winter was his friend—at least now that he'd resurfaced—but he certainly hadn't had Jay's back these past few weeks.

The only friend Jay had ever had like that was Cody. If Jay had been arrested as a spy, Cody would have assembled a ragtag army and stormed the prison without a second thought.

Bertie resumed pacing. "I don't have a choice. I'll go there tonight." His face lit up. "I have a German uniform. I'll pretend to be a guard."

"You don't speak German." Bertie couldn't be serious. But if he was, Jay needed to find another way to get to Brussels. He should probably do that anyway, now he knew Bertie was a British spy.

"Teach me a few phrases. How do I say, 'The prisoners are to come with me'?"

"Bertie, this is a terrible idea. You're gonna get yourself killed. Think about it."

How would he get to Brussels? Maybe he could find a bicycle. Worst-case scenario, he could walk. It would take four or five hours, and it was too late to leave today, but if he left at sunrise—

"Come with me." Bertie's eyes were wild with excitement. "You can wear the German uniform. You'll do the talking, nothing more. I'll handle everything else."

"I don't think—"

"Christ, with that blond hair and those blue eyes, you'll be perfect. This is your chance, Gatz."

"My—"

"Your chance to be a hero. Your chance to make a difference. A relief charity can only do so much. *This* is your chance to really help the Belgians. That's why you're here, after all. Isn't it? Well, that and because you thought it would be an adventure. Isn't that right? Well"—he slapped Jay on the back—"adventure is calling your name, James Gatz."

"I'm sorry, Bertie. I can't."

"Please." The plea in Bertie's eyes was so desperate, he might as well have been down on his knees, hands clasped, begging like a pauper. "Please help me. I can't leave him there. I'll take you to Brussels first thing in the morning, I promise. Come on, what do you say?"

A part of him wanted to help Bertie, and not just for the ride to Brussels. He liked Bertie. He really did. And he could see how painful this was for him. "I—"

"Hell, what am I saying? You don't deserve to be mixed up in any of this. Forget I asked. I've already gotten one good chap into a pinch. Now I'm trying to drag you into this mess. Forget what I said. This is something I have to do alone."

"Bertie, this is a bad idea."

"I have to try. He's American, my friend, Oliver, is. Did I mention that already? They arrested the woman who was with him too. She's . . . well, I've never met her, but she's that reporter, Ella Kaye. You've heard of her?"

Jay nodded trying to make sense of what Bertie had said. "The Germans arrested Ella Kaye?"

"That's right. Apparently, they don't care that she's a woman or that she's famous. They're going to shoot her anyway. They're going to shoot them both tomorrow morning. Unless I do something about it."

Jay sat in shocked silence. How did Ella Kaye know

Bertie's friend? "Why were they arrested?" Jay finally managed.

"I don't know the details. All I know is that I have to do something. I'd never forgive myself for not trying. Look, just help me learn a few phrases."

No one was going to believe Bertie was a German guard. Bertie was going to get himself killed for nothing. And tomorrow Bertie's friend and Ella Kaye would be executed.

"How do I say, 'The prisoners are to be released into my custody'?"

Bertie couldn't do this alone, but Jay couldn't help him. If he saved Ella, he'd be dooming himself. She'd tell Bertie about Teddy Belmont, and that would be the end of him. Bertie wouldn't take him to Brussels in the morning as promised—he'd take him to a Belgian prison. Jay couldn't help Bertie save them. He just couldn't.

"No, that won't work," Bertie said. "Maybe I should tell the guard his shift is over."

"Bertie, don't do this."

Bertie had done nothing but help Jay this entire time. Now, he was going to risk his life to help another friend while Jay selfishly slunk away to Brussels to get paid for stolen bullets. He wasn't proud of it, but that was what he had to do.

He wished Bertie hadn't told him any of it. He needed to focus on getting to Brussels. He needed to get up, leave the room, and figure out how he was going to get there. But Jay didn't move. Something held him back.

And that something, he realized, was Ella Kaye. Now that she was involved, Jay wasn't just turning his back on Bertie, he was turning his back on Cody. Jay had an opportunity to rescue the person Cody had cared about most in his life, and he was turning it down. If Cody could see him now, it would probably be the last time he'd bother to look at him. He'd be disgusted by the lying, thieving, spineless egoist Jay had become.

"I'll bring a gun," Bertie said. "That's what I'll do. How do I say, 'Open the cells'?"

"Forget that," Jay said, looking Bertie in the eye. "If I help, you promise to drive me to Brussels in the morning? No matter what happens?"

Bertie nodded.

"Then, I'm coming with you."

CHAPTER 28

Ella sat on the floor of her small cell with her back against the wall. Beside her, a piece of black bread on a tin plate lay untouched. The afternoon sun streamed through the thin slit of window high on the wall, illuminating the particles of dust hovering in the air.

She didn't know where they had taken Oliver. The rest of the cells in the corridor were empty. She was alone, just as she'd been in the row of cells at Scotland Yard, back when all this started. She had come full circle. At least there was some symmetry to it all.

Otherwise, there wasn't much meaning in any of it. She wasn't even sure why she had agreed to become a British spy. Because of the ridiculous fantasy that a stranger on a boat was really Jay Gatsby? Or because she was so desperate to have her name back on the front page, she would have agreed to anything?

At dawn they would face the firing squad. She had thirteen hours left to live. And that was that. No one knew they were here. No one was coming to save them.

Why should anyone help them? They hadn't done anything to help the Belgians, or the British for that matter. If they'd helped anyone at all, it was the Germans. They'd unwittingly given the Germans carte blanche to slap their names on a series of propaganda pieces. For, after Schnitzer's press department finished editing their articles, that was what they would surely be. And who knew how long they'd continue to use their names for this purpose even after they were dead.

It seemed unlikely the Germans would admit they'd allowed enemy spies to follow the German Army. They'd probably lie and say the two reporters were killed while observing a battle. The world would never know their true fate. Nor would anyone know what they had seen. The town reduced to rubble. Corpses strewn in the debris-filled street. The true price of glory.

Had she had the opportunity to expose the horrors the Belgian civilians were being subjected to by the Germans, at least she could have died proudly. But she hadn't written a single word about any of it. She hadn't done anything to help the Belgians, aside from one feeble attempt to deliver a letter.

The door at the end of the row of cells swung open with a loud creak. A succession of footsteps echoed down the empty corridor. The prison guard approached her cell. He leered at her with a nasty grin as he inserted a key into the lock.

Next to him stood the prosecutor from the trial. What did he want? Was he here to gloat?

The iron door clicked open.

"You have a visitor, Frau Kaye," the prosecutor said. He exchanged a few words in German with a man standing out of view. Then he turned his attention back to Ella. "He says he is an old friend."

It was night now, and the dim bulb dangling from the ceiling hummed with the exertion of lighting her cell. Her visitor having long since departed, she was alone again, trying to make sense of what she had just learned.

This information didn't change anything, at least, not as far as her current predicament was concerned. There was no last-minute reprieve or anything like that. They'd been found guilty. And in a few hours she would be dead.

But at least she no longer had Cody's death on her conscience. That was something. She wouldn't die thinking her selfish actions had killed two men she cared about, just one.

She had spent the last two years convinced Cody's death was her fault. But on the eve of her own demise, she had learned the truth. Cody hadn't killed himself, after all.

There was a modicum of solace in knowing her selfish tantrums hadn't driven Cody to suicide. Of course, that wasn't why Cody's murderer had revealed himself. He hadn't intended to reveal anything. He thought she already knew.

He'd visited her in her cell solely to make sure no one else knew what he had done. He wanted to make sure the secret died with her. And it would. His vile secret would die with her, and there was nothing she could do about it.

The door to the corridor screeched open, and footsteps advanced down the corridor. She sat up in bed. It was the guard. He licked his lips and said something she couldn't understand.

It was well before dawn, hours before the firing squad would end her life. That meant he was here for something else. He unlocked the cell door, pushing it open with a lascivious grin.

She backed into the corner of the cell. There were more footsteps in the corridor. A priest donning a black cassock marched into the cell.

Relief washed over her. The priest couldn't save her life, probably not even her soul. But he could save her from the guard's advances. Perhaps she could convince the clergyman to stay with her until dawn.

A giant cross hung around the priest's neck. It swung to the side as he swiveled around and reached under his robe. At the end of his now-outstretched arm was a gun. A loud *bang* startled Ella into a scream. The guard crumpled to the floor.

The priest spoke with a British accent. "I'll explain everything later. Let's go."

He motioned for her to follow him, but she couldn't move. The room was spinning. Blood trickled out the back of the guard's head, a red rivulet on the concrete floor.

"Come on." The priest waved his arm, urging her to follow him.

She stood in the corner of the cell in shocked confusion.

The clergyman leaned out of the cell and called down the corridor. "I need you to come get her out." He knelt and collected the set of keys from the dead guard. Then he raced down the hall, his cassock fluttering behind him.

In came a man dressed in a German guard's uniform. When Ella saw his face, her mouth fell open. This couldn't be real. Everything that had happened today must be part of one long hellish nightmare. That was the only explanation that made sense.

Cody's murderer had visited her. Then a priest had shot a guard only to leave her with a different German guard—this one with the familiar face that had haunted her these past weeks.

"Come on," the guard said. "We've got to go."

He sounded like him too—like Gatsby or Teddy Belmont, whoever he was.

She felt like she was losing her mind. Like she was one of the women from the madhouse she'd infiltrated all those years ago. A deranged smile crept across her lips. Maybe she *was* one of the women from the madhouse. Maybe she had never left.

"See here, I only want to help." He stepped over the body of the guard with a grimace and held out his hand.

She ignored it. He wasn't here. She was seeing things.

"Ella, we don't have time for this. Please, let's go."

She slumped onto the cell floor, covering her ears and shutting her eyes tightly. But when she opened her eyes, he was still there.

"Who are you? Really? Are you Teddy Belmont or Jay Gatsby?"

He gave a frustrated sigh. "I— Well, I said my name was Teddy Belmont on the boat, but my name's really Jay Gatsby. I used to work for Cody."

"And I'm supposed to believe that you and a murderous priest have come to save me?"

"He's not really a priest. He works for British intelligence. I don't have time to explain."

Maybe Drake *had* sent someone to save them after all. But why was Jay Gatsby here? Something about this was wrong.

"Please, Ella. Let's go."

"Why are you risking your life to save me?"

He took a step back and raised his hands in exasperation. "At this point, I really don't know!" He collected himself. "Because I'm not doing this for you, all right? I'm doing it for Cody."

Ella sat up straighter.

"This is what he would have wanted. And after everything he did for me, I owe it to him. Please." He offered her his hand.

This time, she took it.

Oliver and the man dressed as the priest were waiting in the shadows near the parked car. With a sweep of his arm, the man yanked off his cassock to reveal a suit underneath. He extended his hand to Ella.

"The name's Scott, by the way, Bertram Scott. Call me Bertie."

He unlatched the lid of a rectangular compartment at the back of the car. He tossed in the cassock, spreading it over the bottom. Then he motioned for Ella and Oliver to get in.

The compartment was the size of a large steamer trunk and was riddled with bullet holes.

Ella narrowed her eyes. "I'm not getting in there."

"You're escaped prisoners," Bertie said. "The Germans will be looking for you, and we're breaking curfew as it is. You don't have a choice." He held out the pistol he had used to shoot the prison guard. "Here, take this."

The dark, cramped compartment smelled of old leather, tobacco, and gunpowder. Ella and Oliver sat crouched with their backs at each end, facing one another with their bent legs pressed together. As the car sped out of town, they were jostled and jolted by each imperfection in the road.

Ella spoke in a whisper. "This was all my fault. I should never have sent that telegram. I'm sorry. I—"

Oliver leaned his head closer to hers. "None of that matters."

She reached out to touch Oliver's face, as though to make sure he was real. Then after a moment she said, "I can't believe he saved us."

"Me neither. I had no idea Bertie was even in Belgium."

"No, I mean the man in the German uniform with Bertie. He's Jay Gatsby, the man who used to work for Cody. The one who said his name was Teddy Belmont on the ship."

"Bertie's friend? Really? I thought you said Teddy Belmont was a German spy?"

"I guess Drake was wrong."

"He must work for the British Secret Service with Bertie,"

Oliver said. "That would explain why he was pretending to be Teddy Belmont on the ship."

"But wouldn't Drake have known about him, then?"

"Maybe not. It's a different department." He squeezed her hand. "Who cares. I'm just glad he got you out of there."

There was more she wanted to tell Oliver, but it was difficult to explain, and she was so exhausted.

"Looks like there's a sentry ahead," Bertie called back to them.

A German voice yelled, "*Halt!*"

The car slowed before coming to an abrupt stop that slammed the reporters against the side of the trunk. Jay and someone, presumably a sentry, exchanged words in German. Then the man switched to English.

"Both of you, get out slowly with your hands up."

There was a muffled squeaking of doors and clanking of metal as the two men did as told. Ella picked up the pistol Bertie had given her and gripped it tightly with both hands.

"Who is he?" the sentry asked.

"He's the only person I could find with a car," Jay said. "He's American."

"To where are you going?"

"He's driving me to Louvain."

"After curfew?"

"I'm delivering important documents on behalf of General von der Golz."

"Show them to me."

"They're confidential."

"Very well. Where are your papers? Don't move, we will retrieve them. Just tell me where they are."

"Under the driver's seat," Bertie said in an American accent.

"*Kadet Kemmerich*," the sentry yelled, "*komm her und durch such das Auto.*"

Gravel crunched under boots as the soldier approached. His electric torch caused the bullet holes in the trunk to illuminate like fireflies. A hand thumped around the front of the compartment, searching for the latch. Ella held the gun steady.

"*Nein, Kemmerich. Unter dem Sitz.*"

Oliver touched her arm. The man circled back around the car to open the door. She relaxed.

"What is in the storage compartment of the car?"

"Cigarettes," Bertie answered. "Cartons of them. May I?"

"May you what?"

"Get a sample of the cigarettes for you. I'm a salesman, you see."

"Kemmerich will get them."

Ella raised the gun, certain this time she was going to have to use it.

"Sorry, friends," Bertie said. "I'm afraid the cartons in the trunk are already sold—to your fellow officers in Brussels, as a matter of fact. But I've got a few up front. You can help yourself to those, if you'd like. My treat."

Soon they were driving again. And somehow, Ella managed to drift to sleep. When the car slowed to a stop, she jolted awake, confused by the confining darkness.

The compartment lid flew open.

"Well, don't you two look cozy." Bertie stood over them, a satisfied grin on his face. "You're welcome to sleep here, if you prefer, but I suggest coming with me."

They followed Bertie down a narrow footpath. All around them, tall pines rose into the dark, starless sky. Crickets chirped. A nearby stream gurgled.

"Where are we?" Ella asked. She wasn't sure how long she had been sleeping.

"About ten kilometers south of Louvain," Bertie said.

"Isn't that German-held territory?"

"It is. But don't worry, this place is well hidden."

They came upon a small somewhat dilapidated house. Retrieving an iron key from his pocket, Bertie unlocked the door.

"Whose place is this?" Oliver asked.

"It belongs to the British Secret Service."

Inside, the house was sparsely decorated with an assortment of mismatched old furniture. Grain sacks nailed to the window frames served as makeshift curtains. One of the walls was lined with stacks of cigarette cartons. On another, wooden shelves housed a display of guns and ammunition large enough to equip a small army.

They sat around a wooden table in the kitchen, eating tinned bully beef that Bertie had heated on an ancient iron stove. Ella couldn't help staring at Jay Gatsby. It was really him. It had been him all along.

"Now that I've provided you with sustenance," Bertie said, looking Ella and Oliver over, "can you please tell me how on earth the two of you ended up in Belgium? Wasn't the whole idea to pretend you were spying on England?"

"Well," Oliver began.

"We'll tell you about it later," Ella interrupted. "There's something I need to say first. Something's about to happen. We have to warn them." She paused and for a second questioned whether she had imagined it all.

"I don't suppose you could be a trifle more specific?" Bertie said.

"Antwerp," Ella continued. "He said they're going to bomb Antwerp tonight. And he told me . . ." Her voice trembled.

"Who told you?" Oliver asked. "Who are you talking

about?"

The name wouldn't mean anything to Oliver, but it would to Gatsby. She looked across at Jay. "I spoke to Martin Winter."

CHAPTER 29

The lightbulb hanging above the table in the kitchen flickered, threatening to extinguish. Jay pressed his lips together and tried to think. Was this some sort of trick?

"Who's Martin Winter?" Bertie asked.

"I'm not sure I follow you," Jay said. "You spoke to Martin Winter?" Was Ella trying to get him to admit why he was really here in Belgium? Either that or Ella had lost her mind—and considering her mental state in the prison cell earlier, that was entirely possible.

"He visited me in my cell."

That seemed unlikely. The prison guards must have given her a concussion. She must have hallucinated the event.

"He was supposed to be a witness at the trial," Ella continued. "But he was late, so instead they had him sign a statement. And afterward . . . he came to my cell."

"They let a man in your cell?" Oliver said. "He didn't do anything, did he? You're not hurt or—"

"No, I'm fine," Ella said, turning her attention back to Jay.

Jay tugged at the collar of the German uniform he was still wearing. Speeding toward the prison Jay had learned, much to his horror, that Ella and Oliver worked for the Security Service, the British agency tasked with catching foreign spies. If Ella knew he was working for Winter, he needed to get out of here now, before they arrested him.

"He told me—"

"Hold on," Jay said, certain Ella was about to expose him as a German spy. He glanced around the room frantically. "Just hold on a minute."

He stood up, knocking over his chair. He righted it, trying to think. Sure, he'd helped them escape, but they worked for British Intelligence. So did Bertie. They'd have no choice but to turn him in. They might even decide to get it over with and shoot him on the spot.

They stared at Jay expectantly, waiting for him to finish saying whatever he had been about to say. How far would he get if he made a run for it now? No one at the table had a gun on them. If he took them by surprise, he'd at least make it out the door.

"Martin Winter killed Cody," Ella said.

"What?" That was impossible. Ella was confused. He needed to take advantage of this. He needed to get away before she snapped out of it and exposed him. He shifted his weight and readied himself to sprint out of the house.

"Who's Cody?" Bertie looked back and forth between Jay and Ella, utterly baffled. "Do you two know each other?"

"Cody's an old friend," Jay said, turning back to Ella. He should be running out the door, but he couldn't help it. He wanted to hear this. He sat, scooting the chair closer to the table.

"I thought you said Cody killed himself?" Oliver said.

Ella shook her head. "That's what I thought, but it was Martin Winter."

Bertie's eyes flitted around the table, resting on Oliver. "So, this Martin Winter chap, he was the reason you were arrested?"

"No. We got caught delivering a message for some safety pin man."

"Oh, I see." Bertie cleared his throat, then looked down at the table.

"Martin Winter killed Cody," Ella repeated.

"That's impossible," Jay said. Winter couldn't have killed Cody. Jay was with him that night.

"He poisoned him."

"Arsenic?" Oliver asked.

Ella nodded. "He put it in the bottle of gin in Cody's cabin earlier that day."

"I don't understand." Jay's stomach churned. If this was true, then he had spent the night drinking and laughing with Cody's murderer while Cody lay dying. "Why?"

"For God's sake," Bertie exclaimed. "What on earth are you three talking about? Who the bloody hell is Martin Winter?"

"He works for Krupp," Ella answered.

"Krupp?" Jay's mind was reeling.

"He told Cody he worked for United Copper Works, but the company never really existed. From the start, all the copper intended for United Copper Works went straight to Krupp. Cody found out and was going to terminate the lease. So, Winter killed him."

Jay felt an odd falling sensation, as if someone had shoved him off a ledge and he was plunging into an unending abyss. Winter had killed Cody. Winter worked for Krupp.

How long had Winter worked for Krupp? He searched his mind, trying to recall what the governor general had said about Winter.

"Have you ever heard of the Kornwalzer scandal?" he asked Ella.

"I remember that," Oliver said. "It was all over the papers.

Krupp got caught stealing military secrets from the German Army."

Jay tried to organize his thoughts. "Winter was . . . It's just that . . ." Then he had a sudden realization. He looked at Bertie. "I think Krupp might have other fake mining operations. A French nickel company in New Caledonia. The first time I met Winter, he claimed to work for it." Everything had been a lie from the very start.

"Well, this is certainly something the chaps in London will want to hear about."

"What did you mean when you said they were going to bomb Antwerp?" Oliver asked Ella.

"There's going to be a zeppelin raid tonight. They're going to drop the new bombs from Krupp. Martin Winter said he couldn't wait to watch the light show."

So, that was why Winter had told him to leave Antwerp.

"What time is it now?" Ella asked.

Bertie checked his watch. "A little after eleven."

"The zeppelin isn't leaving Düsseldorf until midnight. We've still got time. We've got to warn them. Is there a telephone here?"

Bertie shook his head. "Even if there were, it wouldn't do us any good. All the lines were severed."

Jay barely registered their conversation. Winter had killed Cody. Winter was a murderer. It all made sense now. Winter had never intended to pay him for the tracers. He'd planned to kill him from the start.

Winter had been the one to give Horst the picture of Jay and Cody. Had the war not upended Winter's plans, Jay would already be dead. He'd have been shot in an empty shop on Caledonian Road by Horst.

He was such a fool. Every single thing he'd done since leaving New York had been for nothing. He slumped in his chair, slack-jawed and miserable.

"Then we'll have to drive to Antwerp to warn them," Ella said.

Bertie shook his head. "Can't do that. We'd have to pass right by those same guards again. Even if they let us through, it's too dangerous at night. There are sentries everywhere, not to mention Belgian mines."

As ruined as his life was, some part of Jay seemed to think it was worth preserving. A voice inside him screamed to wake up, pay attention. Winter may not have told Ella about him, but she wasn't stupid. Both she and Oliver had seen him on the *Oceanic* pretending to be Teddy Belmont.

"What about crossing the border into the Netherlands?" Ella asked.

"Not from here."

Jay couldn't stay. He would wait until they were all asleep. Then, he would sneak out.

"Maybe there's a way to stop it before it gets to Antwerp," Ella said. "They'll use the train tracks to navigate."

Bertie frowned. "How do you propose we do that?"

"With that." Ella gestured to the large cache of weaponry along the wall.

Everyone turned to look.

Jay had his things with him, including the Mauser pistol. He scanned the shelves of weaponry until he spotted boxes of ammunition. He should take extra bullets with him when he left tonight.

"Won't work," Bertie said. "You'd need a large projectile to take down a zeppelin."

"What about those machine guns?" Ella insisted.

"Those won't do a thing. Trust me, I know much more about this than any of you. I've even flown on a zeppelin before—last summer out of Potsdam." Bertie smiled at the memory. "You wouldn't believe the view. The food wasn't half-bad either, considering it was German."

Jay glanced around the room, searching for a compass or a map he could take with him.

"You don't say?" Oliver smirked. "Ella and I also went up in a zeppelin."

"Did you?" Bertie cocked his head to the side. "When?"

"A few days ago, out of Düsseldorf. Although, we weren't served a meal. The German Army's new zeppelin doesn't have a passenger cabin. We rode in the control car with the captain."

"Well," Bertie said, "it sounds like you had quite the adventure, Ollie, old boy, but you still can't shoot down a zeppelin with a machine gun."

Jay would make his way to Rotterdam. He'd get the money Dierks owed him. Then what? He couldn't go back to New York, not without the thousands of dollars he owed the Eastman gang.

"Machine guns could easily create a tear in one of the hydrogen bags," Ella said, crossing the room to examine the large guns resting on the bottom shelf. "And a tear will allow oxygen in."

"So what?"

"A spark won't ignite in pure hydrogen," Oliver said, catching on.

He could go to Ireland and stay with Connor. No. That was ridiculous. Connor didn't want him there. He barely knew him.

"You plan to explode it?" Bertie laughed. "Well, that's brilliant. Except you're rather leaving it to chance, wouldn't you say? Not every bullet is going to hit the metal frame, and even those that do won't necessarily cause a spark."

"But it's possible?" Oliver asked.

"Technically, yes. But the two of you aren't going anywhere."

Maybe he'd go to Brussels tomorrow, after all. He'd confront Winter and avenge Cody.

"We have to do something." Ella let out an exasperated sigh. "What's the point of gathering intelligence if you're just going to sit on it while a city goes up in flames?"

"I didn't save you from the firing squad so you could be gunned down by a zeppelin!"

Too bad Jay couldn't tell Ella about any of this. She'd want to avenge Cody too. Maybe they all would. Why, all four of them could go to Brussels. They'd face Winter together, armed with Bertie's weapons. Jay sat up straighter, invigorated by the fantasy playing out in his mind.

"Besides," Bertie continued, "we've only got half a can of petrol left, and I promised Gatz I'd drive him somewhere tomorrow."

"Who?" Ella screwed up her face.

Bertie gestured to Jay. "James. The man who just risked his life to save you. I'm driving him to Brussels in the morning. He has an important meeting."

"It can't be more important than this," Ella said to Jay.

"What?" he asked, his glorious daydream of vengeance thoroughly interrupted. Was she exposing him?

"Whatever your Secret Service mission in Brussels is, it can't be more important than saving Antwerp."

Jay almost smiled. Ella thought he worked with Bertie.

She gazed at him intently. "We can do this."

"We can?" What was she talking about?

"We can shoot down that zeppelin."

"Wait, what?"

"Leave the kid alone," Bertie yelled. "He's not shooting down any zeppelins tonight, either. He's a bloody relief worker, for Christ's sake."

Ella's brow furrowed. "But I thought—"

"Let's do it," Jay cried out, before she could finish the thought. He brought his palms down on the table with a thwack. "Let's shoot down a zeppelin."

"What the hell's gotten into you, Gatz?" Bertie asked.

"Come on, Bertie," Oliver said. "What do you say?"

"I say you've all gone mad."

Bertie wasn't wrong. To think the four of them might shoot down a zeppelin was insane. But if pretending to go along with it distracted Ella from exposing him as a German spy, Jay was all for it. He'd play along for now. Then, when the time was right, he'd slip away into the night before they figured out who he really was.

"If there's a chance to save Antwerp, we have to try," Oliver said.

Jay fumbled to find the right words. "This is our chance, Bertie. Like you said, this is our chance to help the Belgians. Forget Brussels. Saving Antwerp is more important."

"We can do this," Ella said.

"It's just not possible," Bertie said. "Not unless the zeppelin's flying low enough to be within reach of our artillery. If it is, that means *we're* in range of *its* artillery. Standing out in the open by the train tracks, we're an easy target for the zeppelin's gunners. It's suicide."

An idea flashed into Jay's mind. "How far are we from Pertés? Could we get there tonight?"

"Maybe. Why?"

"There's a church tower right on the train tracks. We could shoot the zeppelin down from up there."

"Well, that's better than standing out in the open. But there's no guarantee the zeppelin would ignite. I'm sorry, but the odds aren't in our favor."

"What if I could change that?" Jay said, having yet another epiphany. "If I could guarantee better odds. Would you agree to it, then?"

Bertie huffed. "I highly doubt you can."

Ella stared at Jay with narrowed eyes. They all did. Jay himself was somewhat mystified by what he was about to do.

If he did this, they would have tangible proof of what he had done. But that didn't seem to matter anymore. An elusive instinct, a force greater than reason, had taken charge of Jay. He reached into his jacket pocket, pulled out the silver cigarette case, and placed it on the table.

CHAPTER 30

Ella stared at the silver cigarette case. It was a gift from Cody. She was sure of it.

"Nice try, Gatz," Bertie said, "but I'm pretty sure that, even from a church tower, flicking a lit cigarette at a zeppelin won't cause it to go up in flames."

"Open it," Jay said.

Bertie flipped open the silver case, revealing six shiny bullets. "Bullets. So what?"

"They're not just bullets. They're tracers."

"What are tracers?" Ella asked. There wasn't enough time to pretend she knew what they were talking about. She had a vague recollection of Millie mentioning something about tracer bullets, but she hadn't been paying much attention at the time.

"They're incendiary bullets," Jay said. "They contain a pyrotechnic charge that ignites when fired from a gun."

Bertie leaned in to examine the shells more closely. "Where did you get these?"

"That's not important." Jay shifted in his chair. "Will they work?"

"They might." Bertie held one of the tracers up to the light, examining it. "Are you a decent marksman?"

"I am," Ella said before Jay had a chance to respond. "I'm

an excellent marksman." It sounded as though she were bragging, but that wasn't her intention.

"Really?" Bertie seemed to find this amusing.

"Yes, really."

Bertie turned to Jay. "How about you? Do you know how to shoot a Lewis machine gun?"

"No. Why would I?"

"I don't know, maybe Annie Oakley over there taught you. It's fairly simple. I can teach you now. It'll be better if we have two rifles and two machine gunners."

"Then, you think it's going to work?" A smile crept across her face.

"I'd say it's worth a shot."

They parked the car on the edge of town and made their way through the dark, deserted streets of Pertés. This wasn't the same town Ella and Oliver had visited with Peters, but it had endured the same fate. Over half the buildings were charred skeletons. Rubble and refuse littered the streets.

In the distance the church tower's narrowing steeple rose into the cloudy night. Ella followed closely behind Bertie. In addition to the rifle slung over his shoulder, he had a series of canvas bags strapped to his back. These contained the ammunition for the Lewis machine guns Oliver and Jay carried.

Something moved in a side alley. Bertie held up a hand, and everyone froze. But it was only a cat picking its way through the debris.

When they had almost reached the church square, Bertie stopped in front of one of the relatively unscathed houses and tried the door handle. It was unlocked.

"You three wait in here. I'll check to see how many guards there are."

Compared to the fire-gutted interiors of most of the

structures in town, the small home was in pristine condition. Still, it had been looted. Most of the furniture was missing, and the cabinets and drawers lay open and empty.

They sat in a circle in the small front room, a single lit candle laid on the floor between them. Squinting in the dim light, Oliver examined the label of an overlooked bottle of brandy he had found on the top of a shelf. He uncorked it and took a long swallow.

"You're much better off without it," he said to Jay.

"What?" Jay's eyes darted around the room.

"The mustache." Oliver offered the bottle to Jay, who shook his head. "It didn't suit you."

Jay let out an uncertain laugh. "Right."

"So how long have you and Bertie been working together?" Oliver took another sip. "You met him in New York, I take it. I'm surprised he never mentioned you to me."

Jay cleared his throat. "Say, what was it like riding in a zeppelin?"

Oliver grinned. "Ella here was terrified, but I loved it."

"I was not."

"They even let me fly the thing." Oliver took another swig of brandy. "I was pretty good at it."

"You don't say?"

"He's joking," Ella said, snatching the bottle from Oliver and recorking it. "Oliver can't drive a car, much less pilot a zeppelin."

"True enough. But, seeing as I have you as my chauffeur, why bother to learn?" Oliver winked at her. "Say, do you have a car back in New York?"

"No. Why?" Was he suggesting that when they got back to New York they were going to go on drives together? Well, she could always buy a car, if need be.

"No reason." Oliver turned to Jay. "I have to ask, does *C*

have you and Bertie dress in disguises often? I mean, that whole Teddy Belmont getup with the dyed hair and mustache, it was a little overboard. Wouldn't you say?"

"I—"

The front door flew open. Ella fumbled for the rifle but relaxed when Bertie entered the room.

"James was right. Aside from two Germans guarding the entrance to the church, that part of town's completely empty, as far as I can tell." Bertie turned to Ella. "I should be able to take them both out, unless you want to help."

Did she want to help shoot down a German guard? Of course she didn't, no more than she wished to shoot her own self in the foot. But if she couldn't do this, how did she expect to shoot down the zeppelin? She wouldn't lose any sleep over the loss of Hauptmann Vogel and his terror campaign, but what of the other men up there? They were just following orders.

"I'll help." Now wasn't the time to consider the moral implications of the situation. This had been her idea, after all.

"In that case, let's all go," Bertie said. "As soon as the two guards are down, you three head to the tower. I'll cover you in case another guard comes forth."

Ella started toward the door, but Oliver put a hand on her shoulder, stopping her. She turned and looked up at him.

He ran a hand through the mess of waves atop his head. "I just wanted to say—" He shook his head and gave a nervous laugh.

"What? What is it?"

"Nothing. I'll tell you later." He smiled. "After we save Antwerp."

On the portion of the plaza opposite the church stood a bronze statue of a caped warrior wielding a sword. The figure was perched atop a rectangular pedestal, tall and wide enough to conceal the foursome from view.

Ella peered around the edge of the pedestal. Two German soldiers guarded the entrance to the church, one on each side of the arched doorway. Both stood so incredibly still, their backs pressed against the stone building, they might have been asleep.

The gun Bertie had given Ella was a short-magazine Lee–Enfield rifle. It was standard issue for the British army. It was also one of the guns Felton had kept for use on his shooting range. Ella had shot thousands of bullets from a Lee–Enfield rifle on that range, but that was years ago. Hopefully she was as good as she used to be.

"Ready?" Bertie whispered.

She nodded.

Oliver and Jay stepped back to give her and Bertie more room. Reaching around the side of the pedestal, she aimed at the guard on the left.

"On the count of three," Bertie said softly. "One . . . two . . ."

Ella dug her feet into the ground and braced herself for the recoil. The loud *bang* of the rifle exploded in her ear. The two guards crumpled to the ground in unison.

Bertie turned to looked at her. Eyebrows raised, he nodded in approval. Then he gestured to the heavy machine guns Oliver and Jay had rested on the ground behind the statue.

"Leave those here for now."

They waited to make sure the gunshots had not alerted any other guards before making their way across the moonlit courtyard. They were halfway to the church when another shot rang out. Ella glanced around wildly, unsure where the round had come from.

"Fall back!" Bertie cried. "Shooter in the tower."

Ella looked up. A German soldier stood in an opening

midway up the tower. His rifle was trained directly at her.

It happened in an instant. Bertie's rifle exploded from behind. The gun in the tower cracked. Oliver leaped in front of her. And the soldier in the tower tumbled forward as Oliver stumbled back.

A scream caught in her throat as they both fell to the ground. An expanding circle of red was overtaking Oliver's shirt.

"Hang on, Oliver." Bertie threw off the canvas bags of ammunition he'd been carrying and tore off his shirt to use as a compress. He knelt beside them, his white undershirt damp with sweat. "Grab his legs, Gatz. Help me carry him behind the building. Ella, make sure that was the last guard."

She forced herself upright. Taking a shaky breath, she raised the rifle and scanned the tower and the surrounding area. When she was satisfied the courtyard was empty, she rushed behind the building.

Bertie knelt on the ground next to Oliver. Jay stood a few feet away, hands shoved in his pockets, a terrified look on his face.

"The bullet's lodged just below his collarbone," Bertie said. "Keep pressure on it." As soon as Ella's hands took the place of his, Bertie jumped up. "I'll be right back with the car. There's a Red Cross hospital twenty kilometers from here. James, keep an eye out for any more Germans."

Oliver attempted a smile. His voice was scratchy. "Guess you'll have to save Antwerp without me."

Ella wanted to say something comforting—that he was going to be okay, that he had to be okay. That she wouldn't be able to bear it if he wasn't, but she just looked at him, unable to find the words.

The car pulled up with a screech. Bertie jumped out. He and Jay lifted Oliver into the compartment at the back of the car. Oliver's eyelids fluttered. He was losing consciousness. Ella reached into the compartment and grasped his hand.

"He'll be okay. I'll make sure of it," Bertie said, as though this were something within his power to promise.

She let go of Oliver's hand and stepped back. The lid of the compartment clicked shut. The car sped away. She watched it disappear into the darkness. Then she stared out at nothing.

Leaves rustled in the thin wind. Somewhere in the distance an owl cried out. Then, for a long time, there was only silence.

Standing there in the dark, deserted city, she had never before felt so hopelessly alone.

"Ella."

She turned to see Jay standing at the edge of the plaza. The canvas bags of ammunition Bertie had been carrying were strapped to his back. In his arms he held one of the Lewis machine guns. He gazed up at the church tower, his profile illuminated by hazy moonlight.

"It's a long walk up," he said, turning back to face her. "We should get going."

Ella picked up the rifle and slung it over her shoulder. She followed Jay into the church and up the tower's seemingly endless stairway. They ascended past the midpoint landing, then up past colossal dangling bells.

As they climbed she willed herself not to think about Oliver. She couldn't. Not now. If she did, she would fall apart. With each step she suppressed all thoughts of him. She compressed them and locked them away like the latched folds of an accordion—songs to be played another day.

When they finally reached the top, it was after midnight. Ella leaned against one of the archways, catching her breath. A gust of wind unsettled her hair as she surveyed the devastation below. How many towns had been destroyed in the wake of the German march? How many soldiers and civilians massacred?

Jay set the Lewis gun on its bipod and loaded it with the ammunition from the canvas bags. Ella exchanged the bullets in her rifle for tracers. Everything was ready. Now, all there was to do was wait.

They sank to the floor, backs pressed against the cool stone wall of the tower. Neither spoke. High above the vacant city, the only sound was the whoosh of wind.

It was Jay who finally broke the silence. "Can I ask you a question?"

When she said yes, he looked down at his lap and frowned before turning his gaze back to her.

"Why didn't you want me to have the money Cody left me in his will?"

"Why would you think that?"

"Your attorney told me you contested that part of the will."

She had no recollection of this whatsoever. In the year following Cody's death, it was as if an invisible barrier had sprung up between herself and the rest of the world. Conversations had the distorted countenance of having traveled through water to reach her. Her memories of that time were even hazier.

"If I did, I didn't mean to, not intentionally." She hadn't wanted anything to do with the will or the obscene amount of money Cody had left her. At the time, it was tainted with too much sorrow and guilt. Her attorney had handled everything. "How much did he leave you?"

"Twenty-five thousand dollars."

She nodded. "I'll speak to my attorney about it as soon as I can. I'm not sure what happened. The money should have been yours. I know Cody wanted you to have it."

"I miss him." Jay gave a sad smile.

"Cody spoke of you often, you know. He . . . Well, I think he considered you a protégé of sorts. He was proud of you."

Jay looked away.

"Was that why you were on the ship? To ask me about the will?"

He let out a short laugh and dabbed at his eyes with his shirt sleeve. "I had no idea you were going to be on that ship. When you showed up at the table that first night, I almost had a heart attack."

"So, why were you on the ship?"

He inhaled sharply through his nostrils. "It was just a job. I didn't know what I was getting myself into, not really. I was desperate, you see. I owe a lot of money to a group of, well, rather unpleasant men in New York."

"Bankers?"

"Gangsters. I—"

A low, droning rumble interrupted the conversation. The silver tip of a zeppelin pierced through a cloud. Ella went to the tall arched opening, rifle in hand. Jay knelt beside her behind the Lewis gun.

She waited until the enormous cigar-shaped dirigible had floated into full view. "Ready?"

Jay nodded. With a deafening *rat-tat-tat*, shots soared from the machine gun, stabbing the darkness.

Ignoring the thunderous roar, Ella pulled back the bolt handle, aimed the rifle and pulled the trigger. The tracer arced upward through the sky, leaving a thin streak of smoke in its wake before piercing the balloon just above the rear gondola. Nothing happened.

"Aim higher," she yelled over the loud, concussive bangs of the Lewis gun.

Ella steadied herself and fired again. Small spurts of flame exploded from the rear gondola. The zeppelin was firing back at them. Bullets slammed into the wall, inches from her face.

She fired again. As the gun recoiled, a smattering of stone hit her shoulder. She fired twice more. Now, the zeppelin was floating upward at an increasingly rapid speed. It would soon be out of their reach.

She fired the last shot and held her breath. The tracer vaulted through the night. This time, when it penetrated the silver fabric, a rosy glow illuminated the long balloon. It looked as though someone had switched on a giant lamp. Then the stern of the airship burst into angry flames. Within seconds, the entire ship was ablaze.

Jay rose and stood beside her. The stench of burning oil and scorched fabric filled the air. A series of loud explosions followed. Brilliant crimson flashes lit the sky.

Ella raised an arm to cover her face as the flaming mass hurtled toward them, and they were hit by a violent blast of heat. The zeppelin was on course to crash into the church tower when a gust of wind, like the sweep of an invisible hand, carried it away. The aluminum frame buckled with a loud shriek, and the fiery skeleton crashed into an open field. They stared down at the smoldering wreckage. Glittery embers and dark plumes of smoke drifted into the sky.

In the absence of the thunderous percussion of guns and the furious crescendo of explosions, it was eerily quiet now. The silence seemed garishly inappropriate. They had just shot down a zeppelin. There should be trumpets blaring, loud cheers, the applause of a boisterous audience.

Or perhaps the silence was fitting. For whatever Ella had expected to feel in this moment—exhilaration or some triumphant sense of achievement—was absent.

CHAPTER 31

Morning light filtered in through the gaps in the ceiling of the Lejeune barn. The animals, like all the other inhabitants of Pertés, had long since departed. But their scent lingered in the hay. Approaching footsteps jerked Jay awake.

Bertie stood over him, grinning widely. "Up and at 'em, Gatz."

He winced. His entire body ached. The feat of climbing to the top of the tower carrying a thirty-pound machine gun with ammo strapped to his back had taken its toll. It felt like the Eastman gang had beaten every inch of him with a lead pipe while he slept.

"Come on. We should get out of here before any Germans show up." Bertie extended a hand, helping Jay to his feet. In the other arm he held a stack of clean clothes. "These are for you. That German uniform won't go over well in Antwerp."

Jay glanced around the empty barn. "Where's Ella?"

"She's in the car—well, in the trunk. Can't take any chances. I'll bet the Germans are scouring all of Belgium for their escaped prisoners."

"And Oliver?"

"He's doing fine. I already told her this, multiple times. But she claims she needs to see him for herself, immediately. So, hurry up and change. I want to hear about last night."

Bertie spent the first half of the ride grinning and shaking his head in astonishment like a boy who'd just witnessed his first magic trick.

"Brilliant!" He whacked the steering wheel with the palm of his hand. "Unbelievably brilliant."

Jay grinned. "You make it sound as though you didn't think we had a chance."

"Of course I didn't. The plan was absolutely mad."

"Then, why—"

"It was obvious Miss Kaye back there wasn't going to take no for an answer. So rather than drive you to Pertés with a rifle pointed at my back, I offered to take you there willingly."

"How gentlemanly of you," Ella yelled from the trunk, her voice muffled.

"That you somehow managed to pull it off is truly shocking—although, perhaps not as shocking as what Oliver had to say about you, Gatz." Bertie winked at Jay before turning his attention back to the road. "Or should I say, Mr. Belmont?"

The proud smile stretched across Jay's face disintegrated. It wasn't that he had forgotten about all that. Of course he hadn't. But he'd managed to push it into a far corner of his mind.

"Well, no reason to discuss that now. Wouldn't want to put a damper on the celebration."

"Celebration?" Jay croaked.

"Oh, it's nothing formal. Just a few chaps from the delegation. They want to thank the heroes who saved Antwerp."

There was a succession of loud thuds, Ella banging on the lid of the trunk. "You told me we were going to see Oliver."

"We are. He's at the Hôtel St. Antoine awaiting our arrival.

I had an ambulance take him there this morning."

They rode in silence for the rest of the drive. Jay desperately wanted to know what Oliver had said about him. Bertie wouldn't be taking him to a celebration if he thought he was a German spy. But he had to suspect he was up to something. Ordinary people going about their business didn't travel under a false identity.

Maybe he could claim he'd used Teddy Belmont's name in order to get away from the Eastman gang. He'd started to tell Ella about all that in the tower last night. But that wouldn't explain the tracers.

He fixed his attention on the empty field on the side of the road, stiff with dread. Maybe there was no celebration. Maybe that was just another of Bertie's cover stories, and as soon as they got to Antwerp, Jay would be arrested.

For an instant he considered hurling himself out of the car. But they were driving incredibly fast, and even if he survived the jump without injury, where would he go?

When they reached the outskirts of Antwerp, Jay crossed his arms and stared gloomily at the dismal panorama—the remains of hundreds of upscale homes as flattened and crushed as his own ambitions.

He'd played the game and lost. There was nothing to be done now but accept his doomed fate. Maybe life in prison wouldn't be so bad. At least he'd have food and a bed. And the Eastman gang would never find him there.

But it turned out Bertie wasn't lying after all. Upon entering the city, he drove them straight to the Hôtel St. Antoine. The restaurant was packed with its usual crowd of Belgian officers and foreign diplomats. Oliver was seated outside in the courtyard at a long table with men Jay recognized as the British diplomats.

For someone who'd been shot the night before, he looked

remarkably well. Only his lack of movement betrayed his injury. Rather than twisting his torso to look at something to the side, only Oliver's head rotated. This movement, in conjunction with the large round spectacles perched atop his nose, brought to mind an owl.

As they made their way to the table, one of the diplomats shouted, "Why, here they are now. Here come the heroes." A succession of enthusiastic handshakes and pats on the back followed.

Ella was still wearing her filthy clothes from the night before. She had a series of scratches on her face, and no attempt had been made to tame her hair. She looked like she had been attacked by a family of crows. But sitting next to Oliver, smiling up at him, she looked incredibly happy.

The hour that followed passed in a happy blur. Jay had never been the center of attention like this before, with everyone patting him on the back and placing drinks in his hand. It wasn't until the courtyard began to empty and Bertie suggested the four of them head up to the room for a private toast that Jay's unease returned.

As they ascended to the tenth floor in the small elevator, an impending sense of doom set in. He considered pulling the lever, jumping out, racing down the stairs and out of the building. But it was too late for that. He should have made his escape during the party.

Up in the room, Ella and Oliver took the two seats at the small table. Jay stood beside them, gazing out the window, attempting to keep a neutral expression on his face.

Bertie crossed his arms. "I think it's time we get our facts straight. Who are you, James? Who are you working for? Really?"

Jay continued staring out the window. Distant plumes of smoke rose above a battlefield.

"Let me put it another way," Bertie said when Jay didn't respond. "Who was Teddy Belmont working for? He wasn't working with me." He gestured to Ella and Oliver. "Or them."

Jay squeezed his eyes shut and bit his knuckle so hard it bled.

"All right," Bertie said. "I'll just say it. Are you a German spy? That's what Oliver told me last night."

"Come on, Bertie," Oliver protested, "I was high out of my mind on morphine. I didn't know what I was talking about, not really. He shot down a German zeppelin. What kind of a German spy does that? Who cares who he works for? The man saved our lives. That's gotta count for something."

"I'm not saying it doesn't. But there are questions that need answering. Where did Gatz get the tracers from, for example?"

Jay flinched, waiting for Ella to expose him.

"Well, James?"

Surely, she'd figured it out by now. But she said nothing.

Bertie sighed. "I'm on your side, but we can't have any more secrets. My hope is that rather than punish you, they'll recruit you to come work for us."

"What if they don't?" Jay said, turning to Bertie.

"I'm sure they'll take everything you've done to help the British effort into account. And we'll all put in a good word for you. You can be certain of that. But I have to turn you in. I'm sorry, old sport, but rules are rules."

"You'll do no such thing," Ella said, rising from the table.

Jay perked up. In the tower last night, he and Ella had come to a new understanding. Or, at least, he'd hoped as much. It seemed he'd been right. They were friends now. Ella was standing up for him.

"He's a German spy," Bertie said. "I don't have a choice."

Ella put her hands on her hips. "If I'm not mistaken, Bertie, you work for the *Secret* Service, not the Security Service."

"What's your point?"

"My point is counterespionage doesn't fall under your jurisdiction. If anyone is going to hand him over, it's me."

Jay trudged away from the window and slumped onto the bed. What was wrong with him? Ella wasn't his friend.

Would he ever stop blindly placing his trust in other people's hands? Just because it had worked out with Cody didn't mean it was ever going to work out again. The fact that Cody liked him had been nothing more than a stroke of dumb luck.

Bertie held up his hands. "Fair enough. If you want to be the one to hand him over to Drake, be my guest."

"I said *if* anyone turns him over," Ella clarified. "And *if* we turn Jay in, I feel it's our duty to turn you in as well, Bertie. How do we know you're not a German spy?"

Bertie snorted. "Don't be ridiculous."

"I'm not being the least bit ridiculous. You've been driving around Belgium with a German spy for close to two weeks. You're even sharing a hotel room."

"Unwittingly!"

"Sure," Oliver said. "But admitting you unwittingly did a German spy's bidding for two weeks isn't going to look great on your record either."

Bertie looked back and forth between Jay, Ella, and Oliver, scowling. "Fine," he finally said. "As this is a Security Service matter, I'll leave it to you two to decide what, if anything, you relate to Drake regarding Gatz's, shall we say, German affiliations."

"Thank you," Jay said.

"I will, of course, have to mention you in my report to the

Secret Service."

Jay's shoulders sagged.

"Oh, don't look so put out, Gatz. I'm not going to mention any of that Teddy Belmont nonsense. Like Ella said, that has nothing to do with the Secret Service. Although, you should probably toss that red notebook of yours. It's rather incriminating."

Jay nodded. He'd forgotten about the description of Teddy Belmont it contained.

"I'll only mention the bits where you helped us out. How's that sound?" Bertie crossed the room and extended a hand to Jay.

"That sounds fine."

"I think *C* will be rather impressed by all we've accomplished."

"Do you mind if Jay and I have a moment alone?" Ella waited until the two men had left the room, then she turned to Jay. "That last night on the ship, when you weren't in your room, you were stealing tracers from Stanley Felton, weren't you?"

Jay gulped. Did this mean she *was* turning him in? "I didn't want to steal anything. I was desperate for money, you see, and—"

She waved a hand in the air, swatting away his words. "I don't care. I was just curious. It all worked out in the end. And if Stanley Felton suffered any discomfort thinking his valuable technology had been pilfered, well, that's fine by me. I can't stand the man."

"Oh. I see."

"I meant what I said last night about the twenty-five thousand dollars. It should have been yours all along. I'm sorry you never got it. Truly, I am."

Maybe it was exhaustion, maybe it was overwhelming relief, but tears filled his eyes.

Ella looked at him, perplexed. "What? Did I say something to offend you?"

He gave a short laugh. "No. You're just being nice is all."

She frowned. "And that's so shocking it moved you to tears?"

"No. I just meant—"

"I'm being nice because, well, you and I are friends now, aren't we?"

He nodded.

"Promise me something." She looked at him intently.

"Okay."

"If you need more money in the future, promise me you'll ask?"

"All right."

"Imagine all the trouble you could have saved if you'd come to me in the first place. In New York, I mean, instead of borrowing money from gangsters."

He raised an eyebrow. "And you'd have given me the money, just like that?"

"Well, no, probably not. Definitely not." She shrugged. "But people change."

CHAPTER 32

Five days later, Ella was back at Ashenden, sitting around the long dining room table with Oliver and Drake. In the corner of the room sat a secretary with a typewriter. As Drake conducted their debriefing, she recorded everything said with an efficient clacking of keys.

In discussing their escape from prison and shooting down the zeppelin, neither Ella nor Oliver made any mention of James Gatz's former alias. Ella kept waiting for Drake to bring up Teddy Belmont. But it wasn't until the very end of the interview that Drake so much as mentioned his name.

"By the way, you were right about that Teddy Belmont chap."

"Oh?" Ella affected a bored tone of voice. "How so?"

"He was a German spy."

"Did you catch him?" Oliver asked.

"Not exactly."

Ella kept her face blank. Had Bertie said something after all?

"He's dead."

"What?" Ella shook her head. That couldn't be right. She had just seen him a few days ago.

"We would have preferred to arrest him and question him,

but it couldn't be helped. He attacked an officer from Scotland Yard. The officer shot him in self-defense."

Why would Jay attack someone? It didn't make sense. Ella felt sick.

"In London?" Oliver asked.

"Rotterdam. It happened a few weeks ago. I meant to tell you earlier. It's a shame, really. Now we'll never know much about him."

There were very specific rules as to what they were allowed say about their time abroad. No mention was to be made of the Security Service or their time working as German spies. And under no circumstances were they to reveal their part in shooting down the zeppelin. They were to stick to the story that had been relayed to the public, that the zeppelin had crashed as a result of an onboard fire while flying over Belgium.

Drake asked them both to stay on as agents of the Security Service. They couldn't serve as German double agents anymore. Their covers were blown. But that didn't mean there wasn't a place for them in the agency. And if they wished to report on the war, the press credentials allowing them to follow the British Army were still valid. Their articles would be censored and revised, this time by the British. But only so as not to give anything away to the enemy.

The two reporters politely declined both offers.

Her spying days were behind her. And if Ella was going to work as a journalist, she wanted *her* words printed. She wanted the truth printed. Allowing any government, German, British or otherwise, to modify her journalism to fit their agenda wasn't worth the spotlight. She could live without the fame and glory. That wasn't important, at least not to her. Not anymore.

A few days later, Ella and Oliver were on a ship steaming across the Atlantic back to New York. They stood side by side on the promenade deck. Elbows resting on the rail, they looked out at the water as the salty air rushed past them.

Oliver turned to her. "Say, I've got an idea."

"If it involves mingling with a bunch of socialites in the smoking lounge, you can count me out."

"It's an even better idea than that, if you can believe it."

"Really?"

"I was thinking, when we get back, we should get hitched."

"What?"

"Married. You and me."

"Have you lost your mind?"

He touched his forehead. "Nope."

Ella rolled her eyes.

"How about it? Ella Engel has a nice ring to it. Don't you think?" He got down on one knee.

"Get up," Ella said in a loud whisper, glancing around to make sure no one was looking at them. "You're making a spectacle."

"I thought you liked being the center of attention."

"Not like this." She tugged at his arm until he stood.

"Give me one good reason why not?"

"Because we barely know each other."

"We've spent every waking hour together for the last few weeks."

"Okay, then because it's crazy."

He pursed his lips and nodded his head repeatedly. "So let me get this straight. Your idea to personally take down a zeppelin with a shotgun wasn't crazy, but my idea to get married is?"

"My idea worked, didn't it?"

"And I got shot. Let's not forget that part. But yes, technically, your idea worked. And so will mine. We're good together. You can't deny it."

"That doesn't mean we have to get married."

"Well, sure." He grinned. "But then I wouldn't get to spend all your money."

She laughed.

"Don't worry." Oliver slung an arm around her shoulders. "I won't go around town bragging to everyone that I married a millionaire. That would be redundant. One look at me in my expensive new suits and diamond-studded cuff links, and it'll be obvious to all of Manhattan."

"You'll get sick of me. We're already partners at work."

The editor of the *Journal* had asked them to write a series of articles detailing their time on the battlefield in Belgium. And he'd offered Ella a permanent staff position at the paper. She'd accepted, but only on the condition she could choose her own subject matter.

"Sick of you?" Oliver said, pulling her closer. "Not a chance."

They'd be back in America in a matter of days, an ocean away from Europe's war. No invading army was torching American towns, but that didn't mean there weren't battles being fought. America was not immune to injustice or unrest. Liberty and equality were, after all, just words. Saying them didn't make them true. But just because words rang false today didn't mean they would tomorrow. Change was always possible. But barriers didn't break by themselves—people like Ella broke them.

CHAPTER 33

Jay had spent the last two weeks playing tourist in London and living at the Savoy—compliments of Ella Kaye. During this time, Ella's attorney had settled his loan with the Eastman gang, and all was forgiven. The remainder of the twenty-five thousand dollars now sat in a bank account in Jay's name.

Having been spared an inquisition by the Security Service, Jay was free to leave England whenever he wished. But something held him back. He would return to New York one day. When he did, he would make something of himself—not by way of luck or happenstance, but by means of his own industry. One day he would make New York his own. This indisputable fact was his inescapable destiny. Only, he wasn't quite ready for all that—not yet.

Not that he planned to continue loafing about and idling away his days at the Savoy. He'd enjoyed the past two weeks, but he was ready to get back to work. In fact, he was on his way now to a job interview.

When Jay arrived at 2 Whitehall Court, a young secretary was waiting for him outside. The ornate stone building overlooking the Victoria Embankment and the Thames housed a block's worth of fashionable apartments. The man Jay was here to meet occupied an apartment on the top floor.

They rode the small lift in silence. When they reached the top, Jay followed the secretary through a mazelike series of corridors, steps, and small rooms. Finally, she left him standing in front of a closed door.

He knocked.

"Come in, then," boomed a voice from within.

A sturdy man in his early fifties, wearing a decorated naval uniform, sat behind a plain wooden desk. He stared at Jay through a large gold-rimmed monocle. The man's name, he would later learn, was Mansfield Smith-Cumming. He was head of the British Secret Service. Today, Jay knew him only as *C*.

"Good morning, sir," Jay said, looking around the room. An assortment of maps, charts and painted seascapes decorated the walls. Other than a large safe and *C*'s desk, the room contained no furniture. As such, Jay remained standing.

"So," *C* finally said. "You're the man who shot down a zeppelin with a Lewis gun. Well done."

"Thank you, sir. I had some help, of course."

"So I hear. Wouldn't mind having *her* working for the Secret Service as well. I'd hire her too, if it wouldn't infuriate *K*. He's the chap that runs the Security Service, of course. Don't suppose you've met him."

"No, sir." Thankfully Jay had not.

"*K* paints some ludicrous picture of me running about town poaching his agents, when really, they've all approached me. It's not my fault my department's more exciting." He flipped through a stack of papers on his desk. "Well then, let's get down to it. Agent Scott informed me you were working for a Belgian charity organization run by that American Hoover." He furrowed his brow. "Or maybe I've confused you with someone else. Either way, it's a good cover story. Let's stick with it." He looked up from the papers. "Are you still enrolled at Oxford?"

"No, sir. That was a misunderstanding. You see—"

"Well, let's say you are. Gives you a reason to be in England."

"But—"

"Consider yourself an Oxford man from here on out. We'll take care of it, get you all the official papers, maybe run you up there for a photograph or two for you to carry around." He swatted his hand in the air as though brushing aside any other impediments. "Point is, it's a brilliant cover. Well done."

"Thank you?"

"I'm told you speak German fluently."

Jay nodded. "My father's family is German."

"Any other languages?"

"Russian."

"You don't say? Study it in school, did you?"

"Oh, nothing like that, sir. My mother was Russian."

"How very American. Ever been to Russia?"

Jay shook his head.

"Miserable place. Or so I'm told. Well, consider Russian another feather in your cap. I'd say you have a rather promising career to look forward to with the Secret Service."

"Thank you, sir."

"But remember, this is a serious commitment. We are at war, after all. War isn't easy, and it isn't quick. They say this war will be over by Christmas, but I don't believe it. Assuming you're up for it, we're happy to have you."

Jay wouldn't realize it until sometime later, but something about Mansfield Smith-Cumming reminded him of Dan Cody. The two men looked nothing alike. And their mannerisms were overtly dissimilar. *C* was much more refined than Cody, who up until his death had remained a miner at heart.

But there was an elusive twinkle in *C*'s eyes that hinted at adventure. And that very much reminded Jay of Cody.

Standing here in *C*'s office, Jay felt the same excitement and anticipation he had felt the day he first boarded the *Tuolomee*. He didn't know where in the world *C* would send him, or what he might encounter when he got there. He knew only one thing for certain. This was the start of a new adventure.

C rose, walked around his desk, and shook Jay's hand with abundant enthusiasm.

"Welcome aboard, Agent Gatz."

ABOUT THE AUTHOR

R.M. Spencer was born and raised in New Orleans. She is the author of *Agent Gatz* and *The Island*. She currently lives in Los Angeles. For more information or to join R.M. Spencer's mailing list visit www.rmspencer.com.

Made in the USA
Las Vegas, NV
12 September 2023